Spoo

Spooked

an anthology

Bridge House

British Library Cataloguing in Publication Data

A Record of this Publication is available from the British Library

ISBN 978-0-955791-09-3

This edition published 2009 by Bridge House Publishing
Manchester, England

Contents

Introduction 6

Late Arrival 7

Awake 18

Call Me 29

Full House 37

Gentleman George 45

Until the Sands Run Out... 53

Hamelin 67

Growing Pains 75

On a Hundred Other Nights.. 88

Kindred Spirits.. 102

Passing on the Road... 112

Prints of Darkness.. 120

Sahib... 132

Web of Fear 144

What Comes Around Goes Around 153

A Ghostly Tale.. 161

Reflection 172

A Ghost of A Conscience... 183

Good Company 190

Now That I've Found You 197

The House... 208

Cheating Death 215

The Ghost of Bony Ridge.. 224

Caroline 232

The Attic... 241

5

Introduction

There's always something a bit scary about a ghost story. Somehow, though, when you read a collection of them you're expecting to meet a spook or two. It takes a little more effort to frighten the reader.

We hope we've managed to do just that with this bunch of tales and our striking cover. We hope as well you'll find the stories as different from each other as they are from the normal ghost story.

You'll come across some old friends amongst the authors in this volume. Bridge House is beginning to establish a brand and we have several writers now who have the measure of what we're looking for. You'll also meet some new names and writing styles. We're sure both will please.

And now to the ghosts.... They too have a life of their own – precisely drawn by our authors. It's that time of year isn't it? When the nights are getting longer, the days are getting shorter, when strange shadows lurk and you begin to hear noises you don't understand. We have traditional ghosts, more subtle ghosts, naughty ghosts, nice ghost, nasty ghost and in one or two of our stories it's a little difficult to work out who is haunting whom.

Stoke up the fire, sit back, enjoy and prepare to be:

Spooked!

Late Arrival

Norah's keys jangled in her shaking hand. "It must be this one," she muttered. She felt vulnerable standing there in her robe and slippers hunched over the uncooperative keyhole. Her guest stood silently by her side, his expression hidden by his hat and the shadows of the dimly lit hall. He had had to wake her. Of course, she had been expecting him, but hours earlier. Norah had retired, assuming, perhaps, he had missed his train. He gave no explanation for his lateness. In fact, he had uttered only a few words and those had been perfunctory and her tired, muddled mind could not retrieve them.

On the tenth try, she heard a click. Norah felt more than saw the man's form flinch at the final yielding of the lock.

"Here you are," she said, standing aside so he could pass. "The lights are there. Water's on the nightstand." His hat sat so low over his brow she couldn't see his face.

"Thank you," he said, stepping into the room. "Goodnight." He closed the door and Norah stood outside a moment, wondering.

As she shuffled back to her own room – down the dark hall, a flight of steps and along the passage that led from the front door to the large kitchen – she thought of Martha and her message: *I've referred a man to you. He needs a place to stay. I have a feeling he'll love Lethe House.*

Norah decided to ring Martha in the morning and ask a few more questions. She went back to bed, letting the strangeness of the midnight escort through the dark, sprawling country manor ebb from her consciousness.

The rooster woke her before dawn. Usually she was grateful for the wake up call, but this morning she felt groggy.

She'd had a fitful night of jumbled dreams – nightmares of fire, smoke, and ruin – and was loathe to get out of bed. But duty called. She put on her pressed dress and tied a clean apron over it; stockings, sensible shoes, and her hair rolled up almost completed the picture. She forgave herself her daily luxury of a pat of blusher, which she daubed on her cheeks while repenting her vanity.

In the kitchen, she perked the coffee, steeped the tea, baked the rolls, sliced the bread for toast, spooned out jam, and laid the table for three of her four guests, Mr. Churchill, Ellie Sanderson, and Bella Eavesblood. The new fellow, Mr... What was his name? Usually her guests gave her their particulars on arrival. But last night had been so ... late.

Mr. Churchill and Ellie were always the first to come down. He liked his coffee hot and black. She took tea. Norah poured it for them as they took their places at the table. Mr. Churchill, predictably, buried his nose in his paper. He took the morning train to the city four days a week but preferred to live beyond the hustle and bustle. He once told Norah he loved draughty old places that faced the wild. She had taken the draughty comment personally and filled any chink she could find – there weren't many – before she realized Mr. Churchill hadn't meant it literally. Besides, Burberry was hardly wild, even if it was out of the way.

Ellie Sanderson chitchatted away in her morning delirium; she had a habit of incomplete sentences prior to three cups of tea. Her other habits involved spending the morning composing and then walking among the hills and dales before coming back all muddy and flushed and full of stories of the wood sprites she had cavorted with. Everyone tolerated her flights of fancy because she was an artist.

8

Norah's third guest, Bella Eavesblood, didn't eat breakfast. Norah took her up a milky coffee, very sugary, at about half past eleven. Bella always came to the door partially clad, reeking of perfume, and looking surprised at Norah's offering. "What a dear," she'd coo. And: "Thank you, luv."

Norah enjoyed tending to her guests, and would have liked to have more, which was why she appreciated Martha's referral. Word of mouth could spread and perhaps one day all thirteen rooms would be let. That count included her own, of course. Although she managed the estate, she also considered herself a permanent guest. Mr. Churchill, Ellie, and Bella seemed to be here to stay, too.

Ellie looked up from blowing on her coffee. "Is there a new guest, Norah? Someone who just…"

"Yes," said Norah. "Got in late, I'm afraid, probably still sleeping. I put him in the end room so you won't disturb him with your playing."

"Oh yes, that makes perfect sense. There was a vibe I felt last night, his presence perhaps, and it made me feel so…" Mr. Churchill peered over his paper to see what the artist would say. But she didn't continue as she began buttering toast and scrambling crumbs across the walnut table.

"Bah," spat Mr. Churchill. Norah watched his moustache twitch, an irritated reaction to Ellie's trailing sentences. He snapped his paper back in front of his face.

Norah refilled his coffee cup as Ellie absently dunked her toast into her milky tea. After taking a soggy bite, she addressed Mr. Churchill.

"You know, if you spend all morning reading your paper, you might end up…"

He turned down one corner of newsprint and scrunched his eyebrows. "Yes?"

9

But now Ellie was gazing out the window. Norah smiled. "I think she meant to say you might miss your train. I'll get your hat for you shall I?"

After Mr. Churchill had set off to the station and Ellie had gone to her room to play piano, there was still no sign of the new arrival, Mr... What was it again? Lightfoot, yes, that was it... or was it Lightroot? Norah suddenly wondered if Ellie's scatter-brained condition was contagious.

She decided to take breakfast up to him. She fixed a plate of eggs, covered them, and added fresh rolls and tea – no, coffee – yes, tea – then decided on both and covered the pots with cosies. She left the tray outside his door at ten and went down to finish scrubbing the pots and pans and to make Bella's coffee.

Bella's room was across from Mr. Leadfoot's – no, that wasn't it – so when Norah took up her coffee at half past eleven she saw that his tray hadn't been touched. Bella, half-dressed in a pink slip and lacy brassiere and puffing on a cigarette, opened her door.

"Really, you shouldn't have, luv," she said exhaling a trickle of smoke.

"I've told you before, Bella, no smoking in the house." She'd already banned the use of candles. She didn't want to risk a fire.

"Oh, yes. My sincerest apologies. My memory isn't what it used to be." She tipped the cigarette into the washbasin. Bella caught her glancing at the door across the hall.

"A new spectre in the night, hmmm? How tantalizing." She reached for the coffee tray. "He smokes a pipe, you know." With that, she winked at Norah and tapped the door closed with her heel.

A pipe? Norah hadn't detected any fragrance of tobacco last night, and she had, after all, stood quite close to him. As soon as he made an appearance, she'd have to apprise him of the house rules.

The rest of Norah's day was busy with chores. Sweeping, dusting, ironing, folding. When it was time to start chopping the vegetables for supper, she frowned at the untouched tray sitting portentously on the counter. Martha hadn't answered when Norah had phoned in the afternoon; she would have to try again later that evening.

Once the vegetables were in the pot, she sat at the kitchen table, near the window, and watched leaf shadows dance across the kitchen floor. Mesmerized by the rippling play of light and dark, she barely registered the creak and thud of the front door.

"Ellie?" She normally got back at this time, mud-caked and full of mirth. Mr. Churchill returned on the five thirty train. Bella, vague and mysterious, came in at unpredictable times, depending on her encounters, and helped herself to leftovers. Norah couldn't hazard a guess at the new fellow's whereabouts.

And where was that Ellie? She usually bounded into the kitchen and nibbled while Norah prepared supper, her incomplete sentences having evolved into incoherent ones, but no one pushed through the swing door.

Norah stepped into the foyer. She saw that the door to her room was ajar. Odd. She never felt a need to lock it, not here, and those darn keys were such a nuisance nobody bothered with them here, but she always made sure her room door was closed before she left to keep out any draughts. She peeked in, noticed nothing untoward, and turned back toward the kitchen. From out of the corner of her eye she saw a pant leg turn at the top of the landing.

"Oh Mr., Mr…" What was his name? Norah wiped her hands on her apron and proceeded up the stairs. Since this man clearly didn't enjoy breakfast she was unsure whether or not to make him dinner.

The upstairs hall was empty when she reached it. Norah decided to try knocking on the man's door, if in fact that had been him. She couldn't be sure that what she'd seen hadn't been just a trick of the light. But just before she reached his room, she heard the bang of the front door and a boisterous, "Ta da!" Ellie.

Norah also remembered she'd left a pot on the boil. Rushing back downstairs, she sidestepped Ellie's fresh-faced exuberance. Ellie followed Norah into the kitchen and she didn't have a moment's rest until they sat down to supper.

Mr. Churchill arrived just after six o'clock and ate ravenously. He set his fork down, looking flushed and content, and dabbed the corners of his moustache with his napkin.

"I think I saw that new fellow down at the station, Norah."

"Funny that," said Ellie. "I could have sworn I saw him in the forest dancing with a satyr and a cheetah."

Mr. Churchill flung down his napkin. "There are no cheetahs in Burberry Forest!"

Ellie turned a shocked tearful gaze on him and said quietly, "Don't tell the satyrs. They'd be devastated."

Mr. Churchill rolled his eyes and then looked at Norah. "How can you stand it?"

Norah laid a protective hand on Ellie's shoulder. "You're sure you saw him, Mr. Churchill?"

"Fine upstanding young man. Looked a bit confused, though."

"I hope he's all right."

"Why wouldn't he be?" asked Ellie.

Mr. Churchill and Norah exchanged a glance but there was no need to answer for Ellie had already stood up and floated out the door.

"He'll come back eventually, Norah. Don't you worry."

After Ellie and Mr. Churchill had retired to their rooms, there was still no sign of Mr. Goodroot.

Norah went to the hall and dialled Martha's number.

"Martha? How are you? Yes, yes, everything's fine here. And how about there? Good, good."

"Thank you for your referral, a Mr. Lightroot? I'm not sure I've got the name right, sorry – you remember him? Yes, yes. Really? ... Are you sure? But ... I see. That could explain ... No, no, I haven't. But I will. I've got it right here. Oh, yes, the children, I hear them; sure I'll let you go. We'll talk next week. Goodbye."

Norah hung up the receiver, bewildered and perplexed. She picked up the remains of Mr. Churchill's newspaper. Martha had said page six. Shaking it out straight and holding it up to the light, she saw it. Not the biggest headline, but bold and clear.

Tragic Train Crash. She scanned the column. *Dozens dead, others seriously injured. Among the passengers, a Mr. L.P. Rightgood, suffered concussion and is in critical condition. His wife and children wait in shock.* There was a small photo of a man wearing a hat and smoking a pipe.

Norah looked down the hall toward the darkened kitchen. A meal, still warm, sat on the counter. She didn't go back in. Instead, she went to her room to retrieve her keys.

Huffing up the stairs and puffing down the corridor, she soon found herself in front of Mr. Rightgood's door. She knocked. No answer. She turned the door handle.

Locked. The first key didn't open it, nor the next, nor the one after that. She went entirely around the ring without any success. Befuddled, she took a step back and by the light of the wall lamp she counted out the keys. Twelve. One was missing. She stared at the locked door, feeling her knees weaken slightly. Then she hurried back to her room.

She stayed up late, waiting for Bella to return. She dozed, but woke abruptly when she heard the front door creak. Poking her head out her door, Norah inhaled the waft of spicy perfume and cigarette smoke that preceded Bella.

"Bella," hissed Norah. "I need to speak with you."

Bella raised her already arched eyebrows and sashayed into Norah's room.

"What can I do for you, Norah?"

Was that how she addressed her clients? But now was not the time to dwell on Bella's clandestine affairs.

"Have you seen him?"

"As a matter of fact—"

"You realize he's a husband and father, Bella?"

"They're always the most difficult to tempt, aren't they?"

"Did he say anything to you?"

"Actually, he did his best to ignore me."

"Can't say I blame him."

"But what's the point in fighting it?"

"He thinks he has something worth fighting for." Norah began pacing. "Martha doesn't usually send me the uncooperative ones."

"Sudden, violent, unexpected?"

"Yes."

"And loved ones still in shock?"

Norah nodded.

14

Bella sighed and patted Norah's age-spotted hand. "He'll come around. Just you wait." She rose to go.

"That's not all."

Bella turned.

"I think he stole a key."

"Oh."

"No one's done that before. I don't know what to do." Norah wrung her hands.

"Doesn't he know we're all free to come and go as we please?"

"He's trying to fight it." It was a desperate act, and virtually impossible to achieve, but she'd been warned it could happen.

"You must get the key back, Norah. If he keeps it, and doesn't cross over…"

"I know, I know."

Martha would close the manor down. Norah had promised to maintain a safe haven. She had sworn it. That was what entitled her to stay and run the manor that she loved so much. A promise broken, an oath transgressed would mean…

"I should call Martha right away."

"Don't sound the alarm just yet," said Bella. "Let's at least wait until morning and see if he shows up. If he loses this fight, he's sure to come back here."

Bella went to wake Ellie and Mr. Churchill. He was rather upset to be roused at such a late hour, but when he understood the import of the interruption, he waddled down to join them in the parlour. Ellie was delighted at the spontaneous soirée.

Norah made a fresh pot of tea and stoked up the fire in the grate. She shivered despite the increasing warmth.

15

"But I don't want to leave Lethe Manor!" said Ellie with wide eyes. She looked so young in her flannel nightgown. She had been young when she had wandered into the deep forest lake that had filled her lungs and swallowed her prodigious musical potential. "No one else would put up with me," she whimpered, putting her face in her hands.

Mr. Churchill laid a gentle hand on her shoulder. She looked up at him. "Why can't he see what a special place this is?"

"It's different when you have your life taken from you accidentally, Ellie." Mr. Churchill had suffered a fatal heart attack upon discovering that his business partners had embezzled and left the company bankrupt. He took the train to the city every day to wander the offices that had once contained his life's work.

"Oddly, it's even more shocking than having it taken by force," said Bella sadly. She had been strangled by a high profile client, who feared his nefarious habits might soon be exposed. He had been caught and sentenced to hang. But those types went elsewhere. Martha referred them to the remoter regions.

"It must be his children he's worried about," said Norah wringing her hands. "So, so sad."

"We cannot protect all the young ones now can we?" said Mr. Churchill tenderly, patting Norah's hand. They all knew she had died trying to save the Lethe children from the fire. To no avail. The flames had blazed out of control destroying everything they touched. Of course, the children had gone over to Martha. And, because of Norah's selfless attempt at rescue, Martha had given her the opportunity to restore the manor, to make it a home once again. If she lost it now, they would all be separated, and sent to wherever Martha could find room.

16

They waited until the wee hours of the morning. As the sky outside turned a sluggish gray, they heard the front door creak.

Mr. Rightgood entered the parlour carrying the early morning paper. He took off his hat and gazed at Norah with dark, sorrowful eyes. He handed her the paper, though she knew what would be in it. She whispered a small prayer for the sad, surviving family.

He offered her his hand, the key an iron stamp within it.

"I take my coffee black. Toast with jam, no butter."

He turned from them and left the room, his footsteps slow and heavy as he walked up the stairs. Norah exhaled a long sigh. Bella came up behind her and placed a gauzy arm around her shoulders.

"Give him time, luv. Eventually, he'll realize we have plenty of it."

Norah nodded and slipped the cold curve of the key into her pocket.

April Bosshard

April lives with her family on an island off the coast of British Columbia, Canada, where she edits fiction, coaches writers, and leads creative writing groups and workshops. She has a keen interest in the supernatural, mysterious, and fantastical, and is presently at work on a fantasy trilogy for young adults.

Awake

It seems that death is not the end. After that, there's lunch.

Lunch is probably too extravagant a term. In reality, there are plates of flaccid, ridiculously small sausage rolls that can't decide on an appropriate 'ideal heat', and so remain at a nauseatingly bland room temperature.

There are also cakes – Mr Kipling has paid a visit and his presence has been felt, in a variety of bright and gay colours.

There was a time, not too long ago, when you used to get steak pie at a funeral. Steak pie, potatoes and veg. Okay, the potatoes were out of a tin, and the carrots were out of a tin, and the steak pie was probably out of a tin, or at least a freezer. But still, it was a decent meal. It warmed your cockles, as they say.

My cockles are bloody freezing, just at the minute.

"She was a darlin', a darlin', son."

Oh Christ, it's Mary's cousin, Bobby. I'd forgotten about him. Bobby the bubble, Mary used to call him. He rumbles towards me, a pint of heavy in his hand and a sloppy, moist smile on his face.

"Uncle Bobby, you're right, mum was a darlin', one of the best," Sean says, putting himself between me and Bobby.

Jesus, it's like he can hear me thinking. My boy Sean. He's given me many reasons to be proud of him over the years, and this is but the latest. I wink at him. He's busy re-directing Bobby and doesn't see me. He knows, though. My boy.

I talk to him all the time, but it's been a while since I saw Sean up close. He lives over in Edinburgh these days, and doesn't get back through as often as anyone would like. He's looking smashing; strong and tall, smart and smiling. He's into his thirties now, but he's still got all his hair; which is more than I could say at his age. He got his looks from Mary, thank God. I like to think he got some of his sense from me.

I drift around the room. I don't know what else to do. Mary's sister, Lesley, is crying, I can see that from ten feet away. They were close, Lesley and Mary. Only three years between them – three years means a lot when you're under twenty, but bugger all when you're over sixty.

Lesley's husband, Fred, is doing a good job. She's a stick of a woman at the best of times, but Fred has his arm round her shoulder, whispering what I'm sure are comforting words.

Fred looks up and I give him a nod. He's doing the right thing, no need for me to get involved. Lesley is hurting enough; she doesn't need me adding to it. I wander on towards the next table.

"– three pigeons, two midgets and a lesbian!"

Anyone who's known Mary's younger brother, Alec, for any length of time develops a smile that's reserved solely for his tasteless jokes. I put mine on at the same time as everyone else at his table. He means well, but there's a time and a place, although I have no idea when and where that might be. Not at my wife's funeral, I know that much.

I change my plans and keep moving past Alec, straining to maintain my grin as I go. Once I'm out of his eye-line I let my face relax and glance back at Alec's wife, Jill. She's still wearing her versions of the 'aye, that was funny, honest' smile as I raise my eyebrows in solidarity. I know Jill would want a chat, but I also know she'd understand why I can't stop.

I'm okay in myself. Everyone knew this was coming for Mary. I know it's an awful thing to say, but there's a

19

part of me that's almost been looking forward to it. I think a part of her was, too. No one likes to see someone suffer; a small sense of relief is only natural. It's been a lonely time for both of us, and now there's a chance we can both move on.

Relations-wise, it's strictly Mary's side. My lot are either long gone or too far away for it to be worth their while travelling. I've only nieces and nephews left anyway. Most barely knew Mary.

I'm almost at the bar. I haven't had a whisky for four years – doctor's orders, initially – but I could fair go a dram today.

As usual, it's mainly the men crowded around the small, wooden shelf they've got the temerity to call a bar. It's really a kiosk, at best. I shouldn't complain; they were always good to Mary and me when we came for the bingo and race-nights. The friendliest social club in the Gorbals, this is. They make up for with a smile what they lack in the way of modern comforts. Still, I've always thought cushioned seats in the lounge and a hand-dryer in the gents wouldn't go amiss.

I cast an envious eye over the half-empty pint and short glasses as they're swung from left to right by their don't-know-how-lucky-they-are temporary owners. Gone are the days, unfortunately.

Sean and his mate Andy are stood at the bar with their backs to me. Known each other since they were twelve, these two; pals right through secondary school. Sean was Andy's best man. I was nearly crying, laughing at Sean's speech.

He read out all the cards from well-wishers, then added a couple he'd snuck in there himself. One was supposedly from Big Tony MacFee or 'Tonto' as he's known round here. Tonto's the local loan shark and, believe me, everyone knew who Sean was talking about when he said the name.

"Tonto writes: Congratulations on your special day to the lovely Josephine and her lucky husband, Andy O'Brian, of 148 St Edward's Drive, bottom left flat, who leaves for work at 7.30am every morning and catches the 38 bus into West George Street, then leaves Pronto-Print at exactly 5.30pm in the afternoon, walks to Union Street where he waits for the 38 bus to take him home, arriving back at St Edward's Drive between 5.50pm and 6.15pm. In recognition of his special day, I am happy to extend to Mr O'Brian the courtesy of an extra week's grace, after which normal leg-breaking practices will be resumed." There were more than a couple of guests at the wedding who owed Tonto a few pennies, but they all laughed. Andy's father looked a bit uneasy, right enough.

Sean and Andy are hunched together, deep in conversation, and I don't want to intrude. I hover, a couple of feet behind them. I don't really mean to eavesdrop. Well, maybe I do, a bit.

"Nah, I'm doing okay," I hear Sean say. "Kelly's been brilliant, she's keeping me going." Kelly is Sean's girlfriend. I've never had the chance to get to know her properly, but she seems like a smasher of a girl.

"Good stuff," Andy says. "But you know where I am if you need a pint or whatever. It's going to be a tough few months."

"It's been a tough few years." Sean laughs. "But cheers, mate. I appreciate it."

"Obviously you're going to feel down and stuff, but don't let it go too far before you ask for help, okay?" He's a good boy, Andy. Mary and I were always glad Sean had a friend like Andy.

"I'll do my best. It's weird to think that's her gone. I know she's been sick, but it's still weird."

"It must be, mate. I'm just glad my mum's still firing on all cylinders."

"Hang on to her, Andy. Hang on to her as hard as you can." Sean's head dips, and I'm about to go to him when I get distracted.

"Where is he?" a voice shouts drunkenly from behind me.

I turn around slowly, dreading what I know I'm going to see.

"Where is he?" Tonto shouts again from the door of the lounge. What the hell is he doing here? I can't imagine anyone invited him. I'm about to go and attempt to sort it out (though God knows what I think I could do) when Sean rushes past me, making it to the other side of the hall in seconds. To the rescue once again. That's my boy.

"Uncle Tony," Sean says calmly, but firmly enough that I can hear him from the bar. I attempt a saunter as I follow Sean's approach, ready to back him up if he needs me. "Uncle Tony, you made it, that's great." He's a master of diplomacy, my boy Sean.

"Sean, son," Tonto says. "There ye' are. C'mere 'n give us a hug."

The whole place falls silent as they watch Sean accept Tonto's bear-hug with good grace. He's a bit of a goliath, Tonto. He never needed to hire any muscle to make a point. Sean's doing well not to collapse under the weight of his uncle's aggressive affections.

Tonto is Mary's other brother, the one she tried to pretend she didn't have. He is by far her wealthiest relative, but neither she nor the rest of her family could ever find a way to be proud of him. I agreed with them. He's a parasite, who's made more than one of my friends' lives a nightmare.

He's looking right through me over Sean's shoulder, but I'm not surprised. We never exactly got on.

"C'mon and get a seat, Uncle Tony." Sean wriggles out of Tonto's embrace and guides him over to an empty table. The two of them sit, and Tonto starts whispering some nonsense into Sean's ear.

I'm inclined to join them for Sean's sake, but then Andy approaches the table and sits beside Sean. Josephine and Kelly get up from Alec and Jill's table and join their men. It's a bit of a frying-pan/fire situation, that. I notice Alec feels no compunction to go and talk to his big brother. I can't really blame him. I'm not exactly jumping hurdles to get there myself.

Andy and the girls manage to separate Tonto from Sean's ear and are soon gabbing away, making sure they keep Tonto's attention. They're like a wee gang, those four; and I mean 'gang' in a good way.

Tonto seems happy enough to stick with the weans, thank God, and I look about the place, wondering where to go next.

I spot Mary's Auntie Val at a table in the corner. She looks like, and might well possibly be, the oldest, smallest woman in the world. Val is Bobby's mother, and he's back sitting next to her. Val has a sherry in front of her, but she's not drinking it.

I slip over to say hello. Just as I reach them, Val says: "Robert, who was that doing all the shouting?" She's never smoked in her life, but her words croak their way out of her tiny mouth.

"Och, nobody, Mum," Bobby says uncomfortably. "Just some drunk that shouldn't be here."

"Are you sure, Robert?" Val's eyes make the effort, but there's no chance she's going to be able to see all the way over to the other side of the room. "It sounded like Anthony."

Bobby starts to sweat even more than usual. "Naw, Mum, it was just one of the regulars who didn't know there was a funeral on today. He's away now, don't worry."

"That's good, love," Val says. "I wouldn't want anyone spoiling Mary's day for her."

She's a lovely old soul, Val. She was good to Mary and me when we were starting out. It was Val who bought us Sean's first cot and pram.

I'm about to sit down when Tonto pipes up again.

"Listen Sean, you're a good boy, but get the fuck out of my way or I'll deck you, I swear to God."

I don't care what it's about; I'm back over there like a shot.

Sean is standing in front of Tonto with his hands outstretched, palms open. Andy is standing too, hovering behind Sean's left shoulder ready to help, sweat pishing off his forehead at the prospect.

"Uncle Tony, this is my mum's funeral. I'm not going to let you do this here. Not today." Sean's voice is strong and clear. He might be scared, but I wouldn't be surprised if he wasn't. Me, I'm keeking my knickers. I've seen Tonto's handiwork firsthand. He doesn't care who you are if you're in his way.

I'm about to step in when I feel a familiar presence at my side.

"Leave it."

"But—" I say.

"Just leave it, it'll be fine. Watch."

I do as I'm told.

"That wee bastard owes me money," Tonto shouts.

"I don't care," Sean says.

"Well I do, Sean."

"And I don't. This is not going to happen, Uncle Tony. Understand?"

Tonto has a good five inches on Sean, but my son stands his ground.

"Sean, do yersel' a favour and get out of my way. I don't want to hurt you, but you're not stopping me."

I instinctively take a step forward, but a gentle hand on my shoulder brings me to a halt. "Just wait."

It occurs to me that I don't know who Tonto is chasing. A quick look over to the bar clears that up – George Connelly, our old next door neighbour, is trying to make himself invisible behind a pillar. Unfortunately for him the pillar is no more than eight inches wide, while George is the proud recipient of the local chippy's 'best customer ever' award. George has never had one decent meal in his life; he always has at least two. His white shirt covered midriff is bulging out from behind the pillar like a bewildered jellyfish.

So George owes Tonto some money. Sad, but not all that surprising. George is a life-long bachelor, and never benefited from someone like Mary to tell him that, now and then, he would just have to do without.

Sean can't have seen George Connelly for ten years, yet he's still putting himself between George and harm's way. I'm proud as anything, but I'm not happy to be a bystander.

"Sean, I'm going to give you three seconds to get out of the way." Tonto isn't joking. He's never been much of a bluff-caller.

"That's your choice, Uncle Tony." Jesus, Sean's a cool one. He didn't get that from me.

I'm champing at the bit to jump in, but I'm pulled back again. "Just wait."

"B—" I don't even get the word out.

"Wait."

I pay heed to the boss once again, and don't move. I'm not happy about it, though.

I stand there and watch as Tonto's face contorts. He's ugly at the best of times, but now he's raging ugly.

Sean doesn't flinch. He stays still as a washing pole as Tonto primes his fist. Sean, I think, almost smiles as Tonto's right fist connects with his face. Sean lifts at least a foot off the floor, arcs backwards and lands on the ancient carpet with a thud.

My mouth opens, but before I can let out the scream that's aching to burst from my throat, that hand is on my shoulder once again.

"Wait. Watch."

"But Sean!"

"Watch."

I watch. Sean is on the floor, bloodied and hurt, and I have to watch.

Tonto flexes the fingers of his right hand and grins. "I warned you, son."

He makes to step past Sean's prone form in search of his real quarry. I can't take my eyes off Sean, but can imagine George Connelly shiteing himself.

Suddenly, Tonto is on the carpet with a blur of black-clad activity on his back. What the…?

Tonto's arm is pulled behind his back and twisted up towards his shoulders. He writhes and wriggles, but he's not getting up from this.

"You are under arrest for serious assault. Anything you say can be used against you…"

It's Kelly. Sean's Kelly. She's perched on top of Tonto, reading him his rights. She's a polis? Why didn't I know that?

"I told you to wait."

"But what about—". Again, I'm not allowed to finish.

"Look."

Sean pushes himself up on to his elbows. The blood is still there, and he's lost the crown from his front tooth. I can see that when he smiles.

Kelly pulls Tonto to his feet somehow, and pushes him face first against the wall. She's obviously a lot stronger than she looks, and manages to keep Tonto restrained with one hand while she makes a call on her mobile.

"Shorry folksh," Sean says to the room. "A bit of un-exshpected police bishness, there. Thanksh for coming along today, I know Mum would have been grateful. I'm afraid I need to go to the dentisht now, but the room'sh booked till five and I've left a bit of money with the bar-staff. Enjoy."

Flabbergasted is far too mild a word for what I'm feeling as I hear sirens and watch Kelly force Tonto out of the club's door, closely followed by Sean. Andy starts clapping, and soon the whole place joins in. There's no one in this city, never mind this room, who'll be sorry to see Tonto locked up.

"Did they plan this?" I ask.

"I don't know, but I wouldn't be surprised. There's neither of them daft."

It dawns on me that Sean must have been the one who invited Tonto (and George) to the funeral. "Why didn't I know Kelly was a copper?"

"You haven't been around. How would you know, really?"

27

"I, just thought, it would be one of those things I would know. You know? Is Sean a polis too, and no one's told me?"

"No, he's still just a plumber with a dentist's bill. Don't worry about him; Kelly will keep him out of bother."

"Okay." It's not me who's supposed to be confused at times like these. I've had two years to get used to it, after all.

"Anyway, thanks for coming to collect me. Where are we going, exactly?" Mary asks.

I smile. "Anywhere you want to. The world is no longer your only oyster."

"Good. I never liked seafood."

Ah, but it's good to have her back. Together again, at last.

Danny Gillan

Danny Gillan's award-winning *Will You Love me Tomorrow* was described as one of the best debut novels of 2008 and he has had several short stories published in anthologies and magazines. He finds pretending to be a writer far less tiring than pretending to be a musician, as he did in his youth, though the fringe benefits don't always compare favourably.

www.dannygillan.co.uk

Call Me

The phone buzzed and rattled next to me like an irritating bluebottle caught by a window frame, just as I'd settled in bed. Sighing, I peered groggily at the screen and pressed the button to release messages.

"Call me."

Huh! I pressed delete. I wasn't calling him at one o'clock in the morning! He probably wanted to tell me what a good time they had after I left and that was the last thing I wanted to hear. It wasn't fair. Everyone else stayed until the end of the party, but I had to leave. I'd be the laughing stock at college on Monday.

I banged the phone down and curled up under the bedclothes burying my head in the pillows. It was cold in the bedroom but the duvet was warm and comforting. I tried to block out the images of Olivia and Nick waving at me as I left, and focus on the kiss Jason had dropped on me as I was rushing to the door.

I was deeply asleep and it only felt as thought I'd shut my eyes for a moment when doorbell woke me. My head felt thick and my eyes were gravely. I squinted but my room was still in darkness so I knew it must be early. Since there was no chance of anyone I knew being up I turned over. I heard the carefully spaced footsteps of someone going down the stairs and then rumble of voices a long way away.

There was a knock at my door.

"Tina love?" Dad stood by my bed, a dressing gown over his pyjamas spotlighted in the glow from the hall-way.

What did he want at this time in the morning?

"Tina?"

"Uuhh?"

29

"Tina, the police are here. They want a word with you."

"Me! Uh, like why?" I scrabbled up, my legs tied by the duvet and grabbed the phone, peering blearily at the screen and trying to keep my hair out of my eyes.

6.05 am

Three more messages.

Dad shifted uneasily from one foot to the other.

"There's been an, err, um, accident. The police will explain..." His words trailed off. I jumped out of bed. What sort of accident? I unhooked my dressing gown from the back of the door and followed him downstairs, a heavy feeling in my stomach and my throat dry.

In the living room Mum was concentrating on the police. She wouldn't look me in the eye and continued to put sugar in a mug and hand it to a large policeman who balanced uncomfortably on our sofa. It was too soft and tried to pull him backwards into its depths. He would have been better off on a hard chair but a policewoman already sat there, her hands wrapped round another mug.

"I'll, err, put the heating on," said Dad, seeing her shiver. "It doesn't come on until 8am at the weekends."

He loped off to the kitchen. He was finding jobs to do that kept him out of the way, I could tell. He looked unsettled and embarrassed.

"Ms Dean?" the policeman asked, looking at me. "Am I right in thinking you were at a party in Meadow Estate last night?"

I looked at Mum, but she was staring into her mug and still wouldn't meet my eye. What was all this about? The police obviously knew where I'd been. Had somebody been busted for drugs or something? I mentally searched through all the rooms at the party, trying to remember if I'd seen anything I shouldn't, but there was

30

nothing. There wasn't even much to drink and I didn't have anything because I knew Dad would go ballistic if he could smell alcohol on me.

I nodded.

"Your father says he picked you up about midnight. Is that right?"

I nodded again.

"And your friends," he looked at his notebook, "Jason, Olivia and Nicholas. Did they leave?"

At Jason's name I felt my heart beating faster. A prickle of fear sprinted through me, tickling like an insect along the length of my limbs and up into my face. What had happened?

"They were still there, in the kitchen when I went out. Livy and Nick waved and Jason... err I guess they were laughing about the fact that Dad insisted on coming..."

"Just as well he did," Mum cut in.

"Why?" I demanded, looking from one to the other. "What is it?"

"There was an accident," the policeman said, gently. He looked at Mum but she was staring into her teacup.

"On the by-pass. I'm afraid at least one person is dead and others are in hospital. We think it happened around 1 am."

I felt weak. My legs wilted and my head was fuzzy. He couldn't mean my friends. Noooooo!

"Who...?" I whispered. I daren't guess.

"We need to know Ms Dean, who was intending to drive?"

"Jason would drive of course," I said. "It is his car, and he wasn't drunk. He'd only had a lager. He isn't stupid." I looked at Dad accusingly. That's why he came to get me. Because he always worried about somebody driv-

31

ing when they were drunk. He wouldn't trust my friends or me.

"OK," said the policeman. "What about the other two? How were they?"

"Fine," I said. I didn't mention the pitying looks Livy gave me as I slunk out, or the grin that Nick gave Jason. "Who…?"

"It's Jason, love," said Mum, reaching out and touching my arm. Her fingers seemed to burn my skin. "Nick and Livy are in hospital. They were all thrown from the car and it is unclear who was driving."

I gasped and struggled to get a breath. Jason! My Jason! I felt as if I was going to be sick, and as I stood my legs slipped from under me as if I was wallowing in mud. I scrabbled up and left the room, my head spinning.

"Tina?" Dad called.

"Leave her," I heard Mum say as I reached the stairs.

It couldn't be. Jason? I felt hot spots building up behind my eyes and then the tears began to flow. I wanted to hit something. Jason? Why Jason? My beautiful, lovely Jason.

Then it struck me. The phone! I'd got a message, surely it was after 1am. They must have got it wrong. It couldn't have been Jason. He had texted. Relief surged through me and gave my legs the shot of power needed to get up the stairs. I raced into my bedroom and grabbed the phone.

Fingers fumbling over the buttons… I'd deleted it! Furious with myself I checked the three new messages. They were all from Jason's phone.

"Call me."

"Call me."

"Call me."

Weak with relief I realised they had the wrong person. They must have muddled Jason and Nick.

I sank down on the bed. Guiltily I hugged myself. Jason was alive. Then I thought of Nick, dear sweet Nick and hot tears came rolling down my face like lava flows.

I pressed redial on Jason's number and listened to the phone ring and ring into a void. Of course, if he was in hospital he was probably asleep. I had to get over there and see him.

Ten minutes later, showered and dressed I half fell down the stairs.

"Tina?" My mother called from the kitchen. "Where are you going?"

"To the hospital," I said. "To see Jason."

"But Jason..."

I didn't hear what she had to say as I pulled the door shut.

Shivering I hurried along the path. I only had on the light jacket that I'd worn to the party and I could smell cigarette smoke clinging to it. It wasn't warm enough for the brisk morning.

I pushed my way into ICU. As I came in from the cold my skinned burned.

The receptionist shook her head.

"No, no one of that name was admitted."

"Yes," I argued. "Preece, p, r, double e, c, e."

"No. We don't have anyone..."

"Maybe he was transferred? Can you check?" I could feel my throat tightening. Why couldn't she find him?

The nurse rustled through papers on her clipboard.

"No, nothing."

"Is Livy, Olivia, here?"

"Olivia Hemmings? She was brought in last night. She is very poorly. You can't see her at the moment. Immediate family only."

I could feel the spots of heat behind my eyes again and the heavy lump was back in my stomach. Why couldn't they find Jason? I blinked hard but more tears began waterfalling down my cheeks.

The nurse took pity on me or maybe she just didn't want somebody blubbering in the corridor on her shift.

"Look, I can show you where she is. Just through the window."

She led me along the corridor and allowed me to peer through a porthole. I could see Livy, propped up by pillows, and tubes going in and out of her mouth, nose and arms like some bizarre chemistry experiment. She was a pale as the sheets and a bandage swaddled the top of her head. Her parents sat either side of the bed stroking her hands, which lay unmoving on the cover.

A phone rang and the nurse turned anxiously, caught between staying with me and answering it.

"It's OK, I'm going," I said, and started towards the door.

As soon as she had disappeared I sneaked back to the next window. No one I knew. I looked in the next.

"Nick!"

I shouted his name, then tried to bite back the word as soon as it was out. I knew then. Tears flowed without control and I pushed my way blindly out of the hospital.

Somehow I made my way home and I threw myself down on my bed, buried my head in the pillow and cried until I felt dried out.

Time passed as I drifted in and out of despair. My body burned and froze in extremes of hot and cold.

I dimly heard knocks on the door and whispered voices. My phone buzzed and vibrated on the bedside table but I ignored it.

Later, much later, my head aching and my eyes scratchy I woke shivering.

6.15am.

I'd lost a day and a night. Ten messages waited on my phone. I scrolled down. All but one were from Jason.

"Call me."

Hopelessly I pressed the dial button.

I heard it ringing into nothingness. The silence from the end of the phone was heavy and menacing. Who was this? Who was playing some horrible trick on me?

I knew I couldn't sleep again so I got up and rinsed my face. Still dressed in yesterday's clothes, I pulled a thick sweater over them, and picked up the purple bear, with "I love you" stitched into its stomach, that Jason had won for me last summer at the fair.

I crept downstairs, unlocked the front door, wincing as it squeaked, and let myself out into the dark. Half running, half walking I made my way to the by-pass. I didn't know where the accident had been but I figured I wouldn't be able to miss it.

There wasn't much traffic. Nobody paid me any attention as I hurried along the verge.

I saw the flutter of yellow and black chevroned police tape first. The grass was gorged deep by ice filled tire tracks ending at a tree, which bore an ugly weeping gash. There were traces of red paint on the bark. The car had gone, but two bunches of flowers were laid against the tree.

Looking round, I lifted the tape, stepped forward and put the bear down by the tree. At that moment my phone vibrated in my pocket.

I looked at the screen.

"Call me."

I stared at it. In the cold, misty morning the last few red and brown leaves clung to life on the trees by a thread. The line between life and death was very thin.

Call me?

Taking a deep breath I shouted into the early morning,

"Jason!"

A curl of mist separated and wrapped around me. I felt my face brushed by cold damp lips.

The phone vibrated again.

I checked the screen. One new message.

"I will love you 4 always."

Sniffing, I whispered,

"Me too," and I pressed 'save'.

And the mist disappeared.

Alyson Hilbourne

Alyson Hilbourne writes short stories in her spare time and has had prize-winning stories printed in UK writing magazines. She writes occasional copy for travel websites, mainly about Asia where she currently lives, and would love to have time to write more regularly.

Full House

It started the Tuesday night after the refurbishment.

Doris took her seat opposite her sister Janice. Glancing round at the bright lights and huge screen declaring 'Bingo is Best!' she stripped off her coat and folded it neatly on her seat. Janice, brown hair hanging in curtains down her face was tucking into a plate of fish and chips.

"They've done a nice job." Doris said, getting out her comb and carefully tidying her own bob of brown hair, "Look, *real* plants."

Janice looked up from her plate, and shoved her large blue glasses back up her nose.

"I think it was better before all these new people came." She muttered.

Doris arranged her game books in order on the table, the blue first and the red last. She took her special Bingo dabbers from her handbag, opened one and blotted it on Janice's napkin.

"I think I shall win tonight." Doris grinned.

"You never do." Janice replied.

She put her plate to one side.

"And I don't like all these fruit machines in here. Too noisy."

"They aren't allowed to play on them while a game's in progress." Doris looked longingly at the brightly lit machines that whizzed, chirped and sang so enticingly.

"Just as well for you." Janice remarked scornfully, "Just keep your mind on the books."

A cheerful melody suddenly played out making Doris jump in her seat and giggle embarrassedly. A man's voice politely coughed and announced the first Bingo game was shortly to begin. Janice pulled a blue pen and a lucky black cat ornament from her bag. She set the cat on the table overlooking her books.

"Lots of luck tonight Mr Twiggles." She chirruped to the cat. "Don't say anything, Doris."

"You speak to that cat nicer than you speak to me."

"That's because he's lucky."

The Bingo caller had taken his place at the podium at the front of the room, just under the big screen.

"I wish we could have persuaded Melanie to come." Doris smiled sadly, "It would have done her good."

"Her loss, now hush!" Janice was intent on her books.

Doris let out a sigh and looked at her numbers. The caller had just announced 53 and 7. She blotted them out with a big blob of red ink. Janice was rapidly scribbling out numbers, within moments her fingers danced across the book, connecting a line of numbers and…

"House!" Janice cried.

Doris sighed softly looking at her own unlucky books. One of the staff came over and checked Janice's winning line.

"Thank you Mr Twiggles!" Janice laughed.

"Perhaps I should get a lucky cat." Doris mumbled.

Janice glanced at her.

"Its a game of chance Doris, no luck involved."

"But…"

Janice waved her into stupefied silence as the caller began again. Doris tried to concentrate hard on her book, focusing all her energy on it, trying to think lucky. She was studying the numbers so hard that when a twinkling music fluttered in the air she jumped nearly out of her skin.

"No playing on the fruit machines while a game's in progress." The caller snapped a little churlishly.

Some people muttered to each other. Doris giggled self-consciously. Then the game continued. Doris had crossed off two more numbers and was only five away from getting two lines when the twinkling, chiming music played again and this time it seemed louder. Everyone looked around in the direction of the sound. A fruit machine was glowing, its buttons flared with the temptations of nudges and holds, its 'start' button beamed hopefully. There was no one near it.

The caller glanced at some of the other staff who shrugged and went back to collecting tea mugs.

"That's the machine that used to be in the foyer." Doris hissed to Janice, "Fred loved that machine."

"Gambled his life away on it." Janice tutted.

"Don't say that, it's heartless."

The caller cleared his throat.

"We'll continue, ahem, all the sixes, sixty..."

The chiming, cheery music played once more. The fruit machine was all aglow, lights blinked on its neon front, the buttons persistently flashed.

"Perhaps someone could unplug that." The caller asked impatiently.

One of the staff complied. The machine fell into darkness.

"Finally." The caller moaned, "All right, let's try this again, all the sixes, sixty..."

The music played out loudly. Everyone turned to look as the machine, still unplugged, flashed with colour and played its jingly-jangly tune. A woman sitting on a table next to it swore and hastily vacated her seat.

"Left over power?" The caller asked the gathered players.

The machine sang in jolliness. People began to look worried.

"We could try playing with the noise." The caller looked desperately at his audience.

"Better do something or this house will never be won!" Someone called back.

There were mutterings of agreement and the game progressed despite the perpetual noise of the fruit machine in the background, it sang all the way through the full house and the next six games. At the interval it briefly stopped, only to start again when the game resumed. Despite that, Janice won £100.

"Not a bad night." She smiled at Doris, "Coming tomorrow?"

Doris was staring at the offending fruit machine that had once more ceased playing.

"Doris?"

"What? Oh, yes, might as well, Eddie's at his golf club meeting."

"Better luck then." Janice left her sister studying the seemingly powerless fruit machine.

Wednesday night and the fruit machine was back in the foyer.

"Made such a ruckus this afternoon." The man on the front desk told Doris as he took her entry money, "Wouldn't stop going off. Manager threatened to take a sledge hammer to it."

Doris made polite, interested noises before she managed to leave and buy her books. Janice was already seated when she found her.

"Fruit machine kept going off again," she told her as she sat down and undid her coat.

"Probably the mechanisms gone wrong." Janice said as she studied a sudoku book.

"I think it would still need electricity." Doris turned to face the door to the foyer, "I wonder if…

"Don't, you'll spook yourself."

They started playing at seven. Distantly they could hear the chiming, joyful melody of a fruit machine acting up, but it was too far in the background to disturb the game. Janice was one number off two lines when it was called. She cursed loudly.

"Never mind." Doris said soothingly.

She glanced over her shoulder at the banks of fruit machines. The hall seemed cold tonight.

The caller continued for the full house.

"One and two, number twel..." A sweet chiming sound interrupted him.

A few people glanced at the foyer but the fruit machine there was obediently quiet. The majority of people had turned to the banks of machines where lights were flashing. The bingo caller grimaced.

"Has someone been messing with them?" He laughed nervously.

Doris looked at Janice, eyebrows raised in a knowing look.

"Nonsense," Janice muttered and stared resolutely at her books.

The caller decided to carry on regardless, but no sooner had he started then all the fruit machines in the hall suddenly jangled, lighting up one after the other as though a surge had swept through them. Lights flashed, music sang and coins tumbled out of the dispensers. Several people jumped from their seats.

"I think we need to keep calm," the caller said into his microphone.

"Calm? The place is haunted!" A woman stood up dramatically in the middle of the room, "I am sensitive to these things and can feel there is a presence in the building."

"Oh please," Janice scoffed.

"There is a man," the woman continued. "He is trapped here. He died here. I feel he has lost something he desperately wants back…"

Yes, thank you," the caller quickly interrupted her, "But no one has died here."

"But they have!" Doris shouted without thinking.

"I think the lady is mistaken." The caller's voice echoed round the hall.

"Fred died here, the night before the refurbishment. You weren't here that night." Doris could feel Janice's eyes burning into her. "It was as they called the full house. Fred called out and then…"

"He never claimed his winnings!" the sensitive said triumphantly.

"The dead can't claim," the caller snapped.

The fruit machines jangled even louder and coins started scattering onto the floor.

"I sense he wants his winnings paid to his wife." The psychic was swaying slightly as she spoke.

"That's Melanie!" Doris called out enthusiastically.

The hall suddenly descended into chaos. The fruit machines rang noisily and players left while the management tried without success to unplug the machines.

"It's no good." One of the managers held a plug in his hand while the machine it was connected to continued to flash. "What do we do?"

"Pay the winnings." The assistant manager glared at the machines, "It wasn't a big house, better that then lose all the customers."

"You can't seriously…" The manager hesitated. "And if it doesn't work?"

The manager felt someone tap him on the shoulder, he looked round. Doris smiled at him.

42

"Would you like me to bring Melanie tomorrow?"
Around them the fruit machines suddenly fell silent.

The manager glanced at them, bemused.

"I suppose." He said, wondering what on earth he was doing.

Doris held Melanie's hand as they entered the hall.

"Friday evenings," Melanie muttered quietly. "Fred loved Fridays."

The manager was leaning against the foyer desk, clearly waiting for them.

"This is Melanie?" he asked.

"Mrs Shuttleworth," Melanie said primly.

"Well Mrs Shuttleworth, though this is rather against my better judgement, I'm here to hand you a cheque for your husband's full house winnings." He handed a signed cheque to Melanie.

Her hand shook a little as she took it.

"Thank you," she said softly.

"And on behalf of Best Bingo, I can inform you that all your books tonight will be free." The manager half smiled. "Enjoy."

He turned and left with a sigh. Melanie held the cheque in her hands and stared at it.

"Come on, its cold by the door." Doris gave her friend a gentle shove.

Melanie walked forward staring at the bright lights and fruit machines as though for the very first time. She pressed the cheque to her chest.

As they passed the fruit machine that had first caused the problem it lit up temptingly.

"Fred's favourite." Melanie was becoming tearful.

The machine chimed and then without warning the barrels started to whirl. The barrels tumbled and the pictures started to line up.

"A bell, two bells, and..." Doris' voice trailed off as the machine finished with a line of bells.

Lights flared, a loud, cheerful tune played out and money flowed like water from the machine and poured onto Melanie's feet.

"Oh Fred!" Melanie sobbed and the money kept pouring.

Doris rubbed her back comfortingly.

"Wish my Eddie would be as thoughtful as that." She grinned.

Sophie Jackson

Sophie Jackson has worked as a freelance writer since 2003 specialising in historical non-fiction. She has three books to her name, *The Curse of Dasenin, The Medieval Christmas* and *The Horse in Myth and Legend.* She is currently working on a book for The History Press on POWs held in Britain during the war.

Gentleman George

"So you're interested in working lunchtimes, plus a couple of evenings a week?"

Heather glanced towards the polished wooden bar. Everything looked and felt so right. Beer pumps stood proudly as if to attention. Sunlight reflecting off coloured bottles on the shelf behind gave the appearance of a stained glass window. On first impressions, at least, the place seemed everything a village pub should be. Not only that, but she'd taken to Jean on sight. Slightly buxom, without being matronly, the landlady had an air of steady patience and understanding of human nature doubtless accumulated over the years, and seemed the sort of person Heather could be comfortable working with.

"Definitely. My youngest child's just started school, you see, and this would fit round them."

"Of course," Jean nodded approvingly. "I remember those days well. And you've recently moved into the village, so that's convenient. Before we take matters further, though, it's only fair you should know something, since it has put a few people off..."

"They're having you on," Steve reassured her when she told him that night. "Practically every pub's supposed to be haunted. It's good for business. Sounds to me more like dodgy electrics and forgetful staff. Anyway, the hours suit and the extra money will come in handy. You'll be fine."

"Don't worry, George is quite harmless," Jean had reassured her. "Well, that's who we think the ghost is. He used to be the landlord here, back in the late forties, early fifties. Ran the place for a good while, I believe, and seems to have been well liked. We think he's just keeping an eye on things. He's certainly never given Dan and me any trouble, and we've been here for six years now." She paused. "Well, not real trouble, as such, though he can be a bit mischievous. Sometimes you'll put something down and find it in a different place a few minutes later. And he likes playing around with the lights. If they do flicker, just say 'Hello George', and he'll be happy."

Despite what Steve said, Heather felt sure that the old stone building, with its solid wooden beams and massive open fireplaces, was just the sort of place you'd expect to have its own resident spook. In the stillness before opening time, she could almost feel the weight of so many lives lived there, so many friendships cemented, and trysts made and broken. The very walls seemed to speak of them. If there had to be a ghost, she supposed, better a benign former landlord keeping an eye on things than some headless horseman or betrayed lover.

Yet the thought still made her nervous, especially as he seemed to be checking on her from day one. Even as Jean was showing her where everything was, the lights started to flicker.

"Say 'Hello, George'," Jean reminded her.

"Hello George." Heather smiled in what she hoped was a friendly manner, though she couldn't help feeling it looked more like a kind of hideous grin. They flickered once more, then stopped.

A few minutes later, when she was filling the ice bucket, there was distinctly cold draught, and not just from the freezer.

"Hello, George," she said again, trying not to let her voice tremble. "I'm just getting some ice, ready for the customers' drinks."

Thankfully, the draught disappeared, presumably satisfied she was doing her job.

"Now, there's no need to worry about complicated orders," Jean explained. "Men mainly have lager or shandy, while the ladies go mostly for fruit juice or diet coke. Watch out for the local ladies' guild on Wednesdays, though. They like their wine, so make sure you have a few bottles of the cabernet handy. George gets distinctly frisky when they're round, the old flirt," she added. "Some of them are just as bad, even the ones in their eighties. Perhaps there is something in the idea that red wine is good for you, after all."

Even though Heather had done some bar work as a student, that had been a long time ago, so it was all a bit nerve-racking at first, trying to remember where everything was and fathom out the working of the till, which seemed to have a mind of its own. Luckily, most of the locals were friendly and patient and she soon got into her stride, feeling able to cope when Jean popped into the kitchen to sort out some food orders.

Judging from the lack of flickering lights and cold draughts, George must have been reasonably happy with her attempts on her first day.

Sam and Amy were all agog for news when Heather collected them from the school playground afterwards.

"Did anyone get drunk and start a fight?" asked Sam, with all the worldly wisdom and bravado of his eight years. He sized up the trees as they walked along, doubtless working out which ones were best for climbing. His uncle Carl had taught him to climb during the holidays, and since then he'd been eyeing up every likely specimen for its potential. Only last week he'd announced his intention to be a famous stunt man when he grew up, and Heather had had to keep checking on him out of the kitchen window every time he went near the garden shed

47

and gazed speculatively at its roof. Thankfully the ladders were safely locked in the garage.

No, they did not," she replied now. "It's not that kind of place, and I dread to think where you got such ideas from."

"Bo-ring," Sam moaned. Even little Amy looked distinctly underwhelmed.

Once she'd settled into her new job and gained some confidence, Heather enjoyed herself and soon began to feel at home. It was surprisingly satisfying, getting a drink just right – especially shandies, with their tendency to froth all over the place if you weren't careful.

She liked the customers, too. Most of them enjoyed a chat in the cosy atmosphere, whether they were just passing through, had escaped from town for a quick snack during their lunch break, or were locals meeting up for a social hour or two. She found out more about the village in the space of a few weeks than she would have expected to over several years. She still felt nervous of George, though, especially when the ice tongs clattered to the floor after she could have sworn she'd left them well in from the edge.

A few of the older regulars remembered him.

"He was a good bloke," Charlie Jackson said. "A real gentleman, firm but fair. The beer was always in good condition, the fire always lit in winter, and this bar was polished till it shone like a mirror. He insisted he should be able to see his face in it."

"I've heard that, too," agreed Dan, stooping slightly to avoid bumping his head on the low doorway as he brought in extra stock from the cellar.

"What did he look like?" asked Heather.

"Well, he wasn't what you'd call a pretty face. His nose was too big and red, for a start. But he always dressed smartly, in a jacket and tie, and kept his hair combed back – what there was of it. It was funny, really."

"In what way?" Seeing Fred Barrington coming through the door, Heather started pouring his pint of Guinness ready for him, giving herself plenty of time to get the right amount of "head".

"Well, he soon sorted out any trouble-makers, make no mistake about that, and yet he was very quiet-spoken. And he was terrified of his wife, even though she was a good foot shorter than him. We used to say he should change the name of the place to *George and the Dragon.*" Charlie took several long gulps of his drink. "She over-heard us one day and gave us a right filthy look, I can tell you – *Whoa!* Hang on, George. I was only joking."

The lights suddenly started flickering frantically. At the same moment, a chill descended. It took all Heather's willpower not to run outside. Even Dan looked alarmed.

"You want to get those electrics checked," someone called from across the room.

"We have, loads of times," Jean retorted as she ap-peared from round the corner. "There's a phone call for you," she told Heather in a quieter voice. "From the school."

As if in response, a glass toppled off one of the shelves, smashing on the floor and making everyone jump.

Heather was still shivering as she stepped out of the car, even though she was wearing a scarf loaned by Jean and had already pulled her coat more tightly round her.

"Thanks again for driving me here," she said.

"No problem," Dan replied. "I had to head up this way for the cash and carry anyway, and Jean can cope. Just so long as your lad's all right. Are you sure you don't want me to come in with you?"

49

Apart from muttering about the traffic as he'd driven, grim-featured and cutting between lanes to save time, they were the first words he'd spoken since setting off. Even if he had said anything, Heather's throat was so tight for most of the journey, she wouldn't have been able to reply.

"It's your son," the school secretary had said on the phone. Heather could have sworn she detected a hint of disapproval. "There's been an accident. We've called an ambulance and they're taking him to the Royal Infirmary now."

Within minutes, she had phoned her neighbour to collect Amy after school and contacted Steve, while Dan got the car started and was waiting for her by the door.

These places always made her nervous. Even the smell of disinfectant instilled a sense of foreboding. All sorts of terrible images flashed through her mind and her heart pounded as she approached the desk. Thankfully, the receptionist directed her and eventually she found her way to where Sam was sitting on a narrow bed, pale and drawn but at least still in one piece – apart from the fact that his right wrist was in a sling.

"Sam!" She ran towards him. One of the classroom assistants from the school was there, together with a young doctor. "What on earth happened?"

"Hi Mum." His face broke into a grin which disappeared as he glanced at the doctor. "I was climbing one of the trees at the edge of the playground. I was doing really well, too, until the stupid branch went and broke."

"Oh, Sam. How many times have I told you...?"

"It's all right, Mum. A man caught me, so I hardly got hurt at all."

"He's been extremely lucky," the doctor put in, sternly. "He fell from quite a height, apparently. It's a miracle he got away with a badly sprained wrist. We've also checked for concussion," he went on, "since he insists on repeating this cock and bull story, when no-one else saw anyone, but he seems fine. It looks like his imagination is as lively as his taste for danger."

"There *was* a man," Sam interrupted. "Honest." He looked pleadingly at Heather. "You believe me, don't you, Mum?"

"We'll talk about it later," she smiled.

The doctor gave her a look as if he also suspected her of possessing an over-active imagination, but apparently decided to leave the subject alone.

"Anyway," he sighed, suddenly looking weary. "I think we can safely discharge the little horror, so long as he promises not to indulge in any further daredevil activities. Otherwise he'll end up in here again, and next time he might not escape so lightly."

"I promise," Sam answered in a small voice.

Chance would be a fine thing, thought Heather. She resolved to give him a very stern talking to once she got him home. It wouldn't be the first time, and probably not the last.

"I'm sorry, Mum," said Sam once they were in the cafeteria, waiting for Steve – who was already on his way – to pick them up. "I hope I didn't cause too much trouble."

She shook her head sadly and ruffled his hair. "You really are going to have to be more careful."

"I know. That's what he told me."

"The doctor?"

"No, the man who caught me. Like I told you."

Heather paused, coffee cup half way to her lips, as the significance of what he had said sank in.

"What did this man look like?"

Sam frowned. "Dunno. At first I thought he was a teacher, because he wore a jacket and tie, but he'd never be heard over our class. Oh, and he had a big nose. When I looked again, he was gone, and no-one believed me."

Heather racked her brains to think of when she might have told Sam about George, or even hinted that the pub might be haunted. She was certain she hadn't, mainly through being careful not to frighten Amy, who only had to watch a few minutes of Doctor Who to have trouble sleeping.

"Oh, I think I know one or two people who who'll understand," she replied, half to herself. Glancing across the room, she saw Steve walking towards them, relief written all over his face.

"Come on," she said, gathering their things. "Dad's here."

As they walked out of the main entrance, Heather slowed down and let the others go on ahead. Good manners demanded some sort of response, she felt, and anyway it was time to make her peace.

"Thanks, George," she whispered. "You truly are a real gentleman. I promise I won't be frightened of you any more. In fact, tomorrow, I'll give that bar an extra good polish, especially for you."

Was it her imagination, or did the lights flicker, just once, before the automatic doors swished shut behind her?

Rebecca Holmes

Rebecca Holmes' short stories regularly appear in women's and general interest magazines and anthologies. She is currently working on her first novel but keeps being distracted by too many ideas and wishes she could invent a way to write more quickly.

Until the Sands Run Out

Do houses soak up the things that happen in them, do you think, storing them away and then letting them slip like fragments of an old person's memory into an atmosphere that you can feel from the time you first walk in the door? I used to think that you could tell when a house had been filled with laughter and sunshine. I used to believe that I'd know if a house had seen awful deeds – that misery and pain would seep from the walls and the floors like ghosts of the past. But that was before we moved into number 37 Wilshaw Drive.

Wilshaw Drive used to be the *nice* part of town. It's a wide, tree-lined street, full of large, old houses set back from the road in their own sprawling gardens. Like grand old ladies sitting around the sunroom of a nursing home, these houses doze in the afternoon's warmth. The mortar might be crumbling and the paint beginning to peel, but there's still the echo of faded elegance.

Most of the houses have been converted into flats, or care homes now, but it's still an expensive place to live, so Adam and I couldn't believe our luck when we saw the advert for a one bedroomed flat on the second floor of number 37. The rent seemed ridiculously low. We were sure it must be a mistake, but the agent confirmed it. The last tenants had left very suddenly and Miss Carmichael, the old lady who owned the house, wanted to let it again as soon as possible. The only condition was that the tenants had to be a young married couple. Well, we certainly did fit that bill. Adam and I had only been married for six months and he was 24, I was 23. Miss Carmichael, the agent told us as he showed us the flat, lived on the ground floor and liked to have young people around her.

There were a couple of damp patches in the corners and the floorboards creaked a bit in places, but I fell in love with the way the sun came in through the bay window in the lounge and with the quirky beams and slanting ceiling in the bedroom. It felt like home if you know what I mean. And it was handy for the station, which was good, because Adam's new job meant he'd be travelling more often to begin with.

We moved in on a Saturday morning in April. Daffodils nodded in the sunshine and the air was full of the scent of hyacinths. Adam's eyes were as sparkling and blue as the spring sky and the air tasted as crisp and fresh as green apples. We were giddy with laughter and the promise of new beginnings. He whisper-kissed the freckles on the cheekbone just below the corner of my left eye as we stood at the bottom of the stairs – something that he knows always makes me shiver with desire for some reason.

"Should I carry you up and over the threshold Mrs Wright," he said softly, his eyes teasing and yet creased around the edges with that look that made the breath catch in my throat and my body lean instinctively into his.

"Ey, we'll have none of that then. Folks'll think you're in love or summat."

We jumped at the sound of the smiling voice. A small, plump woman in her fifties stood in the open doorway on one side of the hallway. Her once dark hair was softened with grey and gently permed and her body was all curves and no angles. Her eyes were velvet brown and her face rosy from the heat of the kitchen. She was as soft and warm and welcoming as a comfortable chair by the fire and she didn't look at all like a Miss Carmichael should look. Adam obviously felt the same.

"Miss Carmichael?" he said, putting out his hand.

"No, love," she laughed, shaking his hand anyway. "I'm Betty Siddall. Call me Betty. Miss Carmichael lives across the way there. I 'do' for her – look after her like. And you must be Lucy and Adam. She's been looking forward to you two moving in. Come on, I've just brewed. I'll make up a tray and we'll take you across to meet her."

She stepped across the hallway and tapped on the door opposite her own.

"Miss Carmichael," she called cheerily, "visitors!"

She opened the door and ushered us into the room.

"Miss Carmichael, this is Lucy and Adam," she said, "and I'll be back in two ticks with the tea."

Miss Carmichael looked up from her book and smiled.

"Do come in, my dears," she said, "I've been hearing your activity all morning and I've been quite longing to meet you. Forgive me if I don't get up; I don't move too well at the moment. Oh, Betty dear, would you turn the fire up a notch before you go? It's a trifle chilly in here still."

To me, the room seemed suffocatingly warm – and dim, with the curtains partly closed. Miss Carmichael sat in a high-backed wing chair by the gas fire with a tartan rug over her knees. Her hair was white and coiled in a neat bun at the nape of her long neck. Her skin had that translucent quality that comes with great age, like a light shining behind blue tinged paper. Her back was still straight, her dark eyes were keen and the way she sat in her chair reminded me of a queen on a throne.

"Come, my dear, sit by me." She motioned me to the corner of the small sofa nearest to her and held out her hand as I sat down. For a weird moment, I thought she meant for me to kiss it, but she just grasped my hand in both of hers. Her hands were cool and dry but I felt as if my hand was trying to slip out of hers for some reason, so I smiled extra warmly.

"So, you are Lucy," she said. "I'm a Lucy too, you know. Lucinda Carmichael."

I couldn't imagine anyone ever calling her anything but Miss Carmichael, so I just nodded and smiled.

"Did you never marry then, Miss Carmichael?" asked Adam, and I wondered how he dared! Miss Carmichael stiffened and turned slowly to look at him and I was afraid that he'd offended her. But then she relaxed and smiled almost coyly at him, a smile that sat very strangely on such a proud, fierce face.

"Indeed no, Adam. Although I was once very much in love. You have something of the look of him in fact. There he is, my Laurence," she nodded over to the portrait that hung above the hearth. "Flight Lieutenant Laurence Armstrong. We were secretly engaged to be married in the summer of 1943."

I went over to look at the portrait. It was of two people dancing, his arm clasped around her waist as if he never wanted to let go, and her hand resting trustingly on his shoulder. The man wore a grey-blue uniform. The woman wore a dark red ball gown. She had dark hair, swept back into an elegant chignon and there were rubies in her ears. The couple looked at one another as if no one else existed in the world. Miss Carmichael had been very beautiful then, and her lieutenant very handsome, but a wistful, yearning quality in the portrait brought a lump to my throat. They danced in a large, empty room. The only furniture in the painting was a grandfather clock. While the colours in the rest of the painting had faded over time, the wood of the clock glowed a rich walnut-brown still. Instead of a face, the clock had an hourglass, with the sands running down.

"Why didn't you marry him, Miss Carmichael," I asked, surprised at my own daring.

"My parents didn't think he was good enough for me," she said flatly. "I don't think that would have stopped me in the end, but, of course, there was the war. He died in 1943, two weeks after we got engaged."

"I'm sorry. I didn't mean to bring back sad memories."

"Not at all, my dear. They're some of my best memories. And we're still together. Until the sands run out."

I thought that was so romantic, but Adam rolled his eyes. I could see him thinking: *maybe she's a sandwich short of a picnic after all.* But even if she was, she still caught the look. We were rescued from an awkward moment by a noise in the hallway. A loud crash and the sound of crockery shattering, followed by a shrill voice:

"Watch out, you stupid cow. God, you've ruined me best top."

We rushed to open the door. Betty stood amid the wreckage of the tea tray, looking on the verge of tears. A couple, about our own age, were brushing drops of tea and cake from the leopard print top the girl was wearing. Its shoestring straps strained alarmingly as they both brushed at her ample chest. Below the leopard print and above the low-slung belt that held up her tight, white cropped jeans was a strip of improbably tanned midriff, with just a hint of the roll of fat that the years ahead would bring if she weren't careful. A white zip-up short top with a faux fur collar completed the outfit.

"Oh leave it alone, Darren," she said, irritably slapping her boyfriend's hands away. She pushed her streaked blonde hair away from her face and turned to Betty.

57

"You've ruined it you have. You'll have to pay for it. It weren't cheap y'know." She noticed Adam and me then. "And what do you think you're lookin' at. Come on Darren!"

She turned and flounced up the stairs. The unfortunate Darren gave us an apologetic grin.

"Watcha mate," he said, "you must be the new people upstairs. I'm Darren and that was Tanya. Don't mind her, daft cow. Good to meet you. We'll have to pop round for a beer, say hello like, when you've settled in a bit."

"We'll look forward to it," grinned Adam.

We helped Betty to clean up the mess.

"Poor Miss Carmichael," she said. "She's not been lucky with her tenants. Most of them don't seem to last long. Just up and go one night, without paying the rent. Or they bring trouble, like Tanya and Darren there. We've had the police round," she continued in a low voice, "asking if we knew anything about stolen goods. Not my cup of tea, to be honest. But they do pay the rent on time, I'll say that for them. Oh, thank you love," she smiled gratefully at Adam, "just pop all the big bits on the tray and I'll hoover the rest up in a minute. You get off now. You two must have loads to do still."

We did. The next few weeks seemed to fly by as we settled more and more comfortably into our new home. Tanya and Darren turned out not to be too bad, as long as we ignored the odd loud argument late in the evening and the slightly dodgy friends that we sometimes met on the stairs. I noticed one of these friends eyeing the lovely old silver in Miss Carmichael's room through the open door one day and worried that they might be planning to rob her.

"Don't you worry, my dear," she said, when I told her I thought she should keep her door locked. "I'm quite able to protect myself still."

We were sat in her warm, dim room having tea. With Adam being away so much during the week, I'd taken to having tea with Miss Carmichael or with Betty when I got home from the school where I taught.

"Of course, if Laurence had lived things would have been very different, but I had to learn to take care of myself after he died and then my parents six months later."

"Oh, I'm so sorry, how awful for you. Was that the war as well?"

"No, no they died in a car crash. But it was a long time ago, and things generally happen for a reason, don't they? Now tell me," she said, obviously wanting to change the subject, "what of your family, and Adam's?"

"Well, Adam was brought up in children's and foster homes, so he never really had a family. My dad left when I was little and my mum brought me up. She was great. It was always, you know, the two of us against the world. But then she died a few years ago. So now it's just me and Adam."

"You poor child. So, you have known great sadness too. Like Laurence and me. And you're all alone now, both of you. Never mind – it couldn't be more perfect now, could it?" She patted my knee with what almost seemed like satisfaction.

I looked at the portrait of Miss Carmichael and Laurence dancing. It was so sad – just the two of them fading away in that empty room, with the sands of time running out behind them. Adam and I *were* lucky to have each other. Then, with a little prickle of unease making me shiver, I looked again. I would almost swear that the sands in the hourglass were lower than before. I gave myself a mental shake. Too much imagination, just like Adam always said.

The next day, sitting in Betty's comfortable, cheery kitchen, I thought of Miss Carmichael and Laurence again, as I looked at all Betty's photos of her children and grandchildren.

"What happened to Miss Carmichael's Laurence, Betty?" I asked. "Was he shot down?"

"Lieutenant Armstrong? No, love – he hanged himself. Well, so they decided at any rate. It was big news at the time, I believe, with people saying he'd been murdered. There was even talk that Miss Carmichael's parents did it, to stop him marrying their Lucinda."

"You're joking!"

But she wasn't. I was so intrigued I went upstairs to the computer and searched for the story on the internet. Sure enough, the story of Flight Lieutenant Laurence Armstrong's death had captured newspaper readers' interest for many months. And it was weirder than I could ever have imagined. In the first reports, his death was seen as a tragic suicide. Then there was speculation that it might have been murder, with the Carmichaels the most likely suspects. Then, most bizarrely of all, came talk of witchcraft and black magic. Scandal grew, and with it the fantastic nature of the stories. 'Carmichaels lead secret coven' screamed the headline of one article, adding that black magic paraphernalia had been found somewhere near Wilshaw Drive. 'Did witches murder daughter's secret fiancé?' asked another, linking the poor Carmichaels with a coven that apparently included every rich or successful person in town. And the centre of all these dreadful activities was supposed to be no 37 Wilshaw Drive. Then, chillingly, came their own unexplained death, driving over the cliffs in their new car.

"There's no wonder Miss Carmichael became a recluse," I told Adam about it later that night, when he returned for the weekend. "Can you imagine it: the man you love hangs himself, and then, as if that wasn't bad enough, your parents are as good as accused of murdering him and hounded by the press until they commit suicide."

"You reckon it was suicide then? It could have been an accident, I suppose – new car, different handling. Creepy though, to think what might have happened here, in this very house."

His eyes widened and he stalked towards me in his best Boris Karloff impersonation and since we hadn't seen one another all week you don't need too much imagination to guess that what happened next took my mind off Miss Carmichael and her story for a while.

I returned to it the next time I had tea with Betty though, when I told her all the details I'd got from the internet.

"That's right," she said slowly, "I'd forgotten about the black magic stuff." She laughed softly. "No wonder my mum was upset when she found out I was coming to work here. Do you know, now that you've mentioned it I can remember them talking about it, my mum and my aunties, when I was little. We'd all get together for Saturday tea and they used to love to gossip about juicy stuff that had happened in the town." She thought for a moment. "There was supposed to be some kind of a foreign doctor involved in it with the Carmichaels. I think it was my Aunty Alice who said she'd heard as how he'd discovered a way of beating death. This doctor could bring souls back to them that loved 'em with his black magic. All to do with sacrifices, it was supposed to be." She shivered. "My mum sent us kids out of the room to play then, so I don't know what else she said. Still, even if you believed that rubbish, it didn't do the poor Carmichaels any good did it?"

I thought about that when I next sat with Miss Carmichael. She was distracted today, looking old and tired. Her hand shook slightly as she lifted the bone china teacup to her lips, which, I noticed, had a blue tinge.

"I'm sorry, my dear, I'm not very good company today. I think the time is almost upon us."

"Time for what, Miss Carmichael?"

"Hmm? Oh, nothing my dear. Just thinking aloud. Thinking about Laurence."

She looked at the portrait and my eyes followed hers. I thought that the figures looked even fainter, almost insubstantial. Then I noticed the hourglass clock. I was sure the sands were lower than before. I blinked a couple of times to clear my eyes. You'd think with the number of times I'd sat in the room and looked at the picture I'd be able to remember where the sands in the hourglass were. I would have to ask Adam when he came home for the weekend. I went over to have a closer look. For the first time I noticed the signature at the bottom of the painting. Ivan Simarov. I'd never heard of him.

"Who was he, Miss Carmichael, the man who painted the portrait?"

"Professor Simarov? He was a friend of my parents. A Russian émigré. I think he was a little in love with me. He gave me the painting just after Laurence's death."

She looked at the painting, her eyes half shuttered and a curious little smile on her lips.

"It became very important to me, my painting. My parents couldn't understand that at first. But they did, in the end."

The heat of the room, and maybe the fumes from the gas fire, were making my heart beat a little harder and my palms felt clammy. Suddenly I wanted to be out of there.

"I'm sorry, Miss Carmichael. I have to go. Adam comes home tomorrow and I need to go shopping for the weekend. Can I get you anything?"

"No, thank you my dear. But please, won't you and Adam come to dinner with me tomorrow evening. It's high time, I think."

"We couldn't possibly put you to so much trouble."

"Not at all." She waved my hesitation away. "I insist. We need some youth and vigour around, Laurence and I."

She laughed, as if to say she was joking about Laurence. I still felt strangely reluctant, but I couldn't think of a graceful way of saying no, not after all her little kindnesses to us since we'd moved in. So, I agreed and went upstairs with a slightly troubled step and the beginnings of a headache.

My headache got much worse as the evening wore on, which is probably why I forgot to tell Adam about Miss Carmichael's dinner invitation when we spoke on the phone that night. It was still there through the next day, pounding my head and making me feel sick and dizzy, so I was in no mood for a fight when he got home. Unfortunately, however, that's what happened. I told him about Miss Carmichael's invitation to dinner. He reminded me that he'd agreed ages ago to meet up with some old friends in the pub. I said my head was in no shape to go to the pub anyway, so we'd meet our friends some other time. He said it was typical that I'd put my arrangements first and I should cancel Miss Carmichael. I said I wasn't going to disappoint an old woman, who was also our landlady. He said I was selfish. I said he was just as selfish and insensitive to boot... well, you get the picture.

After he'd slammed out of the flat to go to the pub, I sat and cried for a while, which didn't do my headache any good. Then I decided to hell with him. I washed my face and brushed my hair and went downstairs. I knocked on Miss Carmichael's door.

"Come in, my dears, it's open."

I walked in. The room was dark, lit only by fat cream candles and the flicker of the gas fire. The table was set for three, with a thick lace tablecloth. Heavy cut glass goblets already held three glasses of a wine so dark it looked thick and almost purple. A heady, musky smell made my headache pound so hard my eyes blurred.

Miss Carmichael wore red taffeta with a cashmere shawl. She looked frail and fragile, like a girl dressed up in her mother's finery. Her eyes searched behind me.

"Where's Adam?" she asked.

I started to explain, but she stopped me after the first few words.

"He's not coming?" There was nothing fragile about her voice. It was like flint. She drew breath. A sudden breeze from the window slammed the door shut behind me and made the candles dance insanely. Even the fire seemed to shrink back away from her.

"No, that cannot be," she spat out each word. "It must be both of you."

Now she was really scaring me. Her eyes gleamed red in the glow of the firelight on her dress. Suddenly, she stopped, as if listening. She looked at the painting above the fireplace.

Then, in a switch so sudden it left me wondering if I'd imagined the last 30 seconds, the old Miss Carmichael was back.

"I'm sorry to hear that, my dear," she said sweetly, "but perhaps some other time, then. There's always another time."

She began to usher me out of the room and I was very glad to go. I don't know what made me look back, at the painting, but I do know what I saw. And I didn't imagine it, no matter what Adam says. The figures of Miss Carmichael and Laurence Armstrong were so faint they were almost gone – and the sands in the hourglass had almost run out.

Later that evening, as I nursed my aching head and waited for Adam to come home, I heard Tanya and Darren clatter past on the stairs.

"But Darren, I don't wanna go," whined Tanya's shrill voice. "Who does she think she is, anyway, the old bag? Inviting us to dinner at the last minute as if she thought we'd have nothing better to do."

"Quiet, you stupid friggin' cow. It's the perfect chance to get a look at the old girl's place. Now shut it, and act nice."

Their voices faded, still arguing, as they thumped down the stairs. Miss Carmichael must have invited them to dinner in place of Adam and me. I wished them the joy of it.

Adam came back before too long and we made up. So thoroughly and enjoyably, in fact, that we hardly stirred from the flat until it was time to go to work again on Monday morning. Which meant it was Monday afternoon before I saw Miss Carmichael again. She called me in for tea as if nothing untoward had happened between us.

What a difference the weekend had made. The flat smelt bright and fresh, and Miss Carmichael looked somehow years younger. Her eyes were bright, her hand was steady and she was walking around with almost a dance in her step. Her skin had lost its blue tinge and looked quite rosy again.

"How are you, my dear?" she asked, as Betty put out the tea things.

"I'm fine, Miss Carmichael. You look very well too."

"She does, doesn't she," chipped in Betty, "and why she should I don't know, when that Darren and Tanya have run off without paying the rent. Disappeared on Saturday night, they did. I knew they were trouble. We've had the police round again, asking about them and their dodgy friends."

"Never mind Betty," said Miss Carmichael, regarding me steadily over her teacup. "Things could be worse."

She looked at the portrait above the fireplace and smiled. Slowly, disbelievingly, I realised that the figures in the painting were brightly coloured and distinct again. And with mounting horror, I realised that the sands in the hourglass were full.

"Yes, my dear," Miss Carmichael nodded, "you and Adam will just have to come to dinner some other time. There will always be another time."

Carol Croxton

Carol Croxton lives with husband, Andrew, and dog, Meg, in North Wales, in a place where the mountains meet the sea, and from where she draws daily inspiration for stories that contain a touch of magic, myth and mystery. She is currently working on her first fantasy novel for children/young adults.

Hamelin

There is nothing for us in Hamelin now. In the quiet patter of the rainy night on the shingles of the roof, Elizabeth and I are leaving our new home behind.

Elizabeth is expecting a child. He would have been our second. She stands watching me load up the car, her hands behind her back. Her lips are drawn together in a grimly patient way that I know very well. She has stood by me faithfully in my recent madness, and believes we are leaving for the sake of my health; but it is to protect her and our child that we are departing tonight.

I know what it is like, to be with a woman who has lost a son. The long weeks of ice and numbness, of sleeplessness at midnight and torpor in the stuffy air of day. The suffocating, crushing ache of it. It must not happen to us again.

* * *

The village seemed so perfect when we first saw its neat little rows of modern houses and its tree-lined walkways. The pavements of Hamelin were cleaner than any I had seen since my childhood. We bought our new home from a rosy-faced couple called Becker. They weren't much older than me, the pair of them; the first signs of a child on the way were beginning to show around Frau Becker's belly. Elizabeth couldn't stop smiling as they showed us round a spacious living room, a wide bright conservatory and an airy kitchen thick with the fragrance of fresh gingerbread. I had missed that smile. Before we left that afternoon I had already worked out which corner would house the piano.

It was only after a couple of weeks in our new home that we became aware of something amiss. Not just the

67

loose shingle on the roof, or the stain on the living room carpet, but something in the atmosphere, in the leafy rustle of the garden and the quiet buzz of neighbours passing to and fro. Something missing.

It was Elizabeth who noticed it first. My own hectic life beyond our home – the bustle of concerts to prepare for, the relentless schedule of rehearsals and the to-and-fro of the daily commute – left me at first with the notion that Hamelin was all dawns and dusks. That clean, peach-tinted sunlight so coloured my vision that for awhile I noticed little else of the village beyond our front doorstep.

Elizabeth had endured inactivity for too long already. Her itch to be back at work again was what triggered our first discovery. There was no school in Hamelin; the nearest was ten miles away, in the city. So Elizabeth telephoned the local newspaper, to place an advert offering private tuition – only to be informed that there was no need for any such service in Hamelin, thank you very much.

There were no children in Hamelin.

I had missed it at first. Hamelin was quiet, but it wasn't uncommon these days for the attractions of the city to draw young families away from the villages. Elizabeth and I were unusual; we preferred seclusion, though there was a reason for our preference. But for there not to be one individual in the whole village below the age of eighteen was clearly abnormal.

Our usually friendly neighbours, the Friedmanns, became icy when we asked them where the children were. At first we found ourselves choked with embarrassment, assuming that they, like us, must have suffered a recent loss. But there were no clues to suggest that the Friedmanns had *ever* had children: no family photographs in the living room, no children's books on the shelves. Every household in Hamelin, as far as we could tell, seemed to be the same.

Yet there was evidence, when we looked for it hard enough, that there *had* been children here, once. Not far from us, in an untended patch of greenery, I uncovered the rusted frame of a swing and the remnants of a roundabout, buried under a mound of convolvulus. I found the school too, eventually, or what used to be the school: a ramshackle shell of a place, hidden behind high grey boarding and rimmed with barbed wire. It was easy enough to slip in through a loose board in the fence, cross the potholed playground, and enter the building through the empty maw of a doorway, into a darkness that reeked of mildew and ammonia. Half believing that the spectres of Hamelin's forgotten children were peering at me through broken classroom windows, I didn't linger. A lone magpie on the high board fence fixed me with a knowing stare as I departed, and rattled a jeer after my retreating back as I hastened homeward.

He was not the first magpie to have followed me about. There was another who used to perch on our garden fence and listen to me rehearsing in the conservatory, where I had the benefit of plentiful light and space. Appropriately, it was the *Thieving Magpie* overture which first drew the creature there. As my flute picked out the familiar theme – *diddle-ee daah, dah dee, diddle-ee daah, dah dee* – he would cock his head on one side and I'd catch a knowing glint in his little black eye.

"Was this written for you, old fellow?" I smiled as the bird flew down to draw closer to the music. "I'd better get it note-perfect, hadn't I?"

The night after my visit to the wreckage of the school, I was awoken by the sound of tapping at our bedroom window. Elizabeth stirred but immediately settled back to sleep. A shiver shot through me, though, and instantly I was bolt upright, clear-headed, and very cold. Heart thumping, I crept out of bed in the dark and pulled back the curtain only to see – nothing. The wind swaying the silhouettes of trees beyond our back garden fence, outlined in the glow of the street lights, that's all. I was naked, and I realised that I was covered in cold sweat.

Disturbed dreams followed this incident. I awoke next morning with a ferocious headache. Dimly, I recalled dreaming I was being chased down the corridors of that abandoned school by someone or some*thing*, in a patchwork robe of black and white that flapped like a magpie's wings.

I couldn't play that day. My fingers and tongue were like clay. My flute wasn't producing music, just a fumbling, strangled imitation of it. The magpie on the fence watched, cocking his head at me as if he had been to blame for disturbing my night's sleep.

The next night, it happened again. Once more, Elizabeth slept through the incident; once more I found myself, naked and sweating, tearing back the curtains on an empty night sky. The night after, I went to bed as usual, but secreted a torch under my pillow. It was almost a relief when the tapping came at last. My torch revealed nothing. A vague hint of something white, a bird perhaps, disappearing into the trees; that was all.

I slept on the sofa downstairs the next night, much to Elizabeth's annoyance. Fragments of the music I was failing to learn kept drifting through my head. At 02.36 (so the clock on the VCR informed me) I was wide awake. There was somebody else in the room.

I saw nothing; but in the darkness I could smell him, a damp, musty smell like the corridors of the derelict school. I wanted to cry out, but my mouth was dry and there seemed to be a knot in my throat. I thought of Elizabeth upstairs, defenceless. Somehow I managed to muster up the strength and spit to scream out, a feeble attempt to frighten away the intruder. The noise broke from my mouth as a ragged yelp; the blood pounded in my temples as if it were about to explode from them; then I must have passed out. When I came to, the clock on the VCR said 02.41, and Elizabeth was standing over me, her face furrowed in concern. There was nobody else in the house; all the doors and windows were locked, exactly as I had left them.

The next morning, I found that my flute, which had been packed neatly away in its case the evening before, had been removed and assembled in the night. I also found a single feather on the living room carpet. A shiny, black and white, magpie's feather.

* * *

I began to fear that I was losing my mind. I no longer trusted Hamelin, with its clean streets and its secrets.

I sought out a psychiatrist in the city. Naturally, she assumed I was suffering from unresolved trauma. The tapping at the window, the presence in the room, and the ubiquitous magpies – all these were manifestations of my grief and longing for the son we had lost, nothing more. I wanted to believe she was right.

I fancied that I was being followed, that a shape in black and white patchwork robes was waiting for me in doorways and around corners. I imagined I could hear music: the echo of the *Thieving Magpie, diddle-ee daah, dah dee,* from behind the hedge in our garden or around the corners of the green walkway.

Elizabeth believed I was having a breakdown. To protect her, I was on the sofa every night now, keeping watch, though often nothing worse would occur than a half-asleep, restless dream. Other nights he would be there, whoever he was: not saying anything, but waiting, with that damp ammoniacal smell about him.

I grew accustomed to his presence, little by little.

*   *   *

I discovered who he was, in the end. The records in the Hamelin village archive had been destroyed in a fire, but I tracked down enough newspaper clippings in the city library to piece together part of the story. Frau Becker knew the rest; and when eventually she agreed to come back to Hamelin and tell me the story, I realised why she and her husband had turned their backs on the home they had made here.

There had been a circus performer ten years ago, a gypsy, who had a certain way with animals. He could charm them all, as easily as some men can charm a lady. The aldermen of Hamelin had paid him to clear the town of rats, and this he had done, ensuring clean and vermin-free streets for years to come. But these were not the only vermin spirited away when the circus performer played his flute in the streets of Hamelin. The corrupt councillor, accused of taking bribes, had gone too. So had the drug dealer who loitered at the school gates, and the former scoutmaster who had molested five young boys in his care.

At first the people of Hamelin delighted in their clean and shameless streets, and the man who had brought them what they wanted. But soon they became fearful of him. Nobody ever discovered what became of those he bewitched.

The day a seventeen-year-old girl went missing, the fear of the villagers turned to hate. They turned on the piper, broke his flute into pieces, broke his back with their stones and sticks, and threw him in the river. Nobody was ever prosecuted for the murder. The gypsy's body floated away and was never recovered. He had been a vagrant, with no family, so there was nobody to search for him.

How it was that the children vanished, no one was ever quite sure. Some accounts told of mysterious music piping through the streets in the small hours of the morning: *diddle-ee daah, dah dee, diddle-ee daah, dah dee*. All that is known for certain is that the children left their beds in the middle of the night, and were never seen again. Since then, nobody has dared bring a child to Hamelin. Those who conceive, leave, as the Beckers had done before us. As we must do now we too have a child to protect.

There are many in Hamelin who cannot leave. The aldermen and the village folk, still bound together by their shameful conspiracy, are growing old. In time the school will crumble into ruins and the people too will crumble, their story forgotten. But Elizabeth and I must leave Hamelin to its fate. We have lost one child already, and cannot allow the piper to claim our second, however patiently he waits.

I do not think Elizabeth understands. She believes I am out of my mind, so she accepts we should leave, before I do myself or her a mischief. We get into the car in silence, start the engine, and pull away.

I glance backwards and notice the magpie, perched upon the street light outside our house: his wings slightly unfurled, his head half cocked in salute. Hamelin is his once more.

A. J. Humphrey

73

A.J. Humphrey is a widely published poet and winner of numerous poetry awards, including five First Prizes in national competitions. His short stories have been published in *Dark Tales*, *Scribble* and previous anthologies from Bridge House and Earlyworks Press. He works as a research scientist and lives in York.

Growing Pains

The changes in her body were already taking place before Jeff left. She noticed her elbow joints were knobbly and there was a small protuberance from her left shoulder. The skeletal projections were put down to a loss of weight. Usually her figure was soft and rounded – it was this that first attracted Edward, then Dean. And it was partly her efforts to eradicate their memory that accelerated her transformation.

She worked as a temp. Her spelling was good and her legs were shapely. Her temporary employers all appreciated that. In her spare time she gardened, growing plants from seed, clambering up trees to prune their branches, slicing the tops of shrubs to titillate their growth. There was a vine that grew round the windows of her house. The more she hacked at the intrusive tendrils, the more they multiplied and clambered up her walls. On occasion, they appeared to be waving to her, even when there was no wind.

She was, by nature, a quiet woman, someone who observed, composted the world around her. This was surprising, as she was pretty with long fair hair and eyes, green, the colour of submerged pond plants. Her face was moon-shaped and her mouth wide. Only by sucking in her cheeks and painting them with blusher could she define her cheek bones. Rarely did she bother. Her faraway expression was one of her ways of dealing with the wandering eyes of her temporary employers, as they observed the curve of her breasts and her comely legs. And it was common for them to believe that because she was temping, she was somehow available as a plaything, that could be discarded, and therefore treated with an element of disrespect. They thought of her as a worker bee, flitting between sources of nectar, extracting pleasure when she saw fit. And in a sense they were right. Several men had passed through her life. None of them had hung around for long. Recently there was Edward from the accounts section of a car-leasing company where she worked as a receptionist. He was a man of extraordinary height. A calculator was a permanent fixture in his top pocket and he was proud of his ability to work out square roots in his head. But there was a problem. His feet smelled. What's more they remained odorous, no matter what. Kneeling to wash them, like some devoted disciple, she failed to dislodge the aroma of foreign cheeses and boiled eggs. All attempts with peppermint foot spray failed. His feet were, as he pointed out, so far from the rest of his body, he was barely aware of their existence.

"Actually," he said. "You know we have a lot in common. For one…" he began to count on his fingers, "we both work in the same office, and secondly you have a caring streak in you and third, I love to be cared for."

"I am no carer," she said. "You've got the wrong idea."

"Perhaps we could have a holiday together. What about Spain? I'll pay. You choose." He stooped and kissed her on the top of his head. "We could even live together. With my connections, I could sort out a mortgage deal."

"I don't want any of that," she said. "I have a fear of settling down, of establishing roots in one place."

Eventually Edward left; manoeuvring his great frame through her doorway, traumatised by her efforts to cleanse his feet. She was up a ladder chopping the vine when he left.

"You're hard," he called out "You have no feelings. Not woman-like.".

After his presence was exorcised, with the help of open windows, sweet-smelling hyacinths and aromatic

76

herb essences, she was moved, by her temping agency, to an estate agent where she spent her time typing up adjectival descriptions of mews cottages and loft conversions.

A senior estate agent, called Dean, regarded her legs, took in her air of independence, and thought her ripe for an extra-marital affair. Dean was a disappointed man, who had discovered too late and with huge debts, that a red sports car and a detached house in a wealthy suburb of London didn't constitute happiness. In her, he thought he would find respite and a woman who would soak up his sorrows. She sat him opposite her in her kitchen, gave him coffee, grown in a small farm in Columbia, and biscuits made from organic flour. She was attracted to him, but knew that it was merely physical. Unusually for a woman, she was able to distinguish between lust and love. It was this that Dean found appealing. And he imagined that it was he, who was falling in love with her, his temporary P.A. He wept and told her of his frustration with the demands of the material world and his greedy wife. Ushering Dean out of her house, she promised she would see him the next day. They both knew she was lying.

After that, she decided to keep herself to herself, for a while at least. Pottering round the garden during the autumn, she cleared away the dead branches fallen from her fruit trees. The travelling vine had doubled in size and was busy exploring the eves. Cutting it back proved harder work than before: the stems tried to wind themselves round her waist.

"You're being awkward," she told it. "You've got a will of your own. I'll have to chop you down."

But she couldn't slice through the stem. It was coarse, would not give, and she was forced to give in to it, to allow the vine to win. Instead, she mowed the lawn, planted daffodils, ready for the spring. As she leant against a sycamore tree that was older than her Victorian house, she put her hands on the trunk to support herself. A splinter pricked her finger.

In her kitchen, she ran her finger under the cold tap, then tried to pluck out the shard. A red circle stained her white hands, where, unknown to her, the tip of the splinter, like the tail of an Australian bush tic, was still lodged, settling under her skin.

As a temp, it was easy for her to take unpaid holidays, to stay at home while everyone else stampeded to the tube or bus stop. Her garden slumbered in the autumn afterglow. The ivy developed suckers, rampant and eager, that prised apart the brick work. A north-easterly wind blew and gardening became an ordeal. A new obsession, jam-making, took over from her work in the garden. The volcanic bubbling of sugar, damsons and raspberries reminded her of the cascades and ripples, the simmering, the boiling eruptions of pleasures she'd shared with the various men she had taken to her bed. The jams were bottled, sealed, labelled, using the names of her ex-lovers, then lined up in descending alphabetical order. The last jam represented a lover, younger than her, a man who was so riotously happy, he made her feel like an outcast, a woman who'd never comprehend the joy of being in love. And reading all the names over, she recalled their pleadings, their declarations of adoration. Hardened by a disparate childhood spent in caravans with her itinerant father (a forester who worshipped the Norwegian spruce), she'd turned them all away.

The wind tore round her house. It moaned and whistled, rattling the jars of jam on the shelf. Next to them, hanging from a hook, dangled multi-coloured beads, feathers rescued from marshes and mud flats, and dried herbs picked from some nearby woods. When a gust forced the door open, the beads rattled while the feathers floated away into the garden. A feral cat howled on her lawn, its cry harmonising with the song of the wind. And it was during this stage in her life that she first became aware of a heaviness in her legs. Ignoring it, she decided instead to return to work. She emerged from her place of safety.

Her agency sent her on a week's placement to a solicitors' partnership. This office was located in a shiny new block with wall-size mirrors in the reception. Footsteps echoed across the marble floor. Voices bounced. Sprinkles of laughter trickled through the murmurs of Monday morning chatter. She sat on a vast black sofa and waited for instructions. She fidgeted: crossed, uncrossed her legs. A woman wearing a snug-fitting black suit clip-clopped across the floor towards her, led her to the lift. A manicured nail pressed the sixth floor button for the top of the building.

"I'll leave you to get on," the woman said when they reached a door at the end of the corridor.

The boss was in court. There was no one to instruct her in her tasks. The morning was spent washing a sink full of dirty mugs, dusting the desk, straightening piles of files, answering his phone. The furniture was minimalist. and the lack of greenery, of living objects, unsettled her, brought about an uneasiness exaggerated by the view from the plate-glass window of similar tower blocks that hid the sky and gave a feeling of swaying, or reeling on a ship, as she peered down to the ground below. A clock on the wall had no numerals, no marks even where they should be. The hands clicked and vibrated on the face. At twelve o'clock she decided to have an early lunch.

Sitting on a park bench in the wind, in the cold of the approaching winter, she snuggled into her coat, shook out the crumbs from her sandwich to the nodding pigeons squabbling at her feet. Jeff sat next to her. Of course she didn't know his name until he sat down, until they'd both waited a few minutes. She was aware of him at about fifty yards. A figure in the distance watching her drink coffee from a polystyrene cup. When he sat on the bench next to her, she averted her eyes, took to studying her finger where the splinter still remained, busy making a home. He moved closer.

"You should drink coffee from a bone china cup," he said. "You have earth in your soul."

She crunched the polystyrene cup and chucked it into the bin. There was half a sandwich spare. She gave this to Jeff. They chatted for a while, as suited men strode to meetings, their ties dancing in the breeze.

"I don't live that far from here," she eventually said.

"Are you ready for this?" he asked. "The changes may be irreversible, you won't be able to go back." He touched her face and the sound of pigeons cooing, the chatter of the workers out for lunch, disappeared, vanished into a vacuum.

They made love in her bedroom with the ivy creeping in through the window. The suckers planted themselves on the wall where the window had been built one hundred and twenty years ago. They made love frequently. The phone rang. She let it pass to her answer phone. She didn't want to return to an office where computers hummed in place of people. When his mobile rang, he switched it off, chucked it across the room. Sometimes their love-making was fierce, a struggle, with cries that could be interpreted as pain. Other times it was soft and harmonious, gentle, like the flowers blooming in her garden.

"We are one," she said. And she asked him the question asked by a million other women of their lovers. Never before had she felt the need to know.

"Of course I do," Jeff said and kissed the length of her body.

They remained locked in each others arms for four days and four nights. They lived on nutty granary bread spread thickly with her homemade jam. The first two jars were consumed: Andy, the lemon marmalade, then Charlie the loganberry jam. She thought she was ridding herself of her past and the lovers who'd misunderstood her bid for freedom. The third jar was Edward, the enormous accountant with the offending feet. He was a tart strawberry jam with pips that were large and chewy. Quite fond of him, she layered an extra helping of jam on her bread. They consumed the bread and jam in between their embraces. Crumbs and sticky jam mixed with their entangled limbs, the secretion of their bodily fluids. Outside, the traffic roared, children sped past on their skateboards, cats fought in the alley. So cocooned were she and Jeff in their own world, they heard nothing. They weren't aware of the vine growing, obscuring the light from the window. Post piled up on the door mat. The bread was getting low.

They talked about their childhoods, their past affairs, their dreams for the future. They gave each other pet names, discreet, childish, ones that no one else would ever know. He was a pavement artist, and had perfected, over the years, accurate copies of Botticelli's Venus. On a good day, he could earn one hundred euros from the chalky replicas.

"My mother was like a sea mist," she said when he'd told her about his. "She appeared, disappeared, returned and vanished. I never knew where she went or why."

She'd never talked like this to the lovers whose ghosts she'd bottled in jars. Reassurance, comfort, these were needs she'd not possessed before. Once she clung to

Jeff so tight, he struggled free and sat on the edge of the bed for a minute.

"Sorry," she said. "I don't want to suffocate you."

Sometimes, when Jeff went to the bathroom, or especially to the kitchen to make more coffee, glutinous with sugar and tinned milk, she imagined he'd gone, left her forever, disappeared into the night. Carefully, she tiptoed to the top of the stairs, listening out for his footsteps back along the hall, the tread of his feet on the lower step of the stairs, not towards the front door as she feared. It was, as she listened out for him, the first time she felt the lump on her shoulder sticking out like a door knob. She said nothing to Jeff as he caressed her face, her neck, but was aware of him hesitating as he slid his hand over the swelling.

By this time, five days had passed. The phone-messaging service had expired from the nagging calls of her staff agency, and between them they'd munched their way through several loaves and eight jars of jam. There was no more bread and the coffee had run out.

"We need milk and coffee," he said. "And champagne to celebrate" Stuffing his mobile phone in his pocket, he left with her order for a Vietnamese take-away. An inkling of an idea formed in her mind then, that perhaps he would never return. Begging him not to leave her, she dropped to her knees as she had for Edward to wash his feet. He lifted her, gently onto the bed and ran down the stairs, closing the door softly behind him. She looked around her bedroom. Like the remnants of a battle fought over territory, there was chaos. The sheets were bundled to her side of the bed, the pillows and duvet to the other. Plates with crusts of curling toast with dollops of jam were strewn across the floor like shells from a cannon, or mutilated bodies across the conflict zone. There was quiet in the house. A sense of normality had resumed. The ivy dropped away from the bedroom and once again took up its position outside the kitchen window below.

She lay amongst the debris for a while before she went down to her kitchen and retrieved two fluted champagne glasses left to her by a great-aunt she'd never met. Two plates, knives and forks were laid side by side, so their arms would touch as they ate. She sat down and waited for the return of Jeff. There was a quarter of the jam left on the shelf. She ate the contents of a damson jam with a silver teaspoon straight from the jar. The jam was labelled Dean, after the senior estate agent, and was smooth, jelly-like, and slipped down her throat with ease.

Perhaps Jeff was trying to phone her. Was the Vietnamese restaurant closed? But he didn't have her phone number. Dreams ran before her eyes. She pictured him returning, arms laden, promises and stories of his search for the perfect dinner, the best champagne available for them to share in her bed.

She waited and waited, sitting at the kitchen table for hours. The day passed. Night fell. Hunger no longer knocked at her ribs. The ivy rapped on the window pane. Her fruit trees nodded. Mouldy apples, worm-ridden pears lay untouched, uncollected at the trunk bases. The feral cats rummaged elsewhere. They knew the signs, recognised the change that was taking place in the one hundred and twenty year old house.

Next day he still hadn't returned. She put her hand to the lump on her shoulder. It had grown, pushing at the surface of her skin as if desperate to escape from the cosiness of her body. As the days passed a veil came across her eyes and she found it difficult to focus on the jam jars on the shelf. It was harder for her to move. Her legs were stiff, the joints elongated and gnarled. When the phone rang, it sounded muffled, far away, and though she thought she should answer it, the idea came slowly, crawling across her mind. Too late, the ringing stopped. With difficulty, she turned her head to attempt to look out of the window. The vine was curled at the tips, with a creeper that sprawled up the wall. It seemed to her to be trying to break in through the window pane as it pressed itself up against the glass.

Her attempt to stand was agony; it was as if she was fastened to an instrument of torture. But she discovered that after she'd raised herself to an upright position, the pain subsided, as did the sensation of stretching and pulling. Once she was standing, she found she couldn't move her feet. Looking down, trying to see through the mist that now almost entirely concealed her vision, she realised there was moss at the roots of her feet. Different varieties, some soft, like velvet, or bristly and sharp; and a rare kind that had self-seeded from the shores of Norway, were establishing themselves, fastening their tiny roots onto hers. For what seemed like an eternity, she tried to move an arm until eventually, it forced itself, despite her attempt to resist, into a position at right angles to her body. The splinter from the sycamore was by now drifting up her veins like a twig caught up in a river current and was heading for her heart. Half way through its journey, it stopped and attached itself to an artery.

Dust gathered on the jars of jam and air seeped in through pinholes. While her trunk expanded to a wide girth, tracking time with rings, her roots grew, reaching, spreading underground. Mould gathered on the surface of the jam, devouring the fruit, the pectin and sugar. The ringing of the telephone continued everyday. Unheard, unanswered by her, the agency gave up, recorded her as unavailable in their spreadsheet and told all the solicitors, the estate agents, the car-leasing companies, that they were sorry, but that unreliability was part of the nature of temps.

Light was what she yearned for most now. Light to complete the transformation and to help her grow. Glass shattered on the kitchen table as the vine pressed and forced its way into the kitchen. Her branch stretched out to touch its suckers. They became entwined like lovers. Together, they reached out, high and distant, towards the faint glow of the sun. By now, her other arm was reaching out towards the shelf of jam. The tip of the branch was green with buds bursting down its length.

The days grew shorter. Snow began to fall. By now, her sight was nearly gone. Only outlines, dark and light, were visible, and the jars, the labels now illegible, were indistinguishable, each retreating to hide in the shadows. An isolation, a realisation of her immortality came suddenly, with a howling moon. On the nights when the frost spread up her branches, when it gripped the core of her trunk, she was frightened.

Then the spring came and with it a pair of swallows. They nested in the crook of a branch, where her breast had been. Her sense of survival fought for its place, a great thirst and a need for sunlight consumed her. Growing tall – taller than the room where she'd first taken root – became the instinctual object of her existence. She burst her way up through the ceiling, into the bedroom where she'd lain with Jeff. But there was no recall of the time she'd shared with him. By now she had neither a sense of being and no memory. And by the end of the spring, he'd moved back to his pavement art in Florence., her memory still vivid in his mind.

The next winter was worse. Ice sheets formed on the rivers, and frost turned the ground into iron. Birds dropped from the sky, unable to fly, their wings frozen, rigid like their stuffed counterparts that sat in museums with glass eyes. Her trunk turned spongy with a sickness brought by winds from the far north deserts that tore across the continent. Disease ate away at her bark; it peeled from her trunk like the skin of a snake and lay curled at her roots. Branches decayed, hanging like broken arms. The vine tightened its grip round the trunk and on the shelf above the beads, ice formed on the mouldy jam and the dried herbs turned to dust.

The spring rains brought a thaw. Builders began to take on work, repairing, renewing the houses in her district. Many were from Eastern Europe with plans for a new life here.

Their task was to gut the house, build it anew, modern fresh and gleaming.

They stared at the tree, at the vine that encircled its trunk. Orange fungus dotted the roots, the branches were splitting and bare, the trunk was stripped of its outer skin.

The youngest one walked round it. "There's a new bud on that branch," he said. He'd just moved over here and shared a maisonette with his work mates. A tiny patch of grass lay to the back of their house. In his country, he lived with his girlfriend in a grey apartment bloc surrounded by concrete.

From the tree, he unwound the ivy. He plucked the green shoot from the tree, took a jam jar from the shelf. After he'd washed the jar out, he placed the cutting in some water.

It took a day and a half for the builders to hack the tree down and pull out the roots. They used a chain saw to attack the vine. It shrank from them, replanted itself in a garden across the road. The workers stopped their toil to rest.

"You hear that hissing?" the youngest one said.

Her spirit joined with the wind and scattered leaves round the kitchen. It perched on the young builder's shoulder and murmured into his ear.

"I saw a feral cat through the window yesterday. Probably that," one of the others said.

The youngest builder knew what the whisperings were., His hand was shaking as he pushed the hair from his eyes. "I have to rest some more," he said.

"We must get rid of it," the other one said He picked up an axe and cut deep into the trunk. "This is a stubborn tree."

The tree oozed green liquid as they cut it down. They built a fire in the garden and the youngest used his strength to split the wood into logs. The tree burnt slowly, it sizzled and spat. And sparks from the fire caught on the young builder's clothes. He ran to the tap, his breath catching in his chest. Her mutterings grew louder, so loud, he put his hands to his ears and he screamed for her to stop.

"You've stolen my soul," she hissed. "You shouldn't have done that."

"No," he cried. "Take it back." He put his hand to his shoulder and felt, beneath the folds of his shirt, a small protuberance starting to grow.

Amanda Sington-Williams

Amanda Sington-Williams writes poetry, short stories and novels. Her poetry has been read on BBC radio and her short stories selected for readings at The Komedia in Brighton. Her first novel, *The Eloquence of Desire* is due to be published by Sparkling Books in 2010. She won an award for this novel from The Royal Literary Fund.

www.amandasingtonwilliams.co.uk

On a Hundred Other Nights

People think I'm a genius, but I'm really not. I only seem so smart because everyone else is so stupid. Hey, I admitted I wasn't a genius but I didn't say I wasn't arrogant.

I'm clever, but my strength is that I see things others miss; obvious, staring you in the face things that most people wouldn't notice even if they were slapping them in the face and screaming at them.

So, that's me. Smart but not as clever as people think, arrogant, but deservedly so, and yes, quite sarcastic. I'm difficult to live with (as my exes will testify) and to work with – hence I work alone. I'm also good at what I do, which is why Nicholas Baker – not his real name – hired me to investigate strange occurrences in a place I'm calling Weathermeade. I'm not going to tell you where these events really happened. The last thing those people need are ghoulish tourists.

So why write this down if it's all fake names and made up locations? Simple, I need to tell someone. I need to because most nights I sleep badly, and sometimes I barely sleep at all because of what happened at Weathermeade Leisure Centre.

I know what you're thinking, a haunted leisure centre? It's true though, not every haunted house is centuries old, nor necessarily even a house.

People assume that ghosts have to have been around for centuries. It's hard to imagine one that's only existed for five minutes, or a week. Ghosts are old, faded photographs of times past… at least that's what our heads tell us.

But if you accept the reality of ghosts, then you must also accept the logic that the ghostly Roman soldier still seen marching two thousand years after death, was likely seen marching only a year after death, perhaps only a day.

Still, before heading to Weathermeade I looked into the history of the site. I don't like to rule anything out, and I figured something had to have been there before the leisure centre, maybe there was something obvious lodged in a newspaper somewhere.

By the time I reached Weathermeade I wasn't much wiser.

It's an anonymous little town that fell into decline long before the colliery closed in 1987, and though the local economy has recently begun to pick up, the streets I drove through seemed grim. Lots of houses were boarded up, and there were for sale signs outside many others. The town was the antithesis of a hive of activity, and aside from a couple of women with pushchairs and a few glum smokers outside a pub, I barely saw any signs of life.

By the time I reached my destination I already felt like I'd passed a hundred haunted buildings, a thousand ghosts, but if I was expecting another dark and rundown edifice I was sorely mistaken.

The building was two stories high, a rounded art deco rectangle, all muted yellow bricks and tinted glass. Still it managed to look desolate. Maybe it was because it looked so out of place, or maybe it was because the car park was empty, save for my Volkswagen and a Mercedes in the distance. In truth my imagination was probably ahead of my reason. I'd been told it was haunted, ergo I imagined it looked haunted.

Something told me to turn around and go home. A feeling I often get when approaching a site for the first time, though it felt stronger than usual. In hindsight I should have listened...

The forecast had said rain, but so far the downpour had held off. I grabbed my battered leather satchel and stepped out of the car.

The sound of the door slamming echoed like a gunshot around the car park, and I turned fast on my heels as a cacophony of shrieks sounded behind me.

A flock of blackbirds rose up from a nearby tree, leaving shaking branches in their wake. I shook my head, embarrassed at just how fast my heart was pumping. *Very spooky*, I thought.

Another door slammed shut, but there were no more birds to startle and, for the moment, my nerves had settled. I walked over to the man stood beside the Mercedes, the car grey as the clouds above.

I was expecting him to be grey too, a middle-aged, middle manager, but Nicholas Baker turned out to be an eager young whippet of a man in a sharp suit. I'm no slouch, but he managed to make me feel like a scruffy old man in my jeans and sweatshirt. Go-getters make me nervous; no one should be that eager about anything except a woman or a pint.

"Mr Hawks?" he asked, hand thrusting forwards like a knife.

I shook his hand "It's Trevor."

"Call me Nick," he smiled. "We should get inside before it starts raining."

"There's no one else here?" I asked as we reached the glass doors and he began unlocking them.

The lock turned, but he didn't open the doors. "No, I sent everyone home at four because I knew you were coming."

It wasn't quite four thirty. "I see your staff don't dawdle when it comes to going home."

"They used to," he said before opening the doors.

We stepped inside. I'd been expected a telltale beeping to begin as we did so, but it was noticeable by its absence. "You don't have burglar alarm?"

90

"We have an alarm, just no point setting it these days." He shrugged. "Nobody's going to try breaking in." He disappeared behind the reception desk. A moment later the lights burst into life, illuminating the main foyer. It was what you'd expect. Tables and chairs; machines dispensing junk food, and a weighing machine. Irony was in abundance in this temple of fitness. No skeletons though, no white sheets…

"You're surprisingly calm," I said when he rejoined me. "When we spoke yesterday I got the impression that you didn't like to be alone here."

"I'm not alone," he joked. "Besides, nothing ever happens till later."

Later, when I'd be alone.

We retired to the staff kitchen upstairs to talk further. The room was cramped, but probably sufficed for quick lunches and tea breaks. He made us coffees and we both sat down. I'd put my satchel on the table, and now I removed a notepad and pencil.

"No Dictaphone?"

I shook my head. "Sometimes the happenings I encounter play havoc with electrics. Nobody and nothing can mess with this," and I tapped the pencil against the notepad.

"So where do I begin?"

"Well, first I'd like to know the origins of this place. I don't mean to pry but it seems…"

Nick smiled. "More upmarket than you'd expect from a council facility?" I nodded. "Weathermeade's had a lean few decades," he began, "but in the last few years industry has returned. One of the firms involved in the regeneration offered to pay for this place; Community relations and all that."

"So, when did the haunting start?" I asked.

He winced at the word. "It began a week before we opened... no, that's not true; it probably happened earlier. We had some itinerant builders working on the project; Poles mostly. A couple of them lived on site in a caravan, acted as security. Anyway, one morning they were gone. No warning, no forwarding address, they'd just up and left."

"Was that unusual?"

"Not at the time, builders came and went throughout the project. It was only once the ... *Occurrences* ... began that I started to wonder. Maybe they were scared off? That's what happened the week before we opened."

"Somebody quit because of the haunting?" I'd decided I rather enjoyed the way the word affected him.

He nodded. "A couple of locals, Brian and Steve Peacock – father and son – were contracted to do some finishing off on the building. They were working alone for several nights but then, quite suddenly, they quit. I tried to get an explanation from them but none was forthcoming."

"Have you spoken to them lately? Do you think they'd speak to me?"

"No I haven't seen much of them. Steve moved away shortly afterwards, got a job in Glasgow apparently. As for Brian... he won't talk about it, but from what I hear he's begun to drink heavily. I can't say I blame him."

"You've experienced it?"

His face went white. His eyes flickered to the wall clock. "Do you..." he hesitated "...want me to tell you about it?" His Adams apple bobbed nervously as he spoke.

I shook my head. "The less I know the better."

He looked relieved so I pressed on with my questioning. So far a dozen people had specifically encountered the haunting, but others had reported feelings of unease. I suspected much of that was psychosomatic.

"I'm amazed you opened, or that you've stayed open."

"It hasn't been easy, but if we'd put back the grand opening there would have been financial repercussions. As for keeping it open, the events in question occur at around eight pm. So far I've used staffing and health and safety issues as an excuse to close up at seven. We've drawn a lot of flak, but it was working ok until a week ago. That was when things started to happen during the daytime as well."

I raised an eyebrow. "The haunting has been experienced during the day?"

He frowned. "Not to the same degree, but..." he paused. "Probably easier if I show you. Need to give you the tour anyway."

We finished our drinks and then he led me out of the kitchen. Passing through an office we found ourselves in a gymnasium. Everything looked new and expensive, yet somehow the lack of people contrived to make the gleaming exercise machines look long abandoned.

Kitchen, office and gym took up roughly half the first floor. The other half comprised a mezzanine viewing gallery that looked down through the open floor to the swimming pool below. As we leaned over the glass barriers and looked down I frowned. I was beginning to understand what Nick had meant.

"Is the water supposed to be that colour?" I asked.

"Not really, no."

The water in the pool was brown, almost a rusty orange in hue.

"We clean and filter the water every morning, but by mid afternoon it's dirty again. We've checked the filters, increased the regularity of the cleaning, even changed the water completely. Nothing makes any difference."

Somewhere within me a thirteen year old was tempted to release a mouthful of spit and see it fall into the dark water below. I resisted. "Can't be good for business."

"It isn't. Right now we're only open mornings. Already rumours are rife about hygiene problems. We've even had the Health and Safety Executive in. They tested the water but found nothing unusual."

I turned and regarded him. "You realise I can't guarantee to clear this matter up, don't you? Some hauntings are ingrained in the very fabric of time itself, there's no real solution."

Nick nodded. "I understand, but frankly you're my last hope. With so many rumours flying around it won't be long before we're forced to close. Our benefactors are already considering writing the place off as a bad job. I've tried everything else, why not a ghost hunter?"

I don't like the title 'Ghost Hunter', but I didn't correct him. Instead I leaned back over the edge and stared thoughtfully at the murky water below.

"I'll see what I can do."

*   *   *

Nick showed me where the light switches were, and put the snack machines on free vend. I asked him to gather up what information he could on the Polish workers; names, acquaintances etc. It struck me there was a good chance they'd either been the first the spot the haunting, or else were the cause of it.

"Are you sure want to be alone here?" He said before he left.

"I've handled worse," I smiled. I'm an idiot sometimes.

The centre had wireless internet, so I set my laptop up in the foyer to continue my researches; Some people might have found it eerie, sitting there alone, the lighting insufficient to sweep the shadows from every corner of the room, but I felt fine.

By seven forty five my shoulders ached, my stomach felt decidedly queasy from too much junk food, and I was no further along in ascertaining whether the haunting pre-dated the construction of the centre.

As far as I could tell there'd been a factory here that had been knocked down in 1985; the site had then lain derelict for two decades. There were no records of ghostly activity, either before or after the demolition.

This didn't necessarily prove anything. People often don't report such happenings, and with the site being abandoned the haunting might have passed by without witnesses, until a load of builders turned up. In truth though, my suspicions were growing that the focal point for the haunting was more recent. Construction of the lei-sure centre had entailed long working hours. It was incon-ceivable that nobody had seen anything.

My thoughts kept returning to those Poles...

It was getting closer to eight, closer to the witching hour. I closed my laptop; in the process knocking an empty coke can off the table. I swore and dropped to my knees. Three hollow taps sounded out as it bounced across the floor.

I was reaching for the can when the fourth tap sounded. On my knees, fingers stretching towards the empty cylinder of aluminium, I froze. The can had been at rest when the fourth tap sounded.

Another tap, a muffled hammer blow perhaps? It had been warm inside the building, but suddenly I felt icy ten-drils slide along my spine. I stood and nervously turned around. I'd been facing towards the main doors, and now looked back towards the entrances to the changing rooms.

I checked my watch. Not quite eight.

Another knock. Even with the echo caused by the empty foyer I was certain that the sound was coming from the changing rooms. Some sixth sense made me reach inside my bag for my torch, and an instant later my precognition was rewarded when the lights went out.

As darkness fell, another knock sounded. The skin at the back of my neck prickled as if some invisible figure behind me was gently blowing at the base of my skull. I fought the impulse to run, and flicked on my torch.

The flashlight was a reliable tool, one that had never let me down, and it didn't now. As the spotlight illuminated the twin doors my breath caught in my throat.

The male changing room door was wide open.

With trepidation I walked towards it. Pausing at the threshold I peered inside, but couldn't see much. A sharp corner ensured the changing area couldn't be viewed from reception when the door was open.

I didn't shout and ask if anyone was there. It could have been someone playing a prank, or Nick come back early, but I knew it wasn't. I stepped cautiously inside, pausing at the bend. My heart was racing, but the adrenalin had kicked in now. This was my territory; I'd experienced things like this before. I stepped around the corner...

And the lights flared back into life, taking me by surprise. I saw movement, shadowy figures hovering in the distance. I held my ground though, blinking to help my eyes adjust, and slowly the room came back into sharp focus, and I turned my torch off.

White tiles covered the walls. Lockers lined each side of the room, and running down the centre were wooden benches. There was nothing out of the ordinary; I was alone. As open as I am to the unknown, I'm capable

96

of realising when what I've seen was just a visual trick, the shadowy figures had been caused by the lights kicking back in, I was sure of it.

There was nothing illusionary about the handful of knocks that sounded then though. It definitely sounded like someone with a hammer, and definitely originated from further inside the changing room. I moved to investigate.

To my right were three toilet cubicles; whilst to my left showerheads drooped from the wall like dead flowers. Ahead a shallow footbath led to another corridor running at right angles to the changing rooms. This led to the pool area.

I was level with the second cubicle now. I'd heard no more knocking, and I wondered if the haunting had run its course?

The cubicle door swung open fast, knocking me backwards. I stumbled but managed to keep my footing. Instinctively I retaliated, shoving the door back hard. Even as it slammed back into its frame I knew that whatever had caused it to spring open was no longer there. I saw no one, but I heard splashing water, and when I stepped forward I discovered fast fading ripples in the shallow pool.

Licking dry lips I stepped across the footbath. On the other side I had a choice; right towards the female changing room, left towards the pool.

I turned left.

It was an eerie sight. Light streamed down from the high ceiling, bouncing off the dirty water in the pool and creating twinkling reflections that glittered across the walls like dancing fairies.

As I walked towards the edge of the pool I swept my gaze around the cavernous space, but could see no sign of anything out of the ordinary… if you didn't count the water. If anything it had gotten dirtier, and orange scum floated atop the surface. It looked like a latrine, although all I could smell was chlorine.

Footsteps echoed behind me. I turned fast but no one was there. Suddenly another sound; coming from the pool. I spun back in time to see the water erupt as if someone had jumped in.

My heart was hammering in my chest now, my eyes saucer wide as I scanned the surface. Concentric circles blossomed outwards as the shockwave dissipated. Silently I began counting. Maybe it was ghost, but maybe it was just a prankster, and if no one broke the surface in the next thirty seconds I was going to have to risk going in. I'm not always the nicest of guys but I couldn't leave someone to drown.

The count had reached ten when it happened. The pool began to boil. First the water began to churn, then bubbles the size of fists began to burst on the surface, and I swore I saw steam rising up.

There'd been no smell until then, but now a fetid, unearthly stench seared my nostrils, and the sudden thought assailed me that I was in over my head; that the centre was home to a demon from hell itself.

Then the scream started.

It's hard to put into words how it sounded. It was the agonised cry of a child in pain, the haunting wail of the bereaved. It was a scream of utter torment.

The noise stuck me as surely as a hurricane, and I physically had to drop to my knees before I fell. The torch clattered to the floor as I clasped my hands over my ears. The act did little to reduce the volume of that terrible noise, but I found horrified distraction in the boiling pool. Was it my imagination, or was something rising from the depths?

The lights went out again, and I was suddenly cloaked in a dark, infinite void, with only that terrible, plaintive scream for company.

The scream... and whatever had been exiting the pool...

I was panic stricken, but not to the point of paralysis. Tearing my hands from my ears I began to scrabble around for the torch.

The scream was all around me, bouncing off the walls and amplifying with each passing second. My fingers touched wetness and I tried not to think about how filthy the water was. Finally I touched rubber, my torch! I was saved.

I flicked it on.

Nothing happened.

The thought of an eternity spent living inside of that scream finally tipped me over the edge, and I let out a cry born of fear; panic; desperation.

For a moment my own wail was lost within the storm, but then it began to break through as the banshee's lament faded, until the only scream that remained was my own.

The lights came back up, and the water was calm once more. Still it was a minute before I stemmed my own cries, and several minutes more that I remained on all fours, staring at the pool. For a while I didn't even notice that my torch was now shining bright.

Eventually I rose and staggered back the way I'd come, trembling as I passed the toilet doors. Nothing happened though. It was over.

I slumped back into my seat in the foyer. Only then did I check the time; eight ten. The haunting had lasted barely twenty minutes, though to me, trapped in that cold, dark scream, it had seemed like hours. My throat was dry, and I stared at the coke machine on the far wall. I was just about to stand when I looked down. My notebook lay on the table. The paper looked damp, and two words had been scrawled below my copious notes. The handwriting didn't remotely match mine.

Help me

Suddenly I wasn't thirsty any more.

*   *   *

Nick returned at nine to find me shaken, but imbued with adrenalin fuelled vigour that he found perplexing until I explained. I'd figured it out.

Despite everything, some part of my mind had remained dispassionate, observing events as if they were happening to someone else.

It seemed obvious now that the haunting was focused on the leisure centre, and hadn't existed before the place had been built. The words written in English seemed to preclude the spirit of a foreigner; Nick confirmed that the pool hadn't been filled until after those builders vanished.

Knowing this the solution was obvious, and the next day we visited Brian Peacock. The old man crumbled before our accusations like a sandcastle before the tide.

Steve wasn't in Glasgow; he was dead, buried behind an abandoned house nearby. All I'd had was a vague hypothesis that seemed logical; Brian was able to fill in the details.

Money was tight for both men, and so Brian had taken to using cleaning products that had sat in his workshop for years. One of these was terribly corrosive – outlawed nowadays.

During the night father and son had begun to argue, and it turned to blows. On a hundred other nights it would have come to nothing, but on that night Brian had knocked a bottle of the outdated fluid against his son, the liquid splashing all over Steve's chest, all over his face.

Panicked, and thinking only that it was corrosive, Steve had rushed to the pool and thrown himself in, hoping to wash the substance off. Instead the chemicals reacted with the water, worsening their effects.

Brian said Steve's agonised scream as he died was terrible, and had haunted him ever since. My skin crawled as I heard it again in my mind.

Steve's body was recovered. Though badly decomposed the coroner was able to determine the cause of death as heart failure from shock. Brian wasn't charged – anyone who looked into his eyes could see that the guilt was worst than any prison cell. Steve was buried once more, properly this time. As for the leisure centre, from the moment Brian confessed the haunting ceased, and the last time I checked the centre was open late every night, and there were no further reports of ghostly activity.

This just leaves me. Though the centre is no longer haunted, in a way I still am. Sometimes I wonder if I will ever forget that terrible scream. Has this helped, putting it down on paper?

Perhaps, if I can pass at least a few of my sleepless nights onto you…

Paul Reginald Starkey

Paul Starkey has spent the last decade pursuing his childhood dream of being a writer. His first novel, a post-apocalyptic horror story, was published this year. He's also written a time-travel thriller, and is currently working on his third novel, a haunted house story with a twist.

www.cityofcaves.me

Kindred Spirits

Make yourself a dress in your own colours.

Ellen sat up sleepily to write down the words. They puzzled her. If only she could remember more of the handwritten list Jim had shown her in her dream. He'd written down the things he wanted her to do for her birthday. There were about a dozen items. One was to go to a concert. Or was it an exhibition? She couldn't be sure. But there was no doubt about the dress. He'd read it out loud to her from his list, pointing to the words to make sure they stuck in her mind.

And then he'd shown her samples of shot taffeta in a range of gleaming evening colours. She remembered seeing delicately woven gold fabric. Fit for a princess, she thought. The kind of gossamer Cinderella had worn to the ball.

Was Jim playing fairy godmother to her? Rescuing her from the dreariness that'd become her everyday life?

There'd been a darkness since she'd lost him. Hard to define but always there, smothering the light. An envelope of sorrow that she wore, day and night.

She rubbed her eyes, hoping it'd help her wake up. And that's when she remembered the other puzzling thing about her dream. Jim had been wearing an evening suit. Jim, who never dressed up.

How handsome he'd looked. As though it was his wedding day.

And he'd looked much younger. About forty.

She couldn't recall him ever looking more handsome. Or more pleased to see her.

Even in her dream, she'd been surprised to see him.

He'd suddenly appeared when she was talking with her friend Linda. One moment she was listening to Linda

102

recounting a problem, the next, Jim was leaning on the counter, smiling at her.

Linda and her problems had flown out of her head.

Light-hearted, she'd looked into his loving face and then wrapped her arms around him. Nothing else existed at that moment.

He'd drawn her to him, as he always did. She'd felt the strength of his arms, and melted into his chest.

If only this moment could last, she'd thought. Being back in Jim's arms, feeling the love that always radiated from him.

She'd missed him terribly these past eighteen months.

And she was aware of all this while she was dreaming.

Somehow she was both in the dream, and looking on. Enjoying his embrace, but realizing he was gone. It only made it all the sweeter.

Which was why it was important to write down these words. They were evidently significant.

She fossicked about in her dressing table. She needed to find her diary. These words would only be lost if she wrote them on a scrap of paper. Like yesterday's to-do list that she didn't find till bedtime.

"I guess this is Jim's to-do list for me," she whispered, as she wrote the words. She added "concert?" underneath.

She looked at the photograph she kept by her bed. Jim was smiling at her, one daughter on each side.

"It was lovely to see you," she said very softly. She wondered whether his spirit was still in her room. For surely this had been a visit? And she'd only just woken up, so perhaps...

A half-smile played on her lips as she decided he might still be around.

"What would you say, Jim, if you were sitting up in bed beside me?"

Ellen smiled as she realized exactly what Jim would've said.

It must be nearly coffee time.

Good idea, she thought. *It'll clear my brain.* She still felt groggy with sleep.

She slipped her dressing gown on and padded into the kitchen.

On the shelf above her cupboards, the stovetop espresso gleamed back at her. Jim always wanted "real" coffee.

She ground the beans dreamily, inhaling the intoxicating rich aroma. It'd been a few weeks since she'd made the effort to have percolated coffee. She only made it for company these days.

Maybe she should change that? "Only the best for my Ellen," Jim had always said.

Tomorrow she'd make herself 'real' coffee again.

And every other tomorrow.

She hadn't been aware till now that this was something she'd allowed to slip.

Sitting up in bed a bit later, sipping the heady brew, Ellen felt a small cloud lifting from her mind.

The envelope had been slit open a fraction and a beam of light had been allowed in.

When she'd showered and dressed, she sprayed herself with 'Romance', his favourite perfume.

Another tentative step.

Another small beam of light.

The phone rang, dragging her back to reality.

Linda's voice sounded troubled. As it often did. "I need your advice on another problem," she began.

Ellen listened as her friend complained about a neighbour who'd heavily pruned a flowering vine that grew on their dividing fence.

Normally she'd allow Linda to talk herself out.

But today she didn't want the next hour to pass in the usual way. She felt herself diluting, the new light ebbing.

So she interrupted after five minutes.

"You should invite Tom in for a pot of tea and talk through your differences," she suggested. "Maybe he isn't aware of how you feel about this."

There was a shocked silence.

Before Linda could resume, Ellen added, "Must fly now. I'm going shopping this morning and want to catch the nine o'clock bus."

She'd decided on the spur of the moment to use some of Jim's superannuation on a new sewing machine. Something he'd often suggested. Her old machine had stood her in good stead over the years, but would need a major overhaul if she wanted it to do anything complicated. Like sewing an evening dress in the kind of fabric Jim had shown her. She'd baulked at the expense of repairing her old machine, and she'd shied away from learning how to use the new ones. Yet this wasn't the real Ellen, was it? The girl Jim had married all those years ago had been a spirited creature, willing to throw her heart at the world and laughing in the face of misfortune.

For a brief moment, as she walked into the sewing centre, Ellen felt a rekindling of that spirit. It was like glimpsing an old friend.

Then a sales girl approached and she felt defensive again.

These machines scared her.

105

"You'll want one of the computerized models." Michelle, according to her name tag, seemed alarmingly unaware of Ellen's love-hate relationship with technology.

"Nothing too complicated," Ellen began.

Michelle sat her down at a large table, in front of a small white plastic machine. It didn't seem nearly as sturdy as her machine at home.

"This is the one we sell to the local high school for home science classes," Michelle explained. "It's easy to learn how to use it, believe me. I used it at school last year myself." And she started pointing out the special buttonhole feature.

Ellen felt the blood rushing to her cheeks. These same school girls also knew how to create My Space identities, email photos to each other, and send text messages. It was unrealistic to compare her with this new generation.

"Is there a beginner's model?" Ellen asked. She flinched as she accidentally bit her bottom lip. How had she become so self-effacing and hesitant? She'd been a dressmaker for years. Till she'd married Jim.

Michelle patted her hand. It felt reassuring.

"I'll give you free lessons on whichever machine you choose," she said.

Ellen released a long gentle sigh. "Really? What if I need a dozen lessons? I'm not very good at anything computerized."

"It's just a matter of learning what to do," Michelle said. "I've taught my gran how to use this model. You couldn't be worse to teach than she was." As she smiled, Ellen noticed that she was wearing braces on her teeth.

It made her feel comfortable. Michelle wasn't perfect either. But she'd taken this step to improve herself. Ellen could make an effort too.

106

Linda was quite put out when Ellen knocked on her front door a few hours later. Her greying blonde hair could do with a cut, Ellen noticed. And there were dark mushrooms under her eyes. If she didn't worry so much, she might get a decent night's sleep.

Then she felt immediately hypocritical. She hadn't really taken very good care of herself either, had she? They'd been acting like a pair of misery bags. That's what Jim would've said.

Over a cup of tea, Linda poured cold water on Ellen's plans. "You should just ask for your money back," she said.

Ellen shrugged. She hadn't mentioned her dream, of course. "It'll be fun to sew again," she said. "I popped in to see if you wanted to come to the sewing classes with me. Michelle said she didn't mind."

A strange sound came from Linda. Ellen couldn't tell if it was a snort or a grunt. "She just wants my money too."

Ellen finished her tea and stood up. "The classes are at ten o'clock every morning. Ring me if you want to come tomorrow."

As she walked down the street she noticed Linda's next door neighbour. Tom was busy spraying his rose bushes. He looked up and waved to her. He seemed very friendly. Why was Linda always complaining about him?

I'll bet she didn't ask you in for a cuppa, Ellen thought.

One of Jim's sayings flashed through her mind. *You can lead a horse to water...*

Ellen felt a bit stronger. There was no need for her to take on any of her friend's despondency.

I'm even starting to dream about her telling me her problems, she realized.

107

To her surprise Linda decided to join her next morning – purely as a spectator, she insisted. By the end of the hour, Ellen was able to sew straight seams and to do buttonholes. The automatic needle-threader was proving difficult but as Michelle pointed out, she'd come a long way in a very short time.

After the lesson she and Linda decided to look at dress patterns and fabrics.

"Something mid-calf, I think," Ellen said, flicking the pattern book open at the tab *Cocktail and evening dresses.*

"You won't get much wear out of that, will you?" Linda said. "An everyday dress in a bright cotton would make more sense."

Ellen didn't answer. This wasn't about being sensible, was it? This was about finding herself. Wear "your own colours", Jim had said. She remembered how handsome he'd looked in the dark suit. She wanted to look her best too. That's what he wanted. She cast a careful eye over the styles. Nothing too short. Nothing too fussy.

And then she saw it. A gypsy style of dress, with a flowing mid-calf skirt, fitted bodice and waist, and a matching jacket. She felt like hugging herself. She'd look pretty in this dress. It was both elegant and fun.

She bought the pattern.

"It's not my place to tell you how to spend your money." If Linda wasn't sixty years old, Ellen would swear she sounded sulky.

"This would look lovely in rich coloured silk," Michelle said next morning. "You could look for cobalt or emerald, maybe shot with maroon."

"You don't think it's too young a style for me?" A few doubts had crept into Ellen's mind after Linda's lukewarm comments. "Mutton dressed as lamb?"

Michelle shook her head. "You've kept your figure. I think it'll really suit you."

And Ellen told her she was planning to go to a concert next month, on her birthday. She hadn't mentioned this to Linda. Her friend had stopped going out at night time since she lost her husband five years earlier, and would no doubt pour cold water over that idea too.

Ellen was planning to bide her time, and wait for the right moment to ask Linda to join her.

Michelle had an idea. "Why don't I help you find the right material?" she said. "It's time for my morning break. And I'll look for some for my gran at the same time."

In the third shop, Lady Luck smiled on them. There was a roll of exquisite shot silk for sale, heavily reduced. They both reached for it at the same time. Michelle held it up against Ellen and beamed. "It's perfect for both of you. You and my gran will look like twins. Would that matter?" Michelle's braces were dotted with lavender plastic, and her grin was contagious. Ellen felt years younger, beside such a light-hearted and generous creature. She'd be more than happy to look like Michelle's gran.

It was only as she lay in bed that night that Ellen remembered that Jim had called her his "gypsy princess" on their first date.

Where had these lovely memories been hiding?

Why had she slipped inside this dark unhappy envelope of despair since his death?

If she wasn't careful she'd turn into someone like Linda.

She put a small swathe of the fabric under her pillow, hoping she might have another dream about Jim.

But dreams aren't always made to order.

109

Besides, Jim would've said she was being very fanciful, she thought, as she ground beans for her coffee the following morning.

Make yourself a dress in your own colours.

So much good advice was in those few words. Jim must've seen her despondency and decided to entice back her fun-loving nature. Take his gypsy girl out of her comfort zone. Open her eyes again to the good things in life. Had he somehow known how she'd been dreading another birthday without him?

The day of the concert drew near. She'd bought tickets for a symphony orchestra performing Beethoven's Pastoral Symphony.

The day before, she took her dress in to show Michelle, and to get her help with some finishing touches.

Michelle was bursting with excitement. Her eyes shone as she carefully worked the delicate fastening on the back of the bodice. Then she noticed a slight shadow on Ellen's happiness.

"Is something the matter?" she asked.

"Linda's changed her mind about coming with me," Ellen said. "She doesn't think it's safe for two women our age to be out at night time."

Michelle shook her head. "Then why is she leaving you on your own, if she doesn't think you'll be safe?"

"I'm beginning to realize how negative she is," Ellen said. "I'll have a good time anyway. Maybe she'll come with me next time, when she realizes the bogey man didn't get me."

"That's the spirit." Michelle added, "You can lead a horse to water…"

Jim's words. And now Michelle's. Surely not a coincidence? It was as though he'd brought this young girl into Ellen's life as a breath of fresh air.

110

Ellen would make sure she was one of the horses smart enough to drink.

The orchestra were everything she'd hoped. Closing her eyes, she felt transported to another realm. Lifted out of herself into a fantasy of sublime sound. Her heart soared with the music.

When she opened her eyes, during a lull in the piece, she had to blink. Surely she was mistaken? Someone had sat down on the empty seat beside her. Someone in a dark evening suit. A handsome man in his forties, who turned to her with eyes radiating love and pride.

As the violins led her into another flight of passion she thought she heard a soft voice beside her and the words "my gypsy princess".

When the lights came on again at the end, the seat beside her was empty. But she thought she noticed a faint hint of the musky aftershave Jim always wore.

She felt very peaceful as she made her way to the foyer for refreshments.

Sipping a glass of chardonnay, she noticed a woman wearing a similar dress to her own. The woman waved brightly and walked up to her. She had her granddaughter's lovely smile and sparkling blue eyes.

"You must be Ellen," she said. "Michelle's told me all about you. I just know we're going to be friends." She clinked her glass against Ellen's. "Here's to happy days."

Ellen took another sip of the wine. "To happy days," she said softly.

Glynis Scrivens

Glynis Scrivens has been writing short stories for magazines for the past nine years. She now writes non-fiction articles on pets and writing as well. Her work is published in Australia, Europe and South Africa.

Passing on the Road

The map slides down onto the bedside mat along with my top, sunglasses and a jumble of receipts accumulated through the day. Shadows, thrown by the lamp, dance mysteriously on the walls. My hand gropes the floor, like a blind person's fumble. To reclaim the landscape of my growing up.

Jim bought the East Anglian Guide, with its 'excellent cartography' plus showy graphics, this morning. The rack of postcards and tourist info rocked in the wind outside a gift shop on the sea front. We'd pulled up for a break from car staleness, just along from Mundesley village.

Inside Jonet's Café, warm and steamy with windows on three sides, we ordered hot drinks and a snack. Jim diverted my thoughts from today's task just by being himself. The familiar sounds of his voice rumbled on, as he discussed local landmarks with the café owner.

"We're touring these parts, enjoying a mini-break."

I was grateful to him for sticking to pleasantries, for concealing the actual purpose of our flying visit to Norfolk. My nerves were jumpy as katydids, even with the personal motives kept private.

"Yes, we plan to take in the Broads." Jim nodded at the polite sight-seeing suggestions of the man in the apron. "Did Yarmouth over the weekend. Blakeney yesterday."

Jim had pursued a mobile inventory of my infant and adolescent haunts with an enjoyment that was reassuring, though I was aware that it was too new an experience yet, to be boring for him. As was Us, he and I as a couple. We were still delighting in discovering each other's personal CV. Taking him on the journey through my past helped to ease that intensity always brought on by memories of family involvements. Jim's down-to-earth comments brought me back to now when unnerving mental figures seemed real again along the way.

"Today?" Jim was answering the sing-song East Coast rhythm of another question from behind the counter, while carefully riding the twinge of alarm which vibrated from my elbow. "We're driving out on the coast road south." My breath sighed out, like a bus exuding steam after a long hill, as he didn't elaborate. The emotions of the past couple of days could remain mine and mine alone.

The pleasing vista from the picture window facing our table, of a seaside stretch, and a warm pool of sun lulled me into forgetting about Auntie. Until, leaning toward me, she made her presence felt.

"Expect you're getting impatient," I whispered guiltily to her. This particular relative, my surrogate mum, never could stand inaction.

We'd set out after breakfast from Cromer, the three of us, through flashes of scenery which were illustrations in my mind diaries. And on here to Mundesley. All the delightful flashback sights made me squeak out references. I was an excited child.

"I came here once with my ole fella." Jim blinked in recognition as we cruised one particular area. "When I was twelve. I remember now." His eyes half closed against the sun as he drove, as he relived his own little chapter of autobiography.

Our fingers steepled together over the gear stick. Another memory stirred, another link between us found. Then a shifting movement from Auntie in the back seat had made me spring back from too much intimacy.

A waitress was hovering, ready to clear our table. I lifted the weight of the canvas holdall, removed from the Vauxhall that Jim bought me for my birthday and that we

113

were using today. We prepared to leave Jonet's, the proprietor having filled two flasks, one coffee, one tea. For later.

Picnics. She was always one for them, my Auntie Vi. So I knew we were right in our destination. We were heading out in the direction of Bacton, along the cliff road, to a particular favourite site that has the remains of countless fresh air meals enjoyed by Auntie, my brother (long emigrated) and me, sunk into its earths. To one side, the gasworks rose like the shadow of a medieval castle in the distance, oddly comforting in their permanence. Then and now.

Mid-climb up a grassy cliff, half an hour later, Jim staggered like a stuntman detached from his ropes. "Have to halt, ladies. Otherwise I can't answer for the condition and functioning of my viscera."

"Sounds painful," I sympathized with my partner, while not wanting to upset Auntie. I hadn't spent as much time as I should in recent years, with the woman who brought me up.

Viscera! Jim's a brainbox as well as being lovely. It's like having my own personal thesaurus and encyclopaedia. I am constantly surprised he's still with me. In comparison I seem as lightless as a twenty watt bulb.

"Not true," he'd protest. "You know about the things which matter. That's special. An extra sense. It's called PSI. Intuitive energy."

He means I'm a people person. I pick up on others' needs even when it might be more comfortable not to. Not that I'm a saint. But it's like when I was there for mum, and my father who died within months of her. I knew he'd go too. No will left at all.

My being there for family, to Jim, qualifies as a degree in caring skills. The only contact he has with any kin are formal printed greetings cards on public holidays. It was especially altruistic of me, he says, since my mother and father hadn't been there for me when I needed them. From babyhood onwards.

"But they were my parents," I explained, puzzled.

"Not their fault they had to work." And missed all my rites of passage.

On the next lap of our climb, Jim ambled slowly along stopping to stare out, and gaze round. I suspected his idea of an appreciation of nature would be from the viewpoint of a country pub. I hoped he wouldn't light up a ciggie. Why any sane person would smoke was beyond Auntie's comprehension. Not to mention the smell.

I felt Auntie's impatience as Jim dawdled. She always nipped along a hundred miles quicker than anyone else, even at seventy plus.

But Jim was important to me. Our hands crept together, my mind transmitting it all, this part of me, to him. My young days at Vi's Cromer bungalow. The holiday trips out in her old mini, to the more secluded resorts She didn't like the gaudy lights of commercial seaside towns. It was all swimming and beachcombing, marathon walks and careless climbs. And below, the white horses gliding up raw sienna shores. When, though I missed Mum and Dad, happenings were simple and enjoyable. Not like later.

Sensing the sudden tension from my body, Jim reached for me as we fought for gravity up the steep path. I drew away.

"What's wrong?" Fear flickered on his features briefly as if whatever it was threatened our togetherness.

"That gorse bush."

Last seen in nineteen seventy something – a flowering piece picked and stuffed in my jeans pocket, a hint of heady bridal bouquets. A bunch of prickles would have been more appropriate.

Jim caught a glimpse of my meaning. We both knew, too well, the hidden barbs in lovers' closeness under surface attractions.

That first wedding. A second marriage. And then Jim. The two of us in the same place, but in a different time zone. We always just missed each other, even holidaying together once, married and with different partners. As friends.

I am adamant that there was a fixed point when we were going to meet and merge, as definite as the vanishing point on the horizon decided in a picture by the artist. So that parallel lines must come together.

Jim says it's just chance. We've just been damned lucky. At last. Odds on. The favourite romped home. For once.

But I've been there before. Listened. Believed. An alcoholic. A womanizer. I wasn't going to count my winnings just yet. They could turn to bad money.

"Better do the deed," Jim suggested, after the ritual of egg and cress sandwiches, and tea.

"Auntie! Yes." I stood up. I felt the scratchy grass against my legs, the wind blasting my arms.

"Here?" I asked as if for her approval. It was a favourite spot. You could see for miles around, the sprawling cliffs, the arc of sand and blue. Images of our family seemed part of the landscape, a DNA imprint. With Auntie like some coastal guide, standing there, sturdy in Clark's sandals, the black and snowy bush of hair raised like a brush by the East Coast gales.

"The beach huts have gone!" My sense of loss was like waking up after anaesthetic and finding a gap where teeth should be.

116

Hadn't she told me? Her memory went AWOL Auntie always joked, as the digits on her personal clock expanded. It must have been the year I didn't visit that the promenade appearance had altered. When my marriage, for a second time, was washed up like unidentifiable fragments left exposed after a stiff tide. And we hadn't been out this way since.

I discarded the holdall and lifted my arms, not believing I could do it. Teeth tapping together, I started to perform the task. Jim shouted encouragement above the gale-like blasts that whipped where we were on the cliff edge.

Afterwards, he joined me.

"There was a lot of her."

There was, for someone petite in the way of those high up the decades ladder. An awful lot of her.

"Let me." Jim offered to relieve me, as the wind did a ferocious u-turn, nearly unbalancing my footing. But I held on to the urn because it gave me the feeling I hadn't quite given her away.

"Bye Vi," I whispered, watching the grey swirl downwards.

We'd seen no one so far. Not that I'd have noticed, my emotions still reeling. But on the way back down the dusty cliff track, a figure appeared round a bend.

"Evening." Don't know who murmured it, if anyone.

Could have been a shadow, I thought, unsettled. They were cast everywhere. I hadn't noticed how low the sun was, head in my memories. The light hung, a pale caramel. And the scape of the beach was shrouded when we came to it, the air filtered to high quality.

"Is Violet happy now, d'you think?"

Jim retrieves the crumpled *Scenic Norfolk* from under the heap of duvet, trailing the bedroom carpet. He knows her story. Another casualty of a pairing losing the way; taking a wrong turn. I hoped she had found something, looking after other people's children.

I slip out of the sheets and pad over to the dresser. Pull open the top drawer. Take out a photo, from under a heap of closeted items. We haven't done that yet. Got to know the other's private places.

I prop up the snap, an old print size. Jim, warm and pyjama-less, chins my shoulder.

"It's him. That chap on the hill path."

A rush of relief makes my toes tingle. Not just my mind tricks then. Jim's description, though making me defensive, affirms this.

"Looked like a vagrant, probably from that care hostel plonked out in the countryside up the road." I remembered Vi mentioning that place. Misfits no one wants on their doorstep so stick them out in the middle of nowhere. People who stood out as different.

He would seem so, the man, of course. Those clothes. Tweed jacket. Cloth cap. The bowl pipe. Collectors items. I read the query in Jim's eyes.

"So how—" He tries to align the stranger with the monochrome likeness in my hand. "You know the gent."

"He's my father."

I'd forgotten. The twin thing. Dad and Vi. That's why he trusted her to be my childminder. And why he came today. To thank me. For the ceremony. And more.

When your existence has resembled a nomadic encampment, mainstay adults alternating, it's hard to know who will stay. Who will bother enough. Whether to commit.

Dad may not have been there for most of my decisions. Physically. But he was firmly in my corner. His presence layered round me like a blanket, testing those I would trust myself to. Not very wisely so far.

But this time is different. He's shown himself. And been recognized.
By Jim.

Sally Angell

Sally Angell writes fiction and poetry, for children, and for adults. In her writing she likes to explore the truth and reality of feelings, the originality of language, and the possibilities of words.

www.sallyangell.firecast.co.uk

Prints of Darkness

It was Tuesday afternoon and already Richard was stuck. He had known it would not be totally straightforward to trace his family tree but having prepared the ground he had not expected to draw a blank so soon. He had watched again his DVDs of the BBC series, in which famous and not so famous people discovered secrets about their families. He had bought and read several books on the subject. He had even attended an event organised by the Hampshire Family History Society, which had been advertised as an introduction to family history; an encouragement to get you started.

All this preparation had convinced him that it was possible to establish the basic facts about your own family back to about 1830 without setting foot in a records office, by using the immense web resources he had been told were available. This is not what the instructors, the books and the DVDs had actually said, but Richard had heard that others had done it and he was a born optimist. He had set aside this week of holiday to have a serious go.

"I'm stuck", he shouted down the stairs from his study. There was no answer. He knew Jeannie was there. "I'm completely stuck", he tried again a little louder this time.

"You've only be doing it two days. You can't be stuck already," came an answering shout from the kitchen, where Jeannie was attempting to study the history of art, whilst also baking cakes for the twins to take to brownies, and peeling vegetables for the dinner party they had arranged for this evening.

"Well come and look," he called, not willing to be denied the chance to explain. He heard her tread on the stairs and prepared to show her his results so far.

"It's being going so well," he began. "I've traced your line back to the beginning of compulsory registration in 1837; before that, if you use the 1841 census data and allow for the fact that the dates of birth could be up to five years out. Did you know your great great grandfather was a blacksmith?"

"That's great. Doesn't sound like stuck at all."

"You're family is quite easy though," Richard explained, "with surnames like Hollingsworth, Tilling, Hollick and Beswetherick, the choices are limited. I've got Richards, Smith, Walker and Miller, which are all fairly common."

"I can see why Smith would be difficult," said Jeannie.

"Actually the Smith line hasn't been too bad. I knew quite a lot from the box in Granny Smith's loft, which got me past 1901. The puzzle is Miller. It should have been easy because I know my Great Grandfather was born in the 1890s. I found his marriage in 1920 and then his birth record from 1896, but I can find nothing about his father anywhere."

Jeannie could sense the frustration beginning to register in Richard's voice. He hated to be obstructed. "Have you tried all the websites?" she said.

"Not all", said Richard, "but the best two that were recommended".

"What's the problem?"

"In 1901 and 1911 I can find Great Grandad Miller, aged 5 and 15, but his father isn't there."

"What about 1891?"

"Not there either. Nor Richard, of course, though his older brother and his mother are. To be missing in one census may be normal but three in a row seems odd. He isn't listed anywhere else either, and at least he had an unusual Christian name, so searching shouldn't be hard."

121

"What was it?"

"Hezekiah."

"Hezekiah? That is odd! How do you know his Christian name if you can't find him?"

Richard thought. How did he know? He was sure he did know, but now he searched his memory banks he couldn't remember how he knew. He'd never seen it written down. Had his Grandfather told him before he died? "I don't know how I know", he answered, "but I do, I definitely know."

"At least try some variant spellings," said Jeannie. "It's basic research really."

"You are so bloody practical aren't you?" he said, smiling, knowing that his wife would always be able to see one step ahead. He turned back to the screen and Jeannie went back to her art and biscuits.

He tried Hez* and Hoz* and even just H, but still drew a blank. He tried guessing his birth date – it must have been sometime between 1855 and 1875 – and searching the births in Devon for those years. There was no Hezekiah Miller. Henry's and Harry's and Horace's and even one Horatio but no Hezekiah.

Then he uncovered a scanned list of births for the last quarter of 1860, listed alphabetically. They were all Millers running from Bernard through to William. His eyes moved immediately to the list of names beginning with H. Between a Hepsibah Miller and Hilda Miller there was a name which had been scribbled over. He moved the mouse and clicked on print. The printer clicked and registered *warming up* on its minute screen. Richard knew it would take a minute and he went downstairs to make a cup of tea. "I think I might just be making a little progress," he said to Jeannie.

On returning to the study Richard immediately noticed that the red exclamation mark had appeared on the printer's tiny screen. Despite this, the machine appeared to have printed the page he wanted, but as he picked it up he felt a second page. The light on the printer went off. The second page was an email printout. There must have been one job left in the print queue, he thought, as he studied the list of names. Under Hepsibah Miller there was more than a smudge. A conscious effort had been made to erase a name. It appeared to have been made with numerous angry pencil marks. Even with a magnifying glass it was impossible to make out anything, even the place of birth.

Disappointed, Richard reached casually for the email that had printed under the list of births. He didn't recognise the sender's address, which was an odd one, unknown1@contraband.com. The message was very brief and very simple. *Don't go there* was all it said. He didn't immediately link the email to his search but was sufficiently puzzled to open up his system and search for the electronic version. Nothing. No email. No history at that address. It was as if the email had come straight to his printer and emerged by itself.

"Darling", he called, "have you been buying anything from a shop called Contraband?"

"No. Why?"

"Just wondered. An email's come through I don't recognise."

"Spam?"

"No. But not on the computer anywhere."

How can you have had an email but not on the computer?"

"Don't know. One of the puzzles of cyberspace I suppose. It's printed itself."

Jeannie laughed from the kitchen. "It's time you came down for a bit of a rest," she said, "it can't print itself. You have to instruct it. It's a machine."

Richard, puzzled and slightly uneasy, came down stairs and sat at the kitchen table opposite his wife.

"No time for sitting", she said. "Would you mind getting the table ready for tonight?"

Richard attended to the table. Jeannie finished the baking for brownies and set the slow cooker to warm some delicious soup. She roasted a large joint of pork, salted to get the crackling going, and added all the trimmings. Aromatic apple sauce, roast potatoes and parsnips and assorted green vegetables. She checked the freezer for ice cream and went through a mental checklist until she was satisfied. The twins (the brownies for whom the baking was intended), had returned from their friend's house, eaten tea, watched some television and were now ready for bed, teeth cleaned, faces washed, pyjamas on and teddy bears secure under each of their arms. Jeannie read them a story, explained gently that Mummy and Daddy had friends coming round for the evening and that they should do their best to sleep tight and not disturb the party.

"Just popping up for a few more minutes before they all arrive," said Richard, climbing the stairs. Before going back to the family research he checked his email account. The mysterious printed email had been bothering him since he went down earlier. He found nothing again. The worry refused to go altogether but he decided to use the time for one last look at the web. He simply googled Hezekiah Miller, not really expecting anything.

To his surprise all the hits were family tree sites. Apparently there were several Hezekiah Millers. None appeared to have any association with Devon, and certainly not Brixham. He was about to exit when he noticed that the last site listed on his screen included something about the Exeter Evening Gazette. It was a site dedicated to old newspapers. He clicked on it and scrolled down the screen. There was a short report from the Exeter Assizes in 1897.

After the ruckus in court yesterday at the sentencing of Hezekiah Miller, the trial of Peter Richardson was a tame affair. Besides his wife there were few people in the courtroom to hear his plea of guilty to stealing six chickens from Parson Glebe.

Richard frantically clicked the flickering screen trying to find a reference to the proceedings in court the day before. He returned to his original search but there was nothing else listed. After a tantalising glimpse of his great-great-grandfather, the trail had gone completely cold. He clicked again, then sighed as he heard the doorbell ring. The guests were arriving. His search would have to wait.

As he left his study at the top of the stairs, he heard a faint whir and a click, and stood rigid. He knew it was the printer, and he knew he had not commanded it to print, or scan or copy anything. It's just going through its maintenance routine, he thought, but the unmistakeable sound of paper creeping through the rollers told him something was actually printing.

Carry on and you'll wish you'd never started.

The email address was the same. The paper was his but it had it had taken on a smell not quite like anything he had ever smelt before. It was not strong, but there was an unmistakeable tang of saltwater, rotten seaweed and decaying fish. It went as soon as he'd smelt it. He clicked open his mail. Nothing. The doorbell went again. He searched his spam, his sent email, his drafts, his archive. Nothing. The doorbell went for a third time. He would have to go down.

He did one last search before supper. *Miller, Dart-moor.* The search engine fired up but the result wouldn't come. "Don't hang on me now," he whispered.

"Richard, everyone's here. Can you get drinks?"

"Damn," he muttered. But he had to go. He took a deep breath and descended the stairs.

"Hello Richard," said Penny, Jeannie's friend, "are you alright, you look a little pale."

"I'm fine," said Richard, aware that he was trembling very slightly. He took the last two stairs very slowly, breathing deeply and reminding himself of his duties as a good host. All these guests were his good friends but they still needed to be welcomed. "I'm very well actually. I am having a holiday I've been planning for several years."

"Holiday at home?" asked Penny's husband, Colin.

"Yes. A whole week to research my family tree. And it's going pretty well. Drink?"

"Gin please. How far back have you got?" said Colin.

"1800 with Jeannie's lot," said Richard, but a bit stuck with my side. It seems there may be a bit of a story." Immediately he said it the smell came back. A sickly, wet, decomposing smell. No one else seemed to notice it but it was noxious. His nose felt poisoned by the stench, and he had to stifle a retch.

"Are you sure you're alright", said Penny. "Jeannie, your husband doesn't look well. He's as pale as a puddle."

Jeannie took one look at Richard and knew he wasn't right, but as soon as the smell had come, it went again. Richard pulled himself together again and finished pouring drinks for his guests. He almost spilt Colin's gin but recovered in time and finally sat down with some relief.

"So, what's this story in your dim and distant family past?" said Colin. "Adultery? Illegitimacy? There was a lot of it about."

"No. I don't think so. But there's something fishy about my great-great-grandfather." Even as he said it – "fishy" – he covered his nose, but the smell stayed at bay. "I was just trying to finish something off when you all arrived, but I have a hunch he did something he wasn't all that proud of."

"Daddy, Daddy," called a voice from upstairs.

Jeannie's eyes lifted heavenwards. "I told them not to disturb us".

"Go back to bed girls", said Richard gently.

"No Daddy, there's someone in the study."

Richard shivered. Beads of cold sweat dripped on to his shirt.

"You're not right at all, are you?" said Penny, looking at Jeannie.

Richard willed strength into his legs and walked to the staircase. At the top of the stairs the twins were entwined, one around each banister. He climbed the stairs slowly conserving his strength and at the top he took a little hand in each of his and led the girls back to their room. He sang them a song as quietly as he could, and kissed their cheeks goodnight.

Out on the landing he paused outside his study. He sniffed the air, but all he sensed was the faint and pleasant smell from the bathroom air freshener. He listened. He could hear nothing. Slowly he opened the door and looked in. There was a pile of paper on the floor. The printer was empty and silent. The screen was still frozen, refusing to carry out his *Miller, Dartmoor* search. He stared down at the papers. Each was identical. A print of an email. He knelt down and picked one up. As soon as he touched it

127

the foulness was driven into his nostrils with almost physical force. The rankness of the odour released by his touching the paper was horrific. It was as if he had been lowered into a vat of decomposing seaweed and rotten fish; a vat that hadn't been opened for years. He gagged and rushed around the corner to the bathroom where he heaved up his supper, and remained retching for several minutes as the smell ebbed away.

Don't push me any further you stupid stubborn bastard.

He had seen the message even as he dropped the paper in revulsion. He washed his face slowly, taking steady breaths, telling himself this must be some kind of weird practical joke. Perhaps it was a computer virus. A worm? He brushed his teeth. He used the tooth mug and drank a long glass of cold water.

"Are you okay?" whispered Jeannie, outside the door.

Opening it slowly and carefully, he said, "fine now, I think, but I just threw up. Sorry."

"You look terrible. Are you okay to come down?"

"Sure. I'll sit in the lounge until coffee".

Jeannie explained to the guests that Richard was indeed ill but that they should all finish the meal. "By the time we are on coffee and brandy, I'm sure he'll be as right as rain".

Richard sat still and composed himself. He controlled his breathing, deliberately timing it against the clock. Breathe in for two seconds, out for three, breath in again. Twelve breaths a minute. He collected his thoughts and resolved a course of action. There had to be a rational explanation, and he would found out what it was, and get to the truth about his great-great-grandfather.

Jeannie was right. As the guests came in to the lounge for coffee, Richard looked calm. He even had a little colour back in his cheeks.

"Can you manage a brandy?" said Colin, who seemed to have taken over the hosts duties.

"I'll have a large whisky", said Richard, grateful for the extra dose of courage he felt he needed. He sipped it, but not so slowly that he couldn't manage a second. His courage rose another tiny notch but he remained shaken. "Colin, I seem to have some kind of problem with my printer. You used to be in the trade sometime ago didn't you? Any chance you could have a look at it for me before you go?"

"No problem old man, happy to help."

Richard knew he had to remain calm and quiet if he was going to get into the study again without blind panic overtaking him. So he sat still observing the others chatting a little woozily over their coffee, their chocolates and their brandies. He fancied he may have heard something from upstairs, but he told himself it was nothing. No one else seemed to have heard. He concentrated hard on keeping calm. Jeannie and Penny were saying goodbye to the other guests. They returned to the lounge.

"One more before you go?" said Jeannie.

"Why not," said Colin, half a second before Penny's, "perhaps not".

"Another whiskey Richard?" said Colin.

"No thanks. I'm ready now."

"Ready for what?"

"Ready when you are," blurted Richard, anxious not to convey any sense of panic to his friend. "Ready to have a quick look at that printer before you go".

"Yes, of course", said Colin, but he wasn't going to hurry his last drink of the evening and he settled into his

129

armchair to chat with the ladies while Richard continued to compose himself.

After what seemed to Richard to be an interminable time, during which he barely managed to keep his panic under control, Colin finished his drink.

"Come on then," said Colin, "let's have a look at this printer of yours."

As they began to climb the stairs, a whiff of burning hit Richard's nose. He instinctively looked at Colin to see if he had smelt it too. He had. "Don't like the smell of that", said Colin, and he bounded to the top of the stairs in three further strides, with Richard following slowly, one step at a time.

Colin threw the study door open. They saw the flames at once, leaping from the printer, in waves of fire far too big for the fuel consumed. The yellow tongues had a life of their own, as if they were materially different from the printer on which they fed. In contortions like a muscled wrestler struggling to lift an opponent the fire now appeared to lift the printer from its place, raise it high in the air and fling it with dreadful accuracy straight at Colin's head.

There was no doubt in Richard's mind that the moment the edge of the printer made contact with Colin's skull, he would never breathe again. He fancied he saw the soft bone cave in and moments later Colin sank to the floor, insensible.

The computer screen was live again. Google had finally done its work. The third item pointed Richard to a list of Dartmoor prisoners in the 19th century. Near the end in 1897 was a one line entry.

Admitted: Miller, H. – Double murderer, twins, Brixham Harbour.

Richard shot like lightening into the twins' bedroom.

"Jeannie," he screamed from the bottom of his lungs, "where are the girls?"

Mark R. Smith

Mark R. Smith writes short stories and articles and is working on a novel about singing, sinning and redemption. He believes that heaven and hell do break into our world from time to time and that creative writing and the other arts are the best way of describing these numinous moments.

Sahib

Hold still, Trishna! Cease your figitations! Do you wish to have knots in your hair? Oh, so the young crow thinks itself *wiser* than its mother now? Then tell me this, oh daughter of mine: what is the price of love? You have no answer? Ah, but of *course* you have an answer! And always the *wrong* one! The price of love is to have a mother who combs your hair every morning and every night, who ensures that in all ways you are cared for, even if that care is neither fully appreciated nor fully understood. *Pain*? Of *course* there is pain! There is a *reason* why your fine hair must be pulled back from your scalp in this way, why the plaits must be as tight as bark to a tree. For without pain how will you come to comprehend my love in all its many facets?

You think me crazy? That I should wish the girl who will shortly present herself at school to look like my daughter and not a raggedy washerwoman? So the whole *school* thinks me crazy now? That you should say such things! Everything I have done for you...

My mother was right. Bringing up a daughter is like watering a neighbour's plant.

Trishna?

Dry your eyes, oh daughter of mine. Life may be topsy-turvy but it is good also, for without it we are dead. These ignorant children have pakoras stuffed between their ears. You should not listen to their lies. This thing they call you, it is an ugly and ignorant word. But then, perhaps I am to blame. How can you possibly know the light from the shadows if always I keep you in the dark?

Let me tell you of your mother. Maybe then you will understand. Know first that she has seen the world from across great oceans. She is neither a spoilt Indian princess nor a middle-class single mum from Brockley, though her life, being tempered by these roles, has acquired a most unusual quality.

Do not interrupt, Trishna. You say you know this story already but what you have heard is only half the truth, just as your grandmother's missives paint our native land in hues of rose-pink.

My story concerns your grandmother also. So – not another word.

Listen.

There was once a time when I was just as headstrong a girl as you and it was my own mother who sat each morning and night combing the knots from my hair, tying it back in just the way I do now.

"This will keep the ghosts from getting into it," she would say. She told me knots were as footholds to these ghosts, who emerged at night to whisper into the ears of their victims, filling their slumber-laden heads with unholy thoughts.

Yes, Trishna. You may well titter. Would you sit patiently as I combed the ghosts from *your* hair? Would that make you behave as a good daughter should? What if I were to tell you that such ghosts are *real*, but that they sit as well on these shores as the superstitions of India's emigrant flock?

This comb – here now in my hand. It is not a good comb. It is cheap; a thing of flimsy plastic. But my mother's comb was most beautiful. It was made of bone, of what animal I could not say and my mother would not say, and it was very old. It had a green patina from many years of use and a hairline fracture across one of its venerable tines. It combed my hair many thousands of times, my mother's and grandmother's perhaps many millions. My sister's – your auntie's – only a little, for she died in her infancy. There, you see? Something you *did not* know.

To lose is to learn, as they say, and my mother learnt only that there are bad spirits who might steal her children away from her.

My mother was combing my hair on the night before we were to leave for London. For both of us, it was a ritual as inappreciably familiar as drawing breath. We were seated on the bed and I asked her what lay in store for me in those barbarous foreign lands, for I was scared of the ghosts who might take me into their unholy confidence. My mother told me not to be scared. She said that there were no ghosts in London. But I could tell that she was scared also, from the way she tugged restlessly at my scalp.

By mischance something happened shortly after she proffered these words that upset her greatly. She took this thing for an omen, I know, though she tried hard to disguise the fact. One of the tines on that ancient comb snapped, the hairline fracture – perhaps decades old itself – finally conceding to decay. She cursed then, the only time I ever heard my mother do so. And yet, after a brief respite during which she plucked the rogue tine from my tresses and slipped it into the twist of her cotton sari, she continued to comb my hair. But she had lost count, you see. Always she would comb my hair exactly one hundred times and always I kept count in my head. But that night she combed my hair only ninety-nine times and for some reason – perhaps for the thrill of even a minor rebellion, I had conformed so in the face of adversity – I stopped short of telling her. Instead I bade my mother goodnight and lay down on my bed to dream of red buses and bowler hats and mild summers and perhaps just a little of what I was leaving behind in the wake of my folly.

As it happened, despite my parents' misgivings, the move was not so bad for them, at least not in the beginning. My father had lived in London as a student, so for him it was a modest homecoming; and while the Victorian townhouse was a great deal smaller than our estates in Malihabad, within her new home at least my mother was still *begum* of all she surveyed.

I was not so fortunate. Before long I fell sick. And as I lay on my bed, believing beyond reason that my sins were great indeed, for my suffering was most profound, I heard Sahib's voice for the first time.

How can I describe it? It was a voice like ancient papyrus unfurling, like a raging sandstorm in a parched well. The hair was stuck to my face with sweat, yet as his words, dry as autumn leaves, worked their way over me I sensed the fever cool and dissipate, leaving my skin stiff with salty residue and the hairs on my forehead to curl inwards on themselves in fright.

"What have you done, Manisha?" he whispered. "Have you no heart? You have taken me away from my home, from my people."

I knew then and there who he was and how he came to be whispering his unholy thoughts into my ear.

"Then you should not have hidden away in my hair," I replied, as bold as you please.

"What else was I to do?" he said. "There was an opportunity – a lock without a weave, a knot in need of attention – and I took it."

"A scalded cat dreads cold water," said I. "Perhaps now you will desist from hiding in people's hair and learn to conduct yourself in a manner befitting one who is dead."

I did not hear another word from Sahib that day; my spirits were even a little lifted and I began to feel myself again. But when night came the shadows took shape at the foot of my bed and I saw him in the flesh.

135

No, *flesh* is a most unfortunate choice of word, for his body had little of it to hold him together. He was a creature of long brittle bones and tender double joints, who moved like a daddy-long-legs, in great lurching fits and starts. Never had I seen a living creature as emaciated, and perhaps that was the point. The thin membrane of skin across his chest was so taut I could see not just the contours but the blush of his sallow ribcage. He was eight feet tall, though the way he stooped he reached only six and a half. He was weighed down by a colossal cranium, you see. Can you imagine such a thing, Trishna? A petrified grapefruit held aloft by a sparse sheaf of bamboo. What a sight!

Truly, he was a terror to behold. Yet most of all I feared the echo left in his body's wake. The awful snapping and cracking and popping of his decrepit joints, it was this infernal racket that came to haunt me more than anything else.

When first I saw him I did not know whether to laugh or cry. He spent a moment parading around the bedroom like a marionette that has had its strings recently cut. Then he reached down; *creak, creak, creak,* he went as he lowered himself into place. His scorched lips drew close to my ear, his hot rancid breath cloying at my cheek.

"You must return to India, Manisha," he implored, "and you must take me with you. What is this place, this great nothingness? Last night I roamed its streets and passageways, its conduits and snickleways, travelling on foot, by bus and train, seeking the life's blood which pumps through the veins of any healthy cityscape. All around me were people and yet they behaved as if they too were ghosts. They drifted from one place to the next, never meeting my eye, never meeting their neighbour's eye, treating me little better than a dog and their city as a third-rate kennel. I want to go back to India, Manisha. You and I both must return before our retiring hearts cease to beat, mine for a second time."

"I cannot go back to India, Sahib," I said to him, "for my parents have done much for me these last months. I have surrendered to their better judgement and I cannot betray their trust."

A great rattling fury consumed his murky presence. "Then I will *break* your heart before it has *time* to wither," he whispered venomously. "I will *shatter* it like *porcelain*. I will *pluck* the hairs from your head and fill your dreams with such *great* sorrow that you will *beg* me to lift you up in my arms and *snap* you in two across my knee."

To which I replied in a small but firm voice: "Then that is as it shall be."

And that is how it was.

Sahib remained true to his word. For me, the weeks and months to follow became a living hell. During the day I was subjected to such heartache that I was often physically sick. During the night I was wracked with such guilt that I sobbed incessantly into my pillow and did not sleep, as all the while Sahib tugged at my hair and serenaded me with his desiccated sighs.

Not for long could I bear this torment. As loathe as I was to further burden my parents, one wet Sunday afternoon I sat in the dining room with my mother and purged myself of Sahib's story. As I described the effect these events had had on my wellbeing my mother's face progressed through a number of distinctly different states, like seasons passing in great haste, before coming to rest in one of the winter months, perhaps a dry and icy January. As she made to speak I shivered before the enormity

137

of my blunder. She told me that I was a selfish child; that it was quite impossible that I should return to India; that I had put herself and my father through enough hardship already; that what haunted my soul was not a ghost from my past but a refusal to embrace the future; that it was time I took responsibility for my actions and behaved as a grown woman should.

My mother believed in ghosts but she did not believe in Sahib, for of course there *were* no ghosts in London.

So I turned my attentions to my father who, as a man of few words – and those used only to paint a rudimentary picture of his thoughts – would need more visible evidence of my profound unhappiness. I borrowed his camera from the top drawer of the writing bureau and, as morning broke, stole Sahib's image just as he slipped away into the last whorl of shadow.

Now a thief is a thief, whether he steals a diamond or a cucumber, and, since Sahib did not consent to my borrowing his image, I had no right to take it. But take it I did, paying no heed to the possible consequences. My father developed the photographs the following week. When he returned from the chemist's my heart skipped several beats. We sat in the living room passing between us undeniable evidence that we were living a new life. Here was the western cut of our clothes; the smiles so forced they turned back down at the edges. Even the quality of light in the photographs seemed somehow different. Then one image held my father's attention longer than the others and pressed a frown to his heavy lips. I tried in vain to peer over his shoulder and it was with tremulous voice that I asked if anything was amiss. He did not respond immediately.

"Look, Manisha," he said at last. "A picture of your pretty new room. What a shame there was a hair on the lens." And he held aloft the picture for us all to see. It was this supposed imperfection that had caught his purist's eye.

"That is not a hair, father," I said quietly.

"Yes it is," he replied, tracing the image with his fingertip. "See the little white halo? That is the end of the follicle."

If he wore a halo then it was only to fool my parents into believing him an angel. But I knew he was no such thing, just as I knew it was no stray hair. It was Sahib.

When next I was huddled beneath my sheets he chose to punish me for borrowing his admittedly unlikely likeness. As he seized his form from the plentiful night I knew at once – here was a spirit in most foul spirits. He flexed and twitched through the gloom of dusk, his joints clicking interminably, his toes tapping a funereal rhythm on the floorboards.

"What more do you wish to take from me, Manisha?" he snapped. Would you have the shoes from my feet?"

"You do not wear shoes, Sahib," I said.

"Never before have I felt the need," he said, "but the ground here is most unforgiving. As far as the eye can see lies a concrete purgatory. I want the moist yielding soils of my mango grove, Manisha, and if you will not allow me to rest in peace I will not allow you a moment's peace either."

That night I did not sleep a wink. I was left a tattered doll, wracked by guilt, swollen with sorrow, yearning for something I could not have. And yet I was sated all the same. For as the pitted channels down my cheeks ran dry – for not a single tear more could I squeeze forth – I planned for Sahib's imminent departure.

The next night was a different story. I was up and out of bed before his creaking limbs had time to fracture the silence.

"You are right, Sahib," I said, standing in front of the dresser and looking through the mirror at the pitching silhouette behind me. "You have been right all along. I have been as stubborn as a goat in this matter. I shall return with you to India this instant. Felicitations, oh persistent one." And I began to comb my hair as if it was the most normal thing in the world to do so in the dead of night.

"That is most welcome news," said Sahib after a moment's pause. I could tell from his tone that my words had come when he was least expecting them, that he was all topsy-turvy. I continued to push my advantage.

"But there is a problem," I said. "You have no passport and I have not the money to buy two airplane tickets. Would you consent to stowing away in my luggage?"

"Am I not too long in the body to stow away in a young lady's luggage?" he asked warily, but he was already as a *musth* elephant who has tasted freedom outside his trap.

"That depends on your outlook," I replied. "There is not an ounce of fat on you, Sahib. You are as skinny as a rake. If I helped you I am sure we could minimise your volume sufficiently. Take this casket for instance –" And I picked up a small decorative ivory casket and deposited its load of jewellery onto the dresser, whereupon I was able to insert three of my digits into its cool interior and still have room for a knuckle. "I believe if you set your mind to it, why this would be more than ample room for a rakelike wraith such as yourself."

"Do you judge me a fool, Manisha?" said Sahib. "That I could occupy such an itty-bitty space?"

"I judge you to be most wise, Sahib," I replied. "That is why I believe you can perform such an impossible feat, where a common household spirit would meet with pitiable failure."

140

That was all my swollen-headed Sahib needed to hear.

"Shall I start with a toe?" he asked. "An elbow? Or a fingertip perhaps?"

Let me tell you now, Trishna, it is no small thing to break a man down so that he fits into an itty-bitty casket. There was a great dearth of blood. His bones snapped like dry twigs. But the rest of his body posed a problem. Tendons had to be knotted, joints twisted and separated, cartilage flexed and scraped and flensed, muscles folded, organs bunched like shoes ready for the suitcase; and his skin, that which seemed so insufficient for the purpose of containing all of this bodily matter, folded away in crisp russet squares to avoid future wear and tear. Finally, there was just enough room to pack in his huge skull, his deep-set eyes all the while surveying my work with a proprietorial eye. It took all the strength I had to tear myself away from that gaze, more so than that required to squeeze shut the casket and to slip the tiny latch. Even then I could not rest, for fear I would begin to question my judgment. Instead I took a pair of scissors from the dresser and severed a thin lock of my hair, with which I bound the casket repeatedly to contain the foul spirit therein. I buried Sahib under the diseased plum tree at the bottom of the garden, deep beneath the ground where, I hoped, in time he would be forgotten, and in perhaps a longer time still – and here I fall foul of wishful thinking – he would forget what I had seen fit to take from him.

I moved on. I tried not to think of the past. My belly filled out. Fearing my skin would tear I basted myself generously with buttermilk. My breasts grew heavy. I took to eating leaves of spearmint. Always have I loved spearmint.

When you entered into my life, Trishna, a beautiful healthy baby girl, I counted my blessings. If you did not possess a considerable amount of hair in your first year, you made up for it in your second. But God gives as he takes away, and my sins were far from absolved. My father was much older than my mother and his health had been in decline for some time. When he died she returned to India. She missed her ghosts, you see. We all have them; she was not a whole person without hers. But I myself could not return. I had not the strength to face mine.

All my life I have lived with the knowledge of my betrayal.

But look! In perhaps a small way he has avenged himself. See here on my head how the life has drained from these forelocks? Exactly one hundred hairs, Trishna, count them if you do not believe me. Two tresses the colour of sallow bone. And I, still a young woman!

What? What is this thing you say? *Ya Allah!* Have you not listened to my story? Of course *Sahib* is not your *father!* Who would think such a thing! Oh, Trishna... I am so very sorry. This thing they call you, the children at your school – it is not true! *This* is what I have been trying to tell you! You are no *bastard* offspring! For truly, you *have* a father and he is made of more substantial fabric than filmy skin and flyaway bones! You must understand, ours was a respectable family. We were landowners. There was a reputation to uphold, unwritten laws of decorum by which to abide...

I buried the ghost of my past and that took courage. But if I had been truly brave there would have been a letter, not a ghost, inside that casket; braver still and I would have placed *myself* in the casket, limb over broken limb, and instead of burying it I would have posted it to a small house in Malihabad, marked for the attention of a common market trader's son – mangos of all things! – a boy who had nothing to his name but his love for a headstrong girl with arms like twigs ensnared in a soft black down.

But I did not and that it how it is...

Off to school now, Trishna. Your fine hair yields no longer and becomes damp with my tears. If I remain standing above you lamenting in this deplorable fashion I fear I shall encourage your great thirst – for you see, that is the meaning of your name. Go. Slake your thirst in the classroom instead. Leave your mother to her delusions and her sodden cheeks and her silly stories. You are right as usual. You are always right. I speak through chimeras when my true voice would suffice. The best way to cross a river is to cross a river. I admit it. In all my life I never met this Sahib.

But answer me this, oh daughter of mine – if there are no ghosts in London why then do they haunt me still?

Adam Bealby

Adam Bealby lives in Worcestershire with his wife and children and the ghosts of a frivolously spent past. His work can be seen in the indie comic book anthology *Fusion*; the award-winning *Red Eye Magazine*; *Ada and More Nano-Fiction* (Leaf Books); and *Dragontales* (Wyvern Publications).

Web of Fear

The guided tour of the old slave fort was over, and on a Sierra Leonean beach a group of African-Americans were weeping and wailing over their enslaved forebears.

"Look at them," scoffed Mark Harris, a student of nineteenth century history from England. "What do you think? Will any of them give up their comfortable lives in the States and rejoin their African brothers and sisters in abject poverty? Slavery's the best thing that ever happened to their ancestors."

"Not for the ones that didn't survive the voyage," said Roger Klein, Mark's colleague from university. "This is a spiritual homecoming for them."

"Pah!" said Mark, dismissively. "And for those left behind by the slave ships, it's more than just a homecoming of their long-lost relatives. It's an opportunity to rip off the ones who made it Stateside."

Sure enough, hordes of souvenir sellers were descending on the grieving African-Americans. One hawker however, weighed down by a dozen drums of varying shapes and sizes, made a beeline for Mark Harris and Roger Klein.

"I couldn't help but overhear your conversation," said the raggedly-dressed Sierra Leonean. "But you must concede that much of West Africa was consigned to destitution by the white man's Trans-Atlantic Slave Trade."

"I'll concede nothing of the sort," said Mark. "It's well documented that rival African chiefs actively promoted slavery."

The African shook his head. "Your great-great-grandfathers profited by enslaving our most precious resource – the young men and women who were the heart and soul of this continent. Your people stole them from

144

our shores. Yet, you fail to admit the great wrong done to us. Where is your conscience?"

Mark held up his hands in a gesture of innocence. "Don't blame me. I'm just a history student, not one of those left-wing loonies with the weight of the world on his shoulders."

Hoping to defuse the situation, Roger offered to buy one of the souvenir seller's drums, a small bongo. Yet once the sale was done, the drum salesman made off angrily down the beach without another word.

"Surly sod," said Mark.

Roger let out a short laugh. "You hardly made an attempt to empathise with him – which you're supposed to do on such a touchy issue."

Mark made a sweeping gesture incorporating all the sobbing African-Americans. "I'll leave the empathizing to these guys."

* * *

That evening, as Roger and Mark relaxed at the round bar beside their hotel swimming pool, they spotted the drum salesman again. This time he was under the guise of a musician, a drummer in the local African band that was entertaining the tourists.

As the souvenir-selling drummer launched into a frenzied drum solo, Roger asked the barman, "Who's the guy over there?"

The barman's brown face suddenly took on a fearful grey pallor. "His name's Karonga," he finally managed. "But they call him 'Spider'. Watch him playing the drums and you'll see why."

Roger and Mark observed the frantic movements as Spider's hands sought out the membranes stretched across the variously-sized drums surrounding him.

145

The longer the two young men watched the frenetic drumming, the greater the illusion that Karonga had more than two hands. His limbs moved so fast, and with such hypnotic synchronicity that they became a blur. It was almost as though he had half a dozen arms – as though his limbs were the legs of a running spider.

After a while, Roger felt himself becoming mesmerised by Karonga's performance, and for a time was unaware that the drummer was staring intently at himself and Mark.

Eventually, with a brisk shake of the head, Roger freed his mind from the strange fogginess invading it. However, this wasn't before having what he later believed was a hallucination. The spider analogy must have become embedded in Roger's subconscious, for Karonga momentarily looked to Roger's suggestive mind like a giant spider, squatting at the centre of a web of drums.

Mark seemed to have been affected worse than Roger and was shaking with fear. It was as though Karonga had somehow got deeper into Mark's subconscious and was punishing him for his unsympathetic opinions on the slave trade.

Eventually Mark clambered down from his barstool, almost falling to the floor in the process. "I'm not feeling well," he announced, and staggered off in the direction of his and Roger's hotel room.

With his head a little clearer, Roger resumed conversation with the barman. "I see now why you call him Spider. He's a very intriguing individual."

"Stay away from him," the barman said bluntly.

Riled by the barman's insolent attitude, Roger said indignantly, "Why on earth should I want to stay away from him?"

The barman leaned forward and said urgently, "Karonga is an *ngozi*, a magician; a practitioner of the black arts. The spider is his familiar, his tribal totem, and he can transform himself into a spider at will. If you or those you love make an enemy of Karonga, he will attach himself to you. Then you and your loved ones will never be safe, no matter where you hide."

Roger involuntarily shivered as he recalled the argument Mark had had with Karonga earlier in the day – an argument which, according to the barman, may have put them both in jeopardy. Roger wanted to pick the barman's brains for some more information on this *ngozi*. However, under Karonga's baleful gaze the barman backed away from Roger and scuttled off to the other side of the round bar.

A few minutes later the evening's music came to an end and the band packed up their instruments.

Shrugging off the superstitious dread he had felt a few moments earlier, Roger climbed off his barstool. Perhaps, like Mark, he too could do with turning in early.

* * *

That night Roger was awoken from a dream of drummers changing into giant spiders by Mark Harris's horrified screams. By the time Roger got to his friend's side, Mark was unable to speak. There were puncture wounds on his neck, as if from a snake's fangs. Already Mark's throat was closing up and his breath whistled in and out in agonized gasps. As the whistling turned to gurgling, Mark somehow managed to sit up in bed. Goggle-eyed, he pointed with a trembling finger towards the hotel room door and to the bongo drum on the floor beside it.

Roger squinted, his eyes searching the gloomy corner of the room; but he saw no movement. If a snake had been lurking there before, perhaps it had now slipped out under the door.

A soft thump brought Roger's attention back to his stricken friend, only to find Mark had fallen back dead on the mattress of his bed.

* * *

Some month's later, Roger resumed his university studies. Since his college was in the same town where his grandmother, Imelda Klein, lived, he was persuaded to board with her – a sensible decision, his family said, that would save money on rent and board.

"I don't believe it," Imelda Klein said one night, as a newsreader appeared on the TV screen.

"Don't believe what?" asked Roger, looking up from a history book.

"A darkie. There's a darkie reading the ten o'clock news, dear."

"She's not the first coloured newsreader you've ever seen, gran."

"I know, dear. But that's not the point. These people are getting everywhere these days. One or two have even turned up at the bowling club wanting to become members."

Roger rolled his eyes. "This is the twenty-first century, gran."

"Don't take that tone of voice with me, young man. If you ask me, you're too keen on these darkies." To emphasize her point, the gruff old lady indicated the bongo drum from Sierra Leone that was sitting on the mantelpiece. "That's why you clutter up my house with all your African junk. Worst thing we ever did was give them darkies independence. They were much better off under the Empire. I just hope you don't bring an Afri-

148

can girl home to meet your parents. It'd break their hearts."

On this occasion Imelda Klein's racist outburst was little more than annoying background noise to Roger. For her mention of the bongo drum on the mantelpiece had taken him back to the awful events surrounding Mark's mysterious death in Sierra Leone.

It all came back; the old slave fort, the argument on the beach, the black magician, Karonga, whose totem was the spider. Most of all, Roger recalled the aftermath of his best friend's death, and of the inconclusive autopsy report which blamed his death on the venom of a snake or a poisonous insect. Suddenly Roger recalled the barman's words about Karonga: *He can transform himself into the shape of the spider at will. If you, or those you love, make an enemy of Karonga, he will attach himself to you. Then you and your loved ones will never be safe, no matter where you hide.*

Imelda Klein's eyes had followed Roger's gaze, and her tirade now switched to the small bongo drum.

"I don't know why you keep that thing here, anyway. On one of the travel shows they said you can get all kinds of nasties from a souvenir like that. You can catch anthrax from the cow skin stretched across the top and you can get woodworm from the body of the drum."

Impatient with his grandmother's bigotry, Roger said, "People don't get woodworm, gran. Furniture does."

"I know that. I was just saying…"

"I know what you were *just* saying."

After this testy exchange with his grandmother, Roger went up to bed. He lay between the sheets for what seemed hours, his mind replaying scenes from his fateful vacation to Sierra Leone; scenes of Karonga, the drum seller-cum-musician-cum-black-magician; scenes

149

of Mark's casual defence of slavery and the slave trade. At one point Roger managed a sad smile at the outrageous thought that Mark and his grandmother were created from the same intolerant clay. Then his smile disappeared, his mood affected by anxiety bordering on fear. What if his gran became the target of the same malicious beast as did away with Mark? Hadn't the barman in Sierra Leone intimated that his loved ones might be victimised, too?

Finally Roger fell asleep, and perhaps due to the bongo drum bringing back memories of Sierra Leone he dreamed of Karonga. The African magician was beating out a tattoo on his drums whilst magically transforming into a giant, malevolent-looking spider.

Roger woke up in a cold sweat and instinctively knew something was wrong. Aware of the telltale hiss of a TV left on after the program schedule had ended, he crept downstairs to the living room.

Gran's fallen asleep in her armchair again, Roger tried to convince himself, but fear lay like a stone in his stomach.

Gran?" Roger called out.

The response was an all too familiar gurgling as Imelda Klein struggled for breath.

When Roger rushed into the living room, he found his grandmother sitting in her armchair, with two small puncture marks on her neck. Her eyes bulged from their sockets, and she was pointing towards the mantelpiece.

This time Roger saw the creature that had killed Mark and which had now mortally wounded his grandmother. The fat, tarantula-like beast was crawling into a hidey-hole opening in the body of the bongo.

"So that's how you managed to attach yourself to me," Roger spat, certain in his mind that the spider was the magically transformed Karonga. When Mrs. Klein gasped her last, Roger knew what needed to be done. He pulled a curtain from its railing, wrapped it tightly around the bongo drum and headed for the kitchen. There he collected a box of matches and the can of lighter fuel they used for summer barbecues.

In the back garden of Imelda Klein's home, Roger doused the curtain in lighter fuel and set fire to it. Almost immediately an inhuman screaming started up. Moments later, engulfed in flames, a beast that could have been a huge spider emerged, struggling, from the inferno.

Shrieking in pain, the creature blundered through the picket fence surrounding Mrs. Klein's garden. Then, still ablaze, it scurried away, illuminating its path as it disappeared down the alleyway at the back of the house.

* * *

Next day, after Mrs. Imelda Klein's body had been removed by ambulance to the mortuary, Roger got a visit from a policeman and a policewoman. They hadn't called about his grandmother, however.

"Did you hear anything strange last night, Mr. Klein?" the policeman asked.

Roger shook his head. "No! Why?"

"Well," said the policewoman. "Earlier this morning, a lady out walking her dog found a man's burned body over at Knesbitt Park. He'd been soaked in lighter fuel and torched."

"Do they know who the man was?" asked Roger.

The policeman shook his head. "He was burned almost beyond recognition. However, from what remains he

151

seems to be of African origin. We reckon the killing could be the work of a gang of human traffickers, as a warning for their victims to stay in line."

"Terrible, isn't it?" said the policewoman. "He came all this way in search of a better life, just to become prey to the modern day slave trade."

Roger nodded dumbly, but didn't venture an opinion.

Paul A. Freeman

Paul A. Freeman is the author of *Rumours of Ophir*, a novel set in Zimbabwe which is on the country's 'A' level English syllabus. He writes crime and horror fiction and has been widely published. His latest book, *Robin Hood and Friar Tuck: Zombie Killers - A Canterbury Tale*, has just been published by Coscom Entertainment. Currently he works in Abu Dhabi, where he lives with his wife and three children.

What Comes Around Goes Around

I was surprised when Katrina handed me an envelope. She had not spoken to me since that silly little incident with her boyfriend. But it was obvious she'd blabbered to just about everyone else. Those dirty looks and behind-the-back snickers said it all. Joni had volunteered to pass messages to Katrina to patch things up, but what was there to say? It wasn't like I had done anything outrageous. Besides, I didn't understand what she saw in the guy, in any aspect other than looks he was a total dud. And one more little detail puzzled me: how had Katrina found out about us?

So what was in the envelope, an angry letter telling me to stay away from her man? For a moment, I was tempted to just toss it away. Nothing good had come from Katrina to me lately. But curiosity won out. I ran my fingers over the thick paper and I felt the outline of a key. It came with a note revealing the address of an apartment and directions. I knew that Katrina had found a small flat a few weeks ago but half the time she had been staying at the dorm to be closer to her boyfriend who lived next door. There was no explanation as to why she would give up the place and pass it on to me, of all people. Maybe there was something wrong with it. Or maybe she just wanted me to be out of the way. I didn't care. Those last few days in the dormitory had been hell. A place of my own was everything I hoped for. I had no qualms about cutting classes that afternoon and eagerly followed the hastily scribbled directions on the sheet of paper.

The neighbourhood was shabby, desperately clinging to an air of respectability. My destination was a narrow three-storey building, set back from the street. A horse-chestnut tree spread its branches over a dark and gloomy yard. Its buds surprised me, not because of the early season, but they seemed to be out of place, looking for sun and warmth in these dreary surroundings. The building looked desolate and empty. The windows facing the street were dark and bare and hadn't been cleaned in a while. I climbed a few steps and forced the heavy door open. I slipped through the gap before it slammed shut. The smell in the hallway nearly made me gag. I flicked the light switch a couple of times before I noticed an empty socket dangling from the ceiling. *What a dump.* I thought. Still, it had to be better than the dorm.

Then I noticed the rainbow of a prism reflected on the upstairs wall. Intrigued by the pretty light I climbed the staircase and found my way to apartment number two. I didn't even have to use the key – the door opened at my touch. When I stepped across the threshold, I left the dreary surroundings behind and was swept into an embrace of sweet sensations. Big windows flooded the room with soft light. Opening them I looked out into a sea of green and drew a breath of deliciously fresh air. An odd assortment of furniture had been left behind. There was a bed without legs, a make-shift desk and two chairs. An old bed frame was propped up and used as a shelf. It held a collection of seashells and a few books. There was a kettle ready to boil and my favourite record was on the turntable. Then I heard it, just a hint of a whisper: *Welcome home, honey!* Or I imagined it.

I did not live in the building alone. There was another flat on the same floor and two upstairs. As for downstairs, I couldn't imagine anyone living next to the hall that was constantly permeated by a foul smell wafting from the cellar door. From inside my apartment I often heard the wooden staircase creak and groan, doors open and shut, and steps passing overhead. But I did not want to

154

introduce myself to my neighbours. I hesitated to plunge into the forced familiarity that had been part of what had driven me away from the dormitory. I revelled in the freedom of being on my own. There was no bickering, no taking sides, no ganging up on one another. I sure didn't miss any of it.

I didn't go out much until I discovered the club. I had been to a couple of second-hand stores browsing through an assortment of curtains and fabric. On the way back I noticed a group of people dressed in black. They were crowding around a side door; there were no ads, no posters. Maybe it was a secret society, I thought, just the thing to pique my curiosity. I lined up. When the door swung open it revealed a long, narrow staircase leading to an underground vault. It looked spooky. Going down the stairs I felt my skin prickle. When I turned the corner I was relieved to be greeted by fragments of music and neon light instead of the sinister trappings of a cult.

The acoustics were great, the atmosphere eerie. I savoured my anonymity and the opportunity to watch people interact without the need to interact with them. As I drifted through the crowd propelled by a pulsing beat, I caught the eye of a tall, good-looking guy. He was dressed in dark jeans and a black silk shirt that accentuated his muscular body. For a moment, his blue-eyed gaze met mine. Then he came over and steered me towards the bar where he bought us both a rum and coke. His words were lost in the noise, but his body sent a strong message. Unable to resist the exhilarating current passing between us, I invited him to come home with me.

He was fun in bed, but extremely self-absorbed. He sought praise for every caress and clearly thought himself to be a great lover. I enjoyed being with him during the course of the night, but when the sun came up, I just wanted him to be gone. But he lingered saying he'd like to take a shower. He undressed and strutted up and down the room showing off his perfect body. Impatiently I turned away. Left without an audience, he stepped into the shower. Then I heard him yell. He jumped out, soap still glistening on his skin. "Someone turned the hot water off!" he said accusingly. I just shrugged. Whatever triggered the cold shower, it had done the trick; it had cooled him down.

After that night I often went to the club. The impersonal atmosphere was less than perfect if you were looking to get to know someone. Yet I managed to meet a few guys eager to take me home. Most of them I never saw again, some stayed acquaintances I nodded to in passing. One odd thing they had in common: They were all treated to a cold shower in the morning.

The old building was in a sorry state of repair and a number of things didn't work very well. The roof had cracks inviting pigeons to nest in the attic and make a smelly mess. The stove smoked. In rainy weather the front door became waterlogged and didn't close. But the water temperature had never troubled me.

Strange things happen when you live alone. The teacup I had just filled was suddenly empty. A different record was playing than the one I had chosen. The light flickered. The tap was turned on when I wasn't looking. In the evenings the door was suddenly bolted and had to be forced open, especially when I was in a hurry to go out. Then there were gentle touches in the night and whispers out of thin air. I dismissed those things easily enough. But the cold showers worried me. I urged my lovers to be gone before breakfast. I discouraged them from taking a shower saying that the water pressure wasn't reliable. Very seldom did I succeed. They were

156

determined to rinse off the odour of love before venturing out into the world.

I was compulsively drawn to the club and felt comfortable in the sleek crowd. And with my short dark hair, pale complexion and green eyes, black has always suited me. I refined my style by spiking my hair and hunted for antique jewellery that made me look sophisticated. The only thing I didn't go for was the monster make-up many of the girls wore. It looked great when I tried it once, but it irritated my eyes. When I wiped away the tears, I smudged the paint job and looked like a sad clown which wasn't the image I was aiming for.

At the club I knew a few regulars by sight and could easily join in a casual conversation. But there was no one to point a finger when I was drinking too much or flirting with the percussionist. It was a lot of fun, until the night Joni showed up. She immediately latched on to me complaining about the dormitory. After I had moved out Katrina suspected Joni of sleeping with her boyfriend and stopped speaking to her. Joni snivelled and suggested that she was of course without blame. *Yeah, right,* I thought, *don't forget that I know you. And I also happen to know that particular lady-killer.* But I offered sympathy and brought her a few drinks. By the end of the night I had found out that it was she who had spilled the beans about Katrina's beau and me.

"Oh, well, that's all water under the bridge now." I assured her. But secretly I wanted to scream: *First you squeal on me, then you come crawling back. Get out!* But she didn't, she kept showing up more and more often. Joni discarded her cheery flower-print dresses and wore tight black pants and platform boots that made her nearly a head taller than me. She freed her thick blonde hair from the restraints of the single braid to let it cascade down her back. Joni immediately stole the show. But she didn't seem interested in picking up guys. She followed me around instead with an endless stream of stories about Katrina, the dormitory and everything I had managed to get away from. She even hinted that she might like to come over to my place for a visit or a sleep-over, to reconnect as she put it. I managed to evade that topic but whenever she was at the club, she ruined everything for me.

Happily, Joni was nowhere to be seen the night I flirted not with the percussionist but with the bass-player. He was just my type and I had my eye on him whenever he was on stage. Tall and a bit quiet, he didn't seem to be the kind of guy who hooked up with a different girl every week. I was ecstatic when he noticed me and invited me to hang out after the show. He even improved on closer inspection; he wasn't only good-looking, but also thoughtful and funny. After the last set, we escaped from the noise of the club and walked along the dark streets hand in hand. We chatted easily and it seemed natural to end up at my place. After spending the night together I was hoping he might stay for a bit. But the cold shower drove him away, just like the others.

That was the moment when I decided that I'd really had enough of this business with the shower. I armed myself with a flashlight and a wrench and ventured downstairs to check the hot-water heater and the plumbing. The heater seemed to be working fine and I couldn't see any leaks or dripping faucets. While I banged on the pipes in frustration I felt an icy breath on my neck.

You were cheating, you slut. How long did you think I would put up with this?

The flashlight flickered. I suppressed a scream and ran upstairs. In my room, it took me several minutes to get my breathing under control. Later I went to knock on my neighbours' doors. There was no response; maybe they were at work. Lying on my bed I listened for footsteps. When I heard them approach, I rushed out only to find the hallway empty. Again I rapped on all the doors; no one answered. "Is there anyone here?" I called out. *Not just anyone, my pet, it's me!* With the answer a cold hand pressed against my cheek. Mad laughter and a gust of icy air followed as I fled back to my apartment. The door slammed shut with a force that threw me to the floor. When I got up and tried the handle, I found it locked. Banging on the door or shouting would not bring any help and the windows were too high to offer an escape route. I was trapped.

To stop shaking I pulled on a comfy old sweater. I put on the kettle and played my favourite record. Sipping the tea calmed me, but it was too cold to sit still. I found a large garbage bag and started filling it with all my fancy clothes. My lacy underwear went first, followed by the tank tops, the skirts and stockings. Of my shoes, I only kept the sturdy ones. Everything with a heel had to go. I added the make-up I had bought, most of it unused. The air in the apartment had grown a touch warmer and I felt relieved. But there was more to be done. I tore the posters from the wall and shredded the programs and autographs I had collected as keepsakes from the club. When the garbage bag was filled, I straightened the room. I dusted the seashells, polished the desk and swept the floor. I was pleased to see the apartment so nice and tidy, almost exactly the way I had found it.

For dinner, I settled on making pasta. While I was waiting for the water to boil, I decided to get rid of the trash. I hardly felt any resistance when I stepped out into the hall and was able to return unmolested. The room had warmed up nicely by the time I sat down to eat my meal.

Now the touch is tender again, the voice sounds caring.

Go to sleep, my love. You need to rest. I'll watch over you, always.

And I close my eyes and pretend to be soothed. Tomorrow morning I will go out to buy milk. And I will never come back. The envelope with the key and directions I will pass along to Joni who was so keen to come here. And she'll be fine, I tell myself, as long as she remains faithful.

Susanne Martin

Susanne Martin lives in a rickety old house on a small island on the Canadian West Coast where the resident ghost often looks over her shoulder and demands an input in her writing. Her work has appeared in various magazines and newspapers as well as *In the Shadow of the Red Queen*, another Bridge House anthology.

A Ghostly Tale

We had always lived in the same small stone cottage. If I had to imagine myself living anywhere else it felt kind of wrong. When I was younger I had loved that the garden backed onto the grounds of the old, abandoned manor house. The manor house had been empty for as long as I could remember and I doubted that was ever going to change. I would climb over our rickety back fence and play in the gardens with my friends. Nobody minded because nobody knew. It was like our own private playground. Hide and Seek was amazing when you had so much ground to cover.

Of course there were whisperings. An elderly neighbour who lived in the cottage next to ours said that one night he had looked out of his window and had seen a light in one of the turrets. He told the story to anyone who would listen. He said that he had seen a flickering light which reminded him of the flame of a candle. When he had looked again and seen a pale face looking back at him he had pulled the curtains closed. After a few moments he had found the courage to peer back out but by then both the light and the face where gone.

I had always heard the rumours about the place. Apparently the family who had owned the place had been subject to a lot of bad luck. The only son of the family married far below his station and his parents only left him the house because there was nobody else. People said that his wife had gone mad, that when he had no longer been able to control her he had killed her to put an end to the humiliation. Nobody knew whether or not that was true. His wife had simply disappeared and soon after so had he. On dark nights when something unusual was spotted near

161

the manor people talked about ghosts and hauntings but to me it was kind of a cliché.

Ghost stories. Old abandoned houses were always going to have ghost stories. But I was sixteen years old and hardly believed in ghosts anymore.

"We have to do something exciting this Halloween, Melinda." Suzie sighed and threw a small toy pumpkin onto the floor sulkily. "Every year we do the same lame things. We walk you kid brother round trick or treating and then we come back here to watch a scary movie before going to bed."

I shrugged. It was kind of a tradition. There wasn't really anything else to do. Some of the boys from school went into the local graveyard and told each other scary stories but then I thought that was kind of lame too.

"Someone has to take Rich. He's got a new costume this year and he's really excited."

Rich was seven. For him Halloween was still all about candy and dressing up. He loved that I still took the time to take him, I was his big sister and he looked up to me. I knew I'd feel really bad if I pulled out at such short notice. He was probably already dressed up with Mum applying his face paints as we spoke.

"He's your kid brother, Melinda! Can't your Mum take him?"

It didn't take a psychic to work out what the problem really was! Suzie had an enormous crush on Tom Stevenson. He was a year older than us and would be off to University soon. Everyone seemed to have a crush on Tom. Suzie, however, knew that Tom would be in the graveyard that night and so obviously she wanted to be there too. If she looked scared enough by his stories then he might offer to walk her home. I doubted it but she seemed to have convinced herself.

162

"Look, Rich will be in bed by eight. We could do something then?"

"The graveyard?" Suzie asked predictably.

I nodded. There was no point arguing. She would make fun of any other suggestion I made until I agreed with her. It was easier to just agree straight out. It saved time.

Trick or treating wasn't the worst thing in the world. Despite being too old to get involved I actually really enjoyed it. Rich would run up to each door, knock several times and then pull his scariest face. The neighbours would all pretend to be terrified. They would take a few steps back in horror and then they would pile candy into his pumpkin shaped collection bowl. When the door closed again he would run back to show me all his treasure.

Suzie dragged sulkily behind. Whenever I glanced back she was examining her nails in boredom. I just loved the grin on Rich's face and no matter how much she sulked I wouldn't have missed it for the world.

"Finally!" She complained as I dropped Rich back at home, hyper on too much sugar.

"Okay, so we go to the graveyard and see if we can find Tom?"

Suzie nodded excitedly. It was the first time that night I'd seen her smile.

"I'm going to pretend to be terrified. I'll cling to his arm and then he'll feel like he needs to protect me. Do you think I should pretend to faint?"

I shrugged. She was going to make a fool of herself but I wasn't in the mood for an argument so decided to leave her to it.

"See how you feel!" Was the only advice I could give her.

There were several of Tom's friends and two other girls from our year already congregated there. Tom was perched on one of the gravestones. He was holding the beam of his torch under his chin and telling some predictable horror story about a serial killer with a hook for a hand. Suzie dropped to the floor close to his feet with an attentive look plastered onto her heavily made up face.

"Great," I whispered finding a seat a little further away. "We all know how this one ends."

I hadn't expected to be overheard. It had been a whisper. Just a joke that nobody was supposed to hear but one of the other girls from my year decided it would be cool to humiliate me instead of letting Tom finish his dumb story.

"Melinda thinks your story is lame." Sally Croft piped up loudly. "Maybe she thinks she's got a better one."

A flash of disappointment passed over Tom's face. Suzie gave me a dirty look for interrupting and I flushed bright red. If I hated anything it was being the centre of attention.

"Of course not. Sorry." I could barely hear my own voice.

"No, go on Melinda! We'd all love to hear one of your stories." Sally continued. "If you think you can do better!"

Sally was completely the opposite to me, she loved attention almost as much as Suzie did. The fact that I had given her the opportunity to humiliate me was probably going to make her night. I sighed. My brain was empty of any scary stories and they were all staring at me expectantly. I wrapped my coat tighter around me and climbed to my feet.

"Don't you think this is a little lame anyway?" I asked, my voice shaking as I waited for the jibes and laughter to start. "Sitting in a graveyard telling stories is for kids. I mean, its Halloween guys! Don't you think we could come up with something a little better than this?"

Tom looked interested. Suzie just looked angry that he was staring at me instead of down at her. After all, she had spent hours applying her make-up and I had come out without any on.

"What do you have in mind?" Tom asked with a look of amusement playing across his face.

I took a deep breath. Why does your mind always going blank at the worst possible moment? I was struggling for an idea, we lived in a small town and there was very little to do on regular nights. When it finally came to me I heaved a huge sigh of relief and looked Tom square in the eyes.

"Stone Manor," I cocked my head to one side as if daring them to keep listening. "The place is haunted, everyone knows that but are any of you actually brave enough to witness it for yourselves... Let's stop telling ghost stories and go and see a real ghost instead. I know how to get in!"

When I glanced around Sally didn't look quite as cocky as she had moments before. She was furiously trying to think of reasons not to go without looking chicken. Tom, on the other hand, looked more than a little interested and I could tell that Suzie was furious it hadn't been her suggestion.

"Let's go," Tom announced loudly to the rest of the group.

I did know a way inside Stone Manor. Like I said before when I had been a child I had played in the grounds numerous times. Once or twice I had actually gone pretty

165

close to the house, never inside but close enough to sneak a look. Some of the windows had been smashed on the ground floor so I knew it would be easy to climb in through one of those.

We climbed the fence near to the road. If my parents had seen me in our garden they would have been angry and made me go inside. Tom walked next to me and Suzie trailed behind looking annoyed and more than a little jealous.

"So how come you're up for a little ghost hunting? Girls aren't usually into that kind of thing?"

"I'm not scared of ghosts Tom." I tried to sound confident. "Are you?"

He laughed. I could see in his eyes that I was gaining his respect with every step closer to the manor that I took. This was my suggestion and I was going to go through with it, no matter how fast my heart was pounding and my head was telling me it was a bad idea.

When I knocked the rest of the glass out of one of the window frames to climb through I heard Sally's squeaky voice behind me.

"I'm just going to wait here guys," she snivelled. "Anne's going to wait with me."

I watched as the two friends held hands and walked a little way away from the house, probably thinking the ghosts might reach out through one of the windows and grab them. I saw some of the boy's exchange looks. They were less than impressed. If Sally or Anne thought they had a chance with Tom now then they were wrong.

I made sure that I was the first one in.

I went in feet first, dropping gracefully to the floor before stumbling over an abandoned stool that had been overturned in the middle of the room. I was terrified. The darkness was suffocating and when I span around to get my bearings I couldn't see anything but darkness ... except ... I thought I saw a flicker of light on the wall outside of the room. Was there someone else in the manor?

"You okay in there?" Tom shouted down to me.

I glanced back at the wall but the light was gone. I shook my head, my imagination was already going wild, what was I going to be like when we actually started exploring the place.

"Yeah, all clear."

Tom dropped down into the room behind me. His hand touched my shoulder as he steadied himself and I shivered. Suzie would die of jealousy if she knew he'd actually touched me. I toyed with whether or not I should casually tell her later.

I led Tom and his friends out of the pantry, which was the room we had entered into, through the kitchen and over to the main staircase. I didn't know my way around the manor at all. I had never been inside until now but I continued onwards with an air of certainty that made them think I knew exactly where I was going.

"Suzie decided to wait outside with the others," Tom said as he strode to keep up with me. "I guess she's not into making a real ghost story."

I nodded. I had known she would chicken out. I also knew that she would be unhappy with me for suggesting this in the first place. She could have happily sat in the graveyard and listened to ghost stories all night. She could have clung to Tom's arm as they walked home and pretended to be terrified. Real ghost hunting was taking things a step too far.

"Follow me." I headed up the main staircase. "If you want to see a real ghost then I know just the place... and just the person who might want to put in an appearance."

167

I could recite the old ghost story off by heart. Tom seemed impressed though. His dumb friends just trailed behind peering into the different rooms and making a lot of noise.

"Who? You got a ghost story for me Melinda?"

Tom's voice was flirtatious. I had him eating out of the palm of my hand.

I'd never really been that interested in Tom before. Most people would say that he was out of my league. He usually went for blonde, athletic girls. I had convinced myself that I found him boring because until now I'd never thought I had a chance.

"Have you ever heard to the story of the Byrom family?" I looked at him as if surprised that he didn't already know the story.

Tom shrugged his shoulders.

"I'm not really into history. Why don't you enlighten me?"

I smiled. My mind was working over time to make the story as scary as I possibly could. I wanted these boys running back to the pantry desperate to get out. At school on Monday they would all be talking about how awesome I was. How brave I was that I wasn't afraid of ghosts.

"The Byrom family built this place back in 1609. The son of the original family married a circus performer. His family were furious and threatened to disown him but as he was their only son they had no choice but to leave him the manor when they died. He brought his wife to live here after his parents had died but most people thought she was completely insane."

I saw the flicker of light again at the top of the stairs. For a moment I was hypnotised by it. I paused and watched as it moved as if being carried across the landing above us. Had someone else had the same idea for a scary Halloween night?

"Go on," Tom encouraged.

"Sorry," I glanced back up but the light was already gone.

Strange!

"His wife was so mad that he had no choice but to lock her in the South turret away from his servants and the rest of the town. Whenever she managed to briefly escape she would run out into the grounds naked and screaming and he was terrified that she would bring shame onto his family if she was seen."

"Naked?" One of the other boys sniggered. "Wish I'd seen that."

"You might get to," I responded quickly and shot him a confident look. "She disappeared one day and the locals believed that her husband murdered her when he became unable to cope with her madness. Legend has it that she walks the grounds looking for revenge on the husband who killed her."

An unexpected bang on the floor above sent us all screaming back towards the kitchens. Tom caught my hand and pulled me after him. I was breathless by the time we reached the window but I clung onto him like a terrified girl that he needed to protect. Suzie's idea worked wonders. He helped me climb out of the window and I saw Suzie glaring at me with utter hatred.

The walk back to the main road was filled with sniggers and attempts by the boys in the group to blame the high pitched screaming on each other. I felt in a particularly good mood because the whole thing had been my idea. The manor had been empty for years so nobody would mind a slight intrusion in the name of Halloween.

As I climbed over the fence to the road I risked a glance back at the house. In one of the top turret windows I could see the light again. It was as if someone was carrying a candle. As it flickered I could make out a shadowy face looking down at us. I shivered.

"You okay Melinda?" Tom sounded concerned.

I took his hand again doing my best to look like I need him to protect me.

"I am now."

Suzie and the other girls left us as the crossroads. Tom insisted on walking me to my front door. I was blushing when he bent and kissed me gently on the lips. I watched him leave after promising that he was going to call me the next day for a trip to the cinema. Suzie would be fuming with envy but she'd have done the same to me. We had a girls' agreement for this kind of situation, it was known as 'each for her own'. It had served us well over our long friendship and on numerous occasions she had used it for her own benefit...

My bedroom window was open when I went upstairs. I remembered closing it before I left but presumed that Mum had opened it to get rid of the smell of burnt pumpkin. I had had a jack o lantern on the windowsill for most of the evening with a candle inside that had burnt away to nothing. I went to close it and risked a brief glance back at the manor. There was no light there now.

It didn't take me long to fall asleep. I was exhausted. In my dream Tom and I were riding a Ghost Train at the annual fair. He was holding my hand and laughing as I screamed. One of the mock plastic gravestones at the side of the track had my name on it.

Something cold brushed against my face, my eyes shot open and as they struggled to adjust to the darkness I saw a flicker, like candlelight on the wall of my bedroom.

I opened my mouth to scream just as loud as I had in my dream but a cold hand clamped down over my lips.

"You came into my house and now I've come into yours." The voice was croaky and unpleasant.

I tried to move but I was paralysed with fear. As the candle guttered out all I had was the darkness and the sound of a mad woman laughing.

My parents still look for me, even though I know people think they should have given up a long time ago. Sometimes I see my Mum in my old bedroom window staring out as if believing that I will suddenly materialise from the shadows. It is her ritual on Halloween to stand there, marking the anniversary of when I disappeared. I light a candle and hold it up in the darkness hoping that she will see.

Boo Irwin

Stephanie Williams, writing as Boo Irwin, has been writing since she was fifteen. She has four short stories due for publication this year and recently won the Flash Fiction competition 2009 by Wyvern Publications. She is currently working on her second teen novel entitled *Myth*.

www.booirwin.co.uk

Reflection

Eve Lambert was dying. She was certain of it.

The cancer that had ravaged her mother's life was gnawing at her from the inside. The thought of it left her sickened, cold.

The mirror had told her so.

*   *   *

It had seemed such a bargain, at first. Just fifteen pounds for a French Art Deco wall mirror with original wrought iron frame. Even by the standard of the auction websites which were now a staple of her business, such a find was astonishing. Eve had to have it. A single bid, not much above the asking price; a few days' wait for the auction to finish; and it was hers. At first Eve had expected a catch: some sort of damage or a botched restoration job that had lowered the value. But the item description said nothing untoward about the condition of her latest prize, and the seller had assured her in a quick, courteous email that there was nothing to worry about.

A sixty mile round trip into the Northamptonshire countryside had secured the mirror, which now had pride of place in the small Art Deco installation in the alcove at the back of Eve's shop. The item description had stipulated "Buyer to collect". Eve had clients in the area, so she had made the journey into a morning's business trip, and met Persephone, as the owner had called herself on the Internet, for lunch.

The mirror had certainly impressed Russell. "I'd be looking at three hundred and fifty for that, minimum," he told her the next time he called round. "And you got it for fifteen pounds? Even your mother never had your gift for spotting a bargain."

"You're not annoyed you missed out, surely?" Eve replied. "You can have it for three hundred and fifty if you like."

Russell smiled at her in the mirror. "It's tempting, my dear. But as your business advisor I'm bound to recommend that you keep it in the shop, for now. And be ambitious. Set the price at four hundred and see what happens."

"Four hundred? Really?"

"Trust me," replied Russell, admiring himself in the shiny glass and stroking his aristocratic chin. "I've been in this business a long time, and I know a sure sale when I see one."

A sure sale. So why had the vendor been so desperate to get rid of it?

* * *

It was always a curious business, meeting Internet contacts in the flesh. But Persephone had seemed a little stranger than most: a pale lady, middle-aged, with thin translucent lips and a restlessness in her wide, watery eyes. Her movements were sharp, her spare body was tense like a bowstring, and the slightest unexpected noise around her seemed to make her start. *Like a frightened sparrow*, Eve had thought at the time. She told Eve that she was closing down a studio, selling off its contents; but Eve's polite request, from one dealer to another, to be allowed a look at what was left of the stock was rebuffed rather coldly. Everything had already been sold, apparently; the mirror which Eve had come to collect was the last piece left.

I should have thought to ask why none of the local dealers, who had cleared out the rest of Persephone's stock, had wanted to touch the mirror. Russell's verdict on

173

the value of the mirror didn't help; it just added further mystery to the whole business. In that condition and at that price, anybody who knew anything about Art Deco would have been mad to pass it by.

* * *

Three days later, the first incident took place. The shop had been quiet all day, and Eve was pottering about the Art Deco display in the alcove. A stray wisp of hair kept floating in front of her eyes as she bent down. After putting up with the distraction for some minutes she straightened up and turned to face the mirror, intent on pinning the strand back into its usual, sensible place. Her eyes met the mirror and it was the face of an old woman she saw looking back at her.

Eve gave a start and jumped backwards, knocking over a decanter which cracked as it hit the floor. Torn between confusion and annoyance at the accident, she blinked and looked again, and everything was normal. As it should be. Her own green eyes looking back at her.

What disturbed her most, she reflected afterwards, was the realisation that it wasn't so much *an old woman* that she thought she had seen in the mirror, but something which seemed to resemble *herself as an old woman*. Deep hollows around the eyes; blotched, sallow skin stretched too far across the long cheekbones; but the same eyes, wide and green and expressive as her own. A face that reminded her of her mother's in the final months, the warm flush of life washed out of it.

The next day, she received a telephone call. Northamptonshire Police, wanting to know about her dealings with a Miss Susan Boothroyd. Eve had been just about to dismiss the caller with an "I don't know who you mean" when she remembered Persephone. "Yes, that's right, of-

174

ficer, I met her four days ago. Business lunch. I'm in the antiques trade too. That's right. A mirror. Art Deco. She seemed really keen to get rid of it for some reason. No, I asked to see her studio but she wouldn't invite me back. Can I ask what this is in connection with? There's no trouble over the mirror, is there?" Not a stolen piece, surely? Persephone hadn't seemed the type.

No. The calm voice of the police officer politely informed her that Miss Boothroyd had died in the night. She appeared to have no family so the police were contacting her recent business clients to establish a picture of the final few days of her life. They'd taken Eve's number from the business card she had handed over with the cash for the mirror. It was just a routine call, and they thanked her very much for her trouble.

Oh. That was sad. Persephone, dead – and so soon after they'd met. Perhaps she'd been ill. She certainly looked ill. Like Mother.

"Still, it's strange they called *you*," said her brother that night, over dinner at their favourite restaurant. It was one of Jamie's regular flying visits. "Normally they'd only do that sort of thing if there were suspicious circumstances. I wonder how she died?"

She found the answer on a local news website, a few days later. Suicide by hanging.

Eve found herself looking at the mirror in the alcove with new curiosity after that. The last relic of a dead woman. She wondered, briefly, if she had been the last person to speak to Persephone before she died. *There* was a chilling thought.

The memory of Persephone played in her mind all that day, and the next. The account books on the desk in front of her became a blur, the figures seeming to shuffle and merge themselves in front of her aching eyes. A couple of times the jangle of the bell on the shop door jarred her back to a semblance of normality; but each time the customer left without buying, without saying a word. Once she glanced up to find a fat-lipped man standing in the doorway, looking at her. Something about the expression in the man's eyes made her squirm. But after her curt "Can I help you?" he shook his head and turned away in silence. The shop door clattered shut; the bell clanged funereally as Eve was left on her own with her thoughts.

Eve was still staring at the account books, much later, when a strange noise from the alcove made her blood turn cold. *Bump* – and a few seconds later, *bump* again – like somebody tapping a ball against the alcove wall. Eve's desk was on the other side of the wall. The sound made her sit bolt upright, suddenly afraid that there was somebody else in the shop with her. Most days the cool, rational part of her mind which dictated her everyday life would have quickly reprimanded her for being so silly – there was no way anybody could have entered the shop without her seeing them – but on this particular evening, other instincts, usually more deeply buried, were asserting themselves. Her skin was prickling, as if a cold draught were moving across her bare arms. She realised with some surprise that it was later than she had thought. Poring over her receipts with the desk lamp and the computer monitor for illumination, she hadn't even noticed that it had gone dark outside. It was night already.

Bump. There it was again.

Eve got to her feet and reached a trembling hand for a letter opener, in case she needed to defend herself. As silently as she could manage on her businesswoman's heels, she crept around the corner to see – nothing. The alcove was just as it always was, empty of people, with the mirror on the far wall reflecting her nervous face. Nothing to see.

Suddenly, it seemed to Eve that the scene in the mirror had changed. The shop, the alcove, and her own reflection had vanished. Instead, there was a bare empty room, almost dark except for something white, suspended from the ceiling and slowly rotating.

It was the reflection of a woman, hanging by a cord from the light fitting in the high ceiling above.

Eve screamed and span round. For a moment she didn't know where she was. Behind her everything was familiar. *Then what had just happened?*

She turned back to the mirror, her heart fluttering wildly. The white, hanging figure and the bare room were gone; all she saw was herself, wide-eyed and pale.

*   *   *

Eve shut up the shop immediately. The accounts could wait one more day. She returned to her quiet little flat above the premises, locked the access door behind her, and spent an anxious night on her own, trying to work out what it was she had seen in the mirror, what it meant. There *must* be some kind of rational explanation; she just didn't know what it was.

She found herself longing for some company. She tried calling Jamie, but he was away from home and wasn't answering his mobile. *It's all very well for him, with his city life and his jet-setting business*, she thought. *He wasn't the one who had to pick up where Mother left off, with a creaky old shop and a heap of debt to be paid off*. There was Russell, of course, but he was out for the evening. All the other people she knew locally were old friends of her mother's; she could hardly go to any of them with a crazy story like this. She realised with a sud-

177

den pang that she'd so wrapped herself up in the business since her mother's death that she'd allowed all of her confidantes from the old days to drift away. They wouldn't even know her now.

She thought, for a moment, of Persephone: solitary, haggard, and starting at shadows. Alone, like Eve was. *Is that what I'm turning into?* she wondered. *A lonely spinster being driven slowly mad by that mirror downstairs...* Maybe it was madness that had driven Persephone to take her own life. Or maybe she'd been sick, dying. Her thin frame could have been nursing a cancer like the one that had carried off Eve's mother. Perhaps that's what had driven Persephone to do it.

Maybe – "Oh God. Maybe I'm ill. Maybe I'm starting to sicken with it too – and *that's* why I'm seeing these pictures in the mirror..."

It was a fear she had been trying to deny for nine years. Diseases like this, she knew, were often passed down through families. If her mother had died of it, maybe she might die of it too. She'd heard of younger women than herself succumbing. Was *that* what the mirror had been trying to show her – that she was dying?

It became almost too painful for her to look in the mirror, after that. When she caught a glimpse of her reflection, out of the corner of her eye, she began to believe that she saw herself older, sickening, worn out by the thing that she imagined was eating her from within. She found that she was losing her appetite. Maybe that was the sickness too – or maybe it was just the fear of the sickness, she could no longer tell the difference. Yet when she found the courage to look squarely at her reflection in the mirror, it was the young Eve she saw – a little pale, and with those early wisps of grey in her hair, but still *her*. Was the mirror mocking her?

178

*   *   *

"You're not at all yourself of late, Eve," said Russell one day over lunch – a salad which she picked at with her fork, hardly swallowing a mouthful. "You've been distracted for weeks, and you don't look a bit well. What is it?"

"I think I've got what Mother had." She spoke the words almost in a whisper, so fearful was she of hearing them admitted to another person; but once they were spoken, the relief she felt was bliss. Russell was calm, understanding; matter-of-fact. He returned to the shop with her and refused to leave until she'd made an appointment with the doctor; then he headed upstairs to make a comforting mug of hot chocolate for her and perched on the edge of her desk as she drank it, her hands wrapped tightly round the mug for warmth.

"What I'm not sure about," he said at last, "is why now? I can understand you being scared, you must have been scared since the day Camilla got her diagnosis. I'm just not sure why it's taken nine years for you to realise."

Feeling foolish, but encouraged by the hot chocolate and a sympathetic ear, Eve told him about Susan Boothroyd, and the mirror. He listened placidly, stroking his chin, then took her arm and led her gently to the alcove. He studied the mirror for a long time, examining it carefully for a clue to its origins, but found nothing.

"I've heard of pieces like this before," he said at last. "They often acquire a certain – reputation, shall we say. Most dealers who hear a whisper of such a thing wouldn't want to go near it. That's why you were able to get it so cheaply. It seems Miss Boothroyd just wanted to be rid of it."

Evening came all too soon, and with it the time for Russell to depart. He let himself out through the front door of the deserted shop, leaving Eve standing in front of the mirror, deep in thought. Her reflection seemed to be mocking her aloneness. She stared at herself for a long time, wondering when the Eve she knew was going to become the sick, haggard old woman she had seen so often in her reflection; wondering, if the cancer had taken root, how far it might have spread, how much of her body was sickening from the disease. A defiant rage welled up inside her breast as she thought bitterly of her mother's last, painful few weeks.

"Damn it," she whispered, "I do not have cancer." Then louder, at the mirror: "*I do not have cancer!*" The words rose in volume until her voice began to crack. In a sudden frenzy to prove to herself that what she said was true, she ripped open her blouse at the neck and began frantically to probe and squeeze the soft flesh beneath her underwear. "There are no lumps. No lumps..."

It was then she realised that there was somebody else in the room.

A strange man, in jeans and a black hooded top, watching her. She could see his reflection in the mirror glass.

Even as she turned to face the apparition, she could hear the rational part of her mind trying to tell her that this was another of the mirror's tricks, another of her hidden fears given visible form for an instant. This time, she was wrong. There *was* a man standing in the alcove, looking at her. The shop door was still unlocked and he must have come in without her hearing the bell ring. A thickset man with fat, stubble-encrusted lips; that was all she could see of him behind his hood.

"Just do as I say, darling, and you won't get hurt."
His voice was rough, coarse.

Eve gave a gasp of horror and stepped back, pulling her blouse across her half-bare bosom with a trembling hand. The man who confronted her was holding a knife.

He took a step forward. There was a stale tobacco smell about him. "Take your top off. *Take it off.*"

Eve was trapped in the alcove, with no room to escape. Behind her was just the wall, and the mirror. As he advanced on her she could feel the heat of his body, tense and hard as a brick wall. Even while the knife continued to threaten her, his other hand reached out to grab at the torn material that she held to her breast. His eyes moved, for a split second, from her bosom to the mirror.

"No..."

The words broke unexpectedly from his mouth and suddenly he was looking away – beyond her, into the depths of his own reflection. His hood fell down and she saw his eyes widen in horror. Sensing that in that moment lay her hope of escape, Eve lunged forward, twisting aside the knife and his arm, and shoving him hard against the nearest cabinet. There was a clatter as clocks and ornaments fell to the floor; then she was free. She could hear him screaming: "No! No!" A second later there was a loud crash; then he was running towards her – past her, flinging her aside – out of the shop door and into the street.

A car's tyres squealed in the road outside. There was a dull thud. Gasping for breath, and with the rush of blood ringing in her ears, Eve staggered to the door to see her assailant crumpled underneath the bonnet of a silver BMW. His neck was bent at a crazy angle, and he did not move.

It was over.

181

*   *   *

Eve never knew what it was the intruder had seen in the mirror glass. Whatever it was, it had put such terror into him that he had picked up a wrought iron statuette and hurled it at the mirror before making his fatal retreat. The mirror glass had cracked like thawing ice. Its frame, twisted and mangled from the force of the blow, was beyond restoration.

Once the wreckage was cleared away, Eve had another job to do. It was time to put the shop up for sale. She had been living too long in Camilla's shadow, shut up here with the dusty old furnishings of a bygone era; afraid to face the present without her. Well, Mother was gone. It was time for a change. She knew that, now.

A fortnight later, a letter from her doctor signalled the all-clear.

A. J. Humphrey

A.J. Humphrey is a widely published poet and winner of numerous poetry awards, including five First Prizes in national competitions. His short stories have been published in *Dark Tales*, *Scribble* and previous anthologies from Bridge House and Earlyworks Press. He works as a research scientist and lives in York.

A Ghost of A Conscience

I saw him again last night.

That man. And, as usual, he was carrying a spade.

It sounds like something out of a gardening programme, doesn't it? Alan Titchmarsh at large explaining to we less green-fingered public how to successfully grow a bluebell. At first I wished that's all there was to it. I wished it had been a programme.

You can turn programmes off.

That was before I knew the whole story.

It all began a few weeks ago. I was leaning out of my window throwing some bread to my feathered friends, as I do every day, when all of a sudden he appeared. Apparently out of nowhere. He gave me quite a shock too, I can tell you. Strolling by as large as life with a spade tossed over his shoulder, making some remark about having eaten already. Funny guy. I was so surprised at seeing him I didn't answer and instead ducked back inside like a cuckoo clock in reverse. What was he doing there in the first place? I hovered about for a few seconds to give him time to pass before I took another look. I was curious as to where he was going with his spade. The beach? Once again I bent down and stuck my head out through the old sash window. The field was empty. He'd vanished. I could see no sign of him or his spade.

In this remote part of the country where my home has stood for years there is in abundance green fields, sea and large spiders particularly during the month of September. Every year it's the same story. Without fail, these eight-legged beasties pack up their belongings and move into my home. Granite, indigenous to the area, is also to be found in abundance. And it doesn't half interfere with my radio reception. I live alone and I have no neighbours apart from the ghostly mists that roll over the Atlantic and the gargantuan spiders particularly during the month of September, so, that evening I locked all my windows and doors and slept with one eye open. Well, not really, I'm joking, but only just. I was familiar with all the noises of the night but nothing unusual occurred. No creaking of the gate or the crunch of someone's heavy boot treading outside my window. No rattling of the door handle. Nothing.

Despite my fears, I slept soundly through the night and lived to see another day as the saying goes. The morning sun streamed in through my threadbare cotton curtains. Well, they are at *least* fifty years old practically an antique. By American standards they would be. Anyway, back to my story. The sky was blue the sea even bluer, the birds were singing their usual song and all was well with the world, tra la!

Right up until the moment when I saw him again.

It happened while I was up to my neck in dirt. Weeding my tubs and pots, home to my colourful mixture of purple flowers and those pretty pinkish ones... well, I never claimed to be a botanist... along with a carpet of primroses interspersed with the odd foxglove that grow wild here in these parts, when all of a sudden – he appeared.

"I do wish you'd stop doing that," I remarked abruptly.

"Sorry." Black eyes pierced the pale greenness of my own. "I mean you no harm."

I stood up and pushed a curl away from my face. My anger dissolved as quickly as it had appeared. I couldn't stay angry with such a good-looking guy even if he did dress like a strange hybrid of scarecrow meets pirate. Interesting look. Russell Brand meets Johnny Depp.

"That's all right. I shouldn't have snapped at you. I'm Tammy, it's short for Tamsyn."

I smiled at him to show there were no hard feelings, but he looked right through me as if I wasn't there.

"Are you all right?" I took a step closer.

"I'm well enough," he replied and turned his face towards the sea. "Thank you for asking, it's been so long." His words faltered as he continued to look at nothing but the vast ocean.

"It's been so long," he repeated quietly.

"What has?" I was so close I could have reached out and touched him. The smell of tobacco mixed with another I couldn't place radiated from his body. I wriggled my nose. I found it curiously disturbing. And he was better looking than I'd first realised with his bronzed skin set off by raven black hair – just like a buccaneer. He made Johnny Depp look almost ordinary in comparison. Johnny, who?

He turned back to face me. "Have you ever wished for something so badly that you would do anything to have it?" he asked.

"Well, no. I can't say I have – why?"

"I did just that and now I'm paying for it. I'm paying for it for the rest of my life."

"What do you mean? Paying for what?"

"Greed, my fine lady, greed and the lust, the aching desire to have all the riches I could carry in my trusty sea chest."

"You sound just like a pirate!" I laughed. "You even look like one."

"That's because I am."

I stopped laughing straight away. Instead I began to feel terrified. There was this growing fear that something was horribly wrong. My throat turned so dry it felt like I'd stuffed my mouth with a ream of paper or my mum's famous scones... they are pretty bad even the seagulls turn their beaks up at them. And my stomach suddenly took it upon itself to churn and lurch as it does before an important interview or exam or when you discover, to your horror, you've been walking around Penzance with your skirt caught up in your knickers.

I turned round to see how far away I was from the front door just in case I had to make a mad dash inside. The man was a lunatic, a good-looking lunatic, but a lunatic all the same. I calculated the distance. Good. Only a few short steps and I'd be safely inside and away from this crazy man with his spade. I turned back to face him.

My eyes gazed upon an empty space. Nothing. He was gone. I nearly fainted on the spot. I looked up at the sky. Then wished I hadn't. The sun was blinding. Sunstroke? No, it was bright, but it wasn't hot enough for sunstroke. Besides, he had to be real. I'd spoken to him. Hadn't I?

I began to shake – like a leaf – I remember thinking. Yes, I know that's not exactly original but it's all I could come up with at the time I'm sorry, so *shoot* me. Had I been suffering from a weak heart I would have been dead for sure. That much was certain.

I urged my shaking legs to move and propelled myself through the front door and into my living room. I slammed the old oak door behind me, shut the bolt across and poured myself an extremely large glass of whisky straight. Then downed another right out the bottle. I disliked both the taste and the spinning of the room, however, it did at least steady my nerves and I was able to stop shaking like a washing machine on its spin-dry cycle.

A pirate? A ghost? Well, I pondered, as I staggered up and down the room, there was no other explanation.

The man was a ghost. Simple. He was a ghost. I'd had a conversation with a ghost. "You should get out more," I muttered to my reflection in the old spotted mirror that hung above the fireplace.

I wobbled over to the window and looked out to sea. It was calm and blue and there was nothing to hint at what had just happened. The sun was still shining and my trowel was lying on the paving stone exactly where I'd left it. Everything looked normal and ordinary except I knew better. At least, I thought I did and then I dismissed it entirely. The whole idea was ridiculous of course. I mean, talking with a ghost? There were no such things as ghosts. Or? Well, if he wasn't a ghost, what was he? Who was he? My mind flitted from one explanation to another back and forth like a ping-pong ball. In the end I didn't know what to think.

I'd always presumed ghosts manifested themselves during the night. Wasn't that when ghosts were supposed to materialise? With chains and things? Scary figures in the dark jumping out at you to go "boo!"

Not so, apparently.

And look at the way he'd disappeared like something out of David Copperfield. No magician is that good, Sooty maybe... no! He had to have been a ghost. There was no other explanation, or was there? Well, maybe if David Copperfield had been around in person there would have been an alternative explanation, but he wasn't. There's never a magician around when you want one.

Well, what did it matter? I could handle it. That's right. I was Cornish through and through. I'd grown up in the land of the fairies or piskies as we call them – nothing fazed me. I don't get in a panic at the mere mention of a roaming spirit... spooks and mystical occurrences are second nature to me, goblins and gremlins, I can handle it all ... water off a ducks bottom ... all right! I'm lying.

Ghosts, manifestations, call them what you will, they scare me half to death and back again. Have you any idea *how* embarrassing that is for a Cornish person to have to admit? It's all to do with tales passed down through my family, something about rogue pirates and suchlike raiding and looting. Along with curses, a werewolf and a handful of vampires thrown in for good measure. These gory tales used to scare me half to death and back again.

Used to? Still do.

Anyway, back to my story.

Days turned into weeks and weeks turned into months and although I kept a sharp lookout for my pirate friend, I didn't see him again.

Not until last night.

It was all over in a matter of seconds. I'd gone outside to investigate a mysterious light on the beach. As I clambered down the jagged path that led from my house to the dunes and the rocks and the sea below, I tripped, fell and banged my head.

I'd caught sight of my gorgeous ghost, spade in one hand, beckoning to me with the other, and that's when it happened. I was so startled by his sudden appearance that I tripped. There and then. The police said it was an accident. But I knew better. It was no accident. It was fate. Karma. Call it what you will.

But it wasn't an accident.

It was an old sea chest sticking out of the ground. That's what I'd caught my toe on and had caused me to go flying through the air like Superwoman. It was an old wooden and iron sea chest when on discovery turned out to be full of treasure. Pewter mostly. And jewellery. Beautiful jewellery encrusted with sapphires, diamonds and rubies. And silks. And, surprisingly, in good condition too. I thought of the threadbare curtains hanging up at my bedroom window and then thought blow that – think clothes. Think lovely new clothes before curtains. I'll stick with the distressed beach thing. It's atmospheric. And what was the outcome of my friend? We won't be seeing him again. His search is over. His conscience is clear. He's at peace. Oh, and he was so cute too. I wonder if he has relatives living close by.

I touched the bandage on my head and smiled. I was grateful. I'd always be grateful. Stealing and looting from my ancestors all those years ago, it had taken a long time, but finally the family riches, such as they were, the treasures had come a full circle.

They'd come back home.

Rosemary A. Bach-Holzer

Rosemary Bach-Holzer is a published writer of articles and short stories. Please visit her on her website at www.rosemarybachholzer.co.uk or visit her blog at www.rosemarybach-holzer.blogspot.com to discover more, particularly if you are fond of cats. And even if you're not, still make a visit... you can be converted. Miaow.

Good Company

The flat smelt of new carpets and fresh paint. Alex looked round the modest living room, admiring the tall windows that let in the spring sunshine.

"It really is perfect, mum." She smiled at her mother who was placing flowers into a vase.

"It makes a change." Mandy sighed, "Never thought I would leave the old house."

"Retirement flats are a good idea, you've got company and someone always on the door to keep an eye out." Alex realised she was sounding preachy, they had had this conversation before.

Down the short hall the doorbell rang.

"That will be Lynn and Mike." Mandy disappeared from the room.

Alex took a better look around now she had the chance. It was odd seeing her mother's familiar possessions spread out in an unfamiliar room. She sniffed the flowers and nudged something with her foot. Looking down she saw a porcelain doll that she didn't recognised. She presumed it was just one more welcoming present.

"It is a bit compact. I had to get rid of a lot," Mandy's voice echoed down the hall, "Downsizing Alex calls it."

Lynn and Mike arrived in the living room and made approving noises.

"Now we're all here I'll make the tea." Mandy ushered her friends to the sofa, "Alex brought a lovely cake."

She indicated a cream sponge cake perched on the coffee table, dishes sitting ready beside it.

"What a pity I didn't bring my camera." Lynn grumbled

"Not to worry, Alex has one of those mobile phone thingies." Mandy nudged her daughter who retrieved a small mobile phone from her bag.

"Why don't I film you cutting the cake, mum?"

"Alex is very technologically advanced." Mandy smiled proudly.

She produced a cake knife and, with Lynn and Mike flanking her, awkwardly smiled at the camera while trying to cut the cake.

"Got it!" Alex grinned.

"Good. Now who wants cake?"

The following Sunday Alex typed an email to her brother Adam who was currently residing in California. She downloaded the mobile phone recording and attached it to the email for her brother to view. She sent it off and went to make some lunch.

That evening there was a new message in her inbox.

"Looks like a fun party," wrote Adam. "Sorry to miss it! Who's the little girl in the film?"

"Little girl?" Alex read the message again. She hadn't viewed the footage properly herself, before sending it to her brother.

She opened the movie file on the computer and played the few minutes of footage the camera had taken. There was her mum, Lynn, and Mike. Mandy was hovering with the cake knife over the sponge, a fixed smile on her face, clearly unaware that the mobile was taking live pictures and not a still shot. The sunshine beamed in through the deep windows, Alex could almost smell the paint.

And then, just as her mum started to cut the cake, she saw her. A little girl in a pale dress and knee-length socks. She was tucked up against Mandy's side and staring straight at the camera, her deep blue eyes seemingly fixed

191

on Alex. Alex couldn't believe her eyes; she played the film again and paused it. The little girl still stared out from the screen. She blinked; perhaps it was a trick of the light? But the girl was so clear, so … solid.

Not sure what else to do she emailed back her brother.

"Don't know who she is." She wrote, "The weird thing is, she wasn't there at the time. What do I do?"

She sent the message then played the footage once more. As she viewed it, her mum smiling and cutting the cake, Mike pulling faces, she realised the little girl was dressed identically to the doll she had seen in her mother's living room. In fact she could just see the doll behind the child and they looked almost like twins.

Alex was not one to jump to conclusions, but the footage had spooked her. Surely there had been no little girl? She felt a knot of anxiety pinch her stomach. Sitting staring at the little girl, she tried to screw up her eyes and make her disappear. But the more she looked the more the little girl felt familiar. Abruptly she realised a stray tear had rolled down her cheek. She brushed it away frightened by the sudden sadness that filled her.

Her mum's flat was new, less than a year old and the site had been barren before they had been built. Nothing more than a decaying warehouse for storing cloth, which the barges had once carried up river. Not a place to find a child. At least not one so neatly dressed.

Her computer pinged. There was a new message in her inbox.

"Must be a ghost then," Adam surmised, "Why not tell mum?"

Alex thought that was a very bad idea and sent a return email stating as much. She stared at the screen a while longer, then turned off the computer with a sigh.

The next morning her mum rang as she was getting ready for work.

"Could you bring the film over this evening?" Mandy asked, "Elaine is coming at seven and I promised I'd show it to her."

"Oh, well it didn't come out that good." Alex mumbled vaguely.

"Adam said it looked all right when I rang him last night. He said you had sent it to him."

"Yes ... well ... okay, I'll bring it after work." Alex cursed Adam under her breath.

"Lovely, I'll make you some tea so you don't have to rush off."

Teatime, Alex stood at her mother's door feeling a sense of dread welling up in her belly. What would her mother say about a haunted flat? Would she want to leave? And after all the hassle it had taken to get her here, Alex could hardly bear the thought.

Mandy opened the door and let her in. There was a smell of roast pork coming from the kitchen.

"Sit down and set up the film. I'd like to see it for myself first." Mandy commanded, before she disappeared into the kitchen.

Alex had burnt the footage to a DVD. She turned on the telly and loaded the disc. Out of the corner of her eye she could just see the doll. It made her shiver.

"Is it all set?" Mandy settled herself on the sofa.

"I guess." Alex pressed play and hoped her mother would watch the film and not notice the child.

The short piece of film flickered on the screen. Mandy watched solemnly, her lips were set in a grim line of determination as though she was being forced to watch something horrid and was going to get through it no matter what. When the footage ended the screen went blank.

193

"Just as I thought." Mandy sank back in the sofa and sighed.

"Mum?" Alex sat beside her and clutched her mum's hand.

Tears were slowly rolling down Mandy's cheeks.

"It was just a party." Alex said, hoping despite all evidence that her mum hadn't noticed the child.

"I had to see it for myself. Your brother said she was there."

"Adam?" Alex whispered. "You knew all along..."

"He told me on the phone. Said I should watch the footage. He said he just knew it was Rachel." Mandy took a deep breath and concentrated steadily on the wall and not her daughter.

"Who is Rachel?" Alex asked.

"Who was, would be a better question." Mandy suddenly let out a sob and squeezed Alex's hand tightly, "I didn't want you to know. I thought it would upset you."

"Upset me?"

"But your brother found out while he was doing that silly family tree project for school. I had to explain everything and make him promise to not say a word to you."

"Whatever for?"

Mandy pulled herself up in the sofa and sniffed.

"I didn't want to frighten you. You used to have such nightmares as a child, I thought if I told you it would make everything worse." Mandy stroked her daughter's face tenderly, "Besides, it was hard to talk about."

"Please, tell me now." Alex begged.

"You were not my first child." Mandy tried to wipe away the tears that welled in her eyes, "I had a little girl, Rachel, back in the 60s."

"Oh." Alex didn't know what else to say.

"It was a bad decade and I did some silly things. I ended up in a bed-sit with her. She was five. I used to let her sleep near the fire where it was warmest, the place was so cold and damp." Mandy fell into silence.

Alex clutched her hand tighter.

"I woke one night and felt so sick." Mandy shut her eyes with the memory, "I was dizzy and there was this smell. The gas fire was leaking. I picked up Rachel and ran downstairs to where there was a phone, but it was too late. The ambulance man said she died in her sleep."

Alex could feel tears welling in her own eyes as she saw her mother's pain and distress.

"I should never have shown you…"

"No, don't say it." Mandy managed to smile at Alex. "I kept her clothes, her nicest dress and socks and shoes. I bought a doll and I dressed it in them."

Alex's eyes drifted to the doll.

"But I soon found that wherever the doll stood Rachel would appear there. Now I'm not much of a believer. But that little girl followed the doll wherever it went, I swear." Mandy struggled with the words, "Before you were born I didn't mind, I liked seeing her even. I supposed it was grief. But when you came I was frightened you would be scared by it so I moved the doll and hid it in my wardrobe."

"That's why I had never seen it before." Alex said.

"I'd almost forgotten, but she hadn't."

"It wasn't your fault."

"I know that." Mandy smiled, "You know, I'm not so sad now, I had left so many memories behind, but one of them was determined to come with me."

They both stared at the doll. In the kitchen a timer buzzed.

"That will be dinner." Mandy got from the chair and wiped her eyes dry.

She looked as though nothing had happened. Alex watched the doll as her mother went into the kitchen. It seemed inanimate as it should. She relaxed a little.

"Will you be happy living here, now you know?" She called through.

Mandy appeared at the kitchen door, smiling sadly.

"Oh yes." She said, "Rachel always was good company."

Sophie Jackson

Sophie Jackson has worked as a freelance writer since 2003 specialising in historical non-fiction. She has three books to her name, *The Curse of Dasenin*, *The Medieval Christmas* and *The Horse in Myth and Legend*. She is currently working on a book for The History Press on POWs held in Britain during the war.

Now That I've Found You

The girl moved back and forth on the child's swing, moving her feet rhythmically. He couldn't work out if she hadn't noticed him or was just pretending she hadn't. She'd made Craig feel uneasy at first. But then he told himself she had no right looking so superior. Because if he was here, at the park, just next to the cemetery, at nine o'clock in the morning, when he should have been at school, then he wasn't the only the one wagging it.

He kicked a bit more sand about in the sandpit, just to show he wasn't bothered about being stared at. But this was the first time he'd done anything like this in life and he didn't think he was that convincing at acting nonchalant. If his dad found out he wasn't at school, he'd kill him.

Or he would have done at one time. Today Craig was banking on it that if the school rang dad later to tell him Craig had failed to register with his form teacher, he wouldn't even bother answering the phone. He'd just let it go to voice mail while he remained slumped in his chair, staring straight ahead at the telly and, as usual, failing to take in anything that was being broadcast.

That's if he'd bothered to get out of bed this morning. When Craig had left, stuffing the abundance of pound coins dad had put out the night before into his trouser pocket – his dinner money – there'd been no sign of him. Dad didn't have a clue how much dinners cost, and Craig, who'd never been so well off in his life, had no intentions of clueing him in.

Mum always used to make sandwiches for him. There'd be a piece of fruit too, and orange juice and a little pack of raisins. She liked to send him off every morning well on his way to his five a day, she used to say.

Sometimes she'd even leave a note for him. *Have a nice day*, it would say. Or *Work hard!* Or even a joke some times.

"Hiya."

Craig, lost in memories of his mum, hadn't noticed the girl creep up on him till she was standing over him. She'd be about his age, he guessed. Small and skinny, her hair invisible under a woolly hat. Pale face. Big staring eyes. She looked a bit like ET, he thought.

Craig returned the greeting with a nod. Until he knew what she was up to he had no intentions of wasting any words on her.

"You on your own?" she said.

He turned his head all the way round to the left, then all the way round to the right, in an exaggerated manner, before his gaze finally came to rest on her strange, pale face. What do you think, his expression read. He'd set out to embarrass her, but all she did was sit down next to him on the edge of the sandpit.

"I'll come with you if you like," she said. "if you're thinking of going to the cemetery."

Craig frowned. "I'm not thinking of going any-where," he growled.

Except going to the cemetery had been exactly where he had been thinking of going. Just not yet, that's all.

"Course, if you don't want to go just yet, we can stay here a bit. Or we could go for a walk if you liked."

What was it with girls that they always seemed to be able to read your mind? Mum had been an expert at it. She knew if he'd been fighting, or lying or if something had upset him. She could guess if there was a girl in his class he liked or if he'd lost his football kit or got in trouble with his teacher.

Funny, but though she was an expert at sniffing out his feelings and persuading him – in the end – to get whatever it was off his chest because she knew that he'd feel better if he did – she was rubbish at spilling out her own troubles.

It's nothing, had been her catch phrase, right from that first visit to the doctor's. *Just routine* had been another. Phrases that squatted like a line of fat ugly toads blocking the way to ever finding out his mum's true feelings.

Dad was the same. Worse, if anything. All that rubbish about mum being right as rain once she'd had her treatment. He'd stopped being quite so jolly though after her second bout of treatment. He'd dropped the mask completely when they'd been told that still more was necessary.

"I know a secret way into the cemetery if you're interested," the girl said.

"How come?" He was interested, in spite of himself.

"Just do, that's all," she said. "It's where I hang out."

She got up and started to walk away.

"My name's Tracey, by the way," she said.

Craig mumbled his own name back. It took him aback, this sudden curiosity he had about her. If she'd asked him why he'd decided to go with her after all, he'd have said that he'd suddenly decided that he might as well, because he had nothing else planned. But she didn't ask him. She didn't even look behind to check he was following. Cocky, Craig thought, not without admiration.

The cemetery was vast. Rows and rows of graves, some untended, some well cared for. It was a maze.

"Do you know where you're going?" the girl said.

There she went again – reading his mind. But coming here had weakened him. It was like he'd lost the strength to fight her.

"No," he said. "I've never been here before."

The girl shrugged. "Well, it wouldn't be top of many people's Days Out lists," she said.

"It's my mum's grave I'm looking for."

There. He'd finally admitted it. To himself and to all the world. All the world except his dad.

"I don't want to go to the funeral," he'd said, the morning he'd stood in the middle of the living room while his dad struggled to tie the tie around his neck.

The suit itched and he wasn't used to wearing proper shoes. You weren't allowed to wear trainers at funerals, Gran had told him, so she'd taken him out to buy these awful black lace ups, along with the itchy suit and the white shirt with the button round his neck that was too stiff, and this tie that his dad was making a proper mess of tying.

He didn't think his mum would mind if he wore trainers or carpet slippers, frankly. She was dead, wasn't she? If there was a heaven then she'd be sitting on a cloud, strumming a harp and waiting for her wings to grow.

But he didn't really think there could be one because there was definitely no God. God would never have made his mum get sick and die.

"I want to stay at home," he'd said again.

"I understand, son," his dad replied. "I know it'll be hard for you. But it's an opportunity to say goodbye, you know?"

Craig *didn't* know. He'd said goodbye a long time ago. When it dropped into his head from nowhere that the woman he went to visit in hospital, wrapped up in tubes and plugged into this and that machine, wasn't his real mum at all.

His real mum smiled with her eyes, not just with her lips. His real mum couldn't have borne the idea of lying so still either and she certainly never closed her eyes and fell asleep just as you got to the bit in your story when you'd got possession of the ball and were about to pass it to Banksy, who went on to score the blinder that put your team in the lead.

He'd given up going to the hospital after that. When she insisted on coming home, less than a week before she died, Craig stayed out of her way completely, right up until that last visit to her room, where even the combined perfume of flowers and plug-ins failed to mask the sour and desperate scent of mortality.

He was adamant he was going to stay away from her funeral too. In the end he'd stayed home with Gran and Dad had gone alone. He'd kicked up such a fuss that he'd frightened them – frightened himself too. He'd never in his life been a one for tantrums. But maybe that was because up till this point nothing much had ever gone wrong in his life.

The girl was weaving her way in and out among the graves, providing a running commentary as she did so – the name of the dead person, their age, the inscription, occasionally an expression of sympathy at the shortness of their life or, at the opposite end of the scale, amazement that they'd lived so long.

Every now and then she'd disappear behind a headstone and Craig panicked till he could see her again. There was something comforting about the sound of her voice and her closeness.

"Elsie and Harold Turner," she said. "Oh, look! They died within two months of each other. *Holding hands into eternity*. Aaw, how lovely!"

Then, a moment later: "Amy McNulty. December 1982 - March 1983. *Safe in the arms of Jesus.* God, that's rotten that is, innit?"

Craig didn't answer. He got the feeling she'd be prattling on like this even if he hadn't been there. There was something weird about her. Like she wasn't solid, not a proper human being. And that stupid woolly hat. Mum used to wear one like that, to cover the fact that underneath she no longer had any hair. She must have been his age. Yet she looked – not old – but ageless.

"Tell us your mum's name, then," the girl said, suddenly sticking her head from behind a huge marble cross and making him jump.

"Julia May Bellamy," Craig said. "Née Barton."

"Nay Barton? Three surnames? That's a bit of a mouthful!"

The smile crept up on him, unawares. Carefully and slowly, he explained what née Barton meant. He liked knowing something the girl didn't know. It wasn't that she was a smart Alec, but she had an air of confidence he envied. She didn't seem remotely afraid of anything. Not being discovered in the park when she should have been at school. Nor of anyone in uniform whose job it might be to patrol the graveyard looking for people who looked like they shouldn't be there. Not even of these graves and the dead people that lay inside them. He shuddered just thinking about them.

"We'll never find her," he said. "This place is massive."

He was beginning to regret coming here. What good would it do anyway, even if he found mum's grave? *She* wouldn't be waiting by it, would she, holding out her arms to him, tall and straight and beautiful like he remembered, not a tube or a machines or a woolly hat in sight?

"We can't give up so easily," the girl said. "We've only just got here."

Craig stuffed his hands in his pocket and kicked a stone hard. It made a pinging sound as it hit one of the gravestones. He felt the familiar anger boil up him in, never far away these days, since mum had gone. Who did she think she was, this girl? Latching on to him like they had stuff in common. He'd had enough. He was going home.

She let him stride off without following him. He wasn't used to being ignored. Usually, these days, they all ran after him. His teachers, his dad, his gran. *You miss your mum, that's all,* they'd say, once they'd caught up with him. *I know how hard it must be for you.*

That just made him more angry. Because they didn't know how hard it was. They couldn't know. They weren't him and there was no way they could possibly guess how he felt inside. How could they when he didn't know himself?

He thought he'd been walking towards the exit, but he must have got lost. Hadn't he been past this grave already? He recognised the names. Elsie and Harold Turner. And that great big statue of an angel in white marble, wings outstretched, looking down on them. He turned round and walked in another direction, a way he didn't think he'd been before.

He couldn't believe it but there she was again. Sitting on the ground, this time, like she was waiting for him, next to a gravestone that looked like it hadn't been there long. There was a bunch of dead flowers in a vase nearby.

"I've found your mum," the girl said. "Pity about them though."

She inclined her head towards the flowers, brown and shrivelled, hanging their heads piteously in a glass vase that was covered in green scum.

203

Craig darted forward and snatched the vase from the ground. It wasn't fair! It was *his* mother's grave, not *hers*! He should have been the one to find it first. He hurled the object as hard as he could at his mother's headstone. The glass shattered and the dead flowers went sailing through the air before plunging to the ground with no noise but the faintest rustle.

Horrified at what he'd done, Craig stood, mesmerised, as a thin film of water trickled like tears down the headstone's inscription. *Julia May Bellamy, née Barton, beloved wife to Michael and devoted mother to Craig. Light of step and heart.*

"I'm going now," the girl said, getting up slowly and adjusting her woolly hat. "This bit's private. But you mustn't be ashamed of being angry with her."

Craig didn't see her go. His eyes were blinded with tears. Tears of such rage that he hadn't known one person could contain. He threw himself forward and with both arms tried to wrench the headstone out of the earth. For death to exist there had to be a grave, didn't there? If only he could rip this grave out of the earth and destroy every trace of it then everything would be all right again, wouldn't it?

He tugged and tugged until he was drenched with sweat and had no more strength left in him, sobbing tears of fury all the while and cursing his mother for leaving him on his own like this. How could she do it to him? He was only just thirteen, he had his whole life ahead of him and she'd just turned her back on him and left him to sort it all out on his own.

"Stupid! Selfish! I hate you!" he screamed. "I hate you!"

On and on he went, yelling, swearing, with an occasional kick directed at the headstone, until finally he collapsed in soundless sobs. He must have fallen asleep. When his father found him, he was still holding onto the headstone, only now he held it in a comforting embrace.

He woke to see his father standing over him, his face awash with tender tears. It took Craig a moment before he realised where he was. The memory of all that had just happened flashed through his brain. Had he really shouted and screamed and kicked up such a fuss? His eye caught one of the dead flowers on the ground, a piece of glass, and then another.

"Dad," he said. "What are you doing here? How did you find me?"

"They phoned me. Said you hadn't turned up at school. Don't ask me how I knew I'd find you here. Just a feeling. You know?"

He looked around him at the dead flowers and the broken vase, his expression bewildered.

"What happened here?" he said. "Do you want to tell me?"

Craig shrugged. He couldn't explain. But whatever demon had got into him had left. He tried to remember the last thing the girl had said before she left. That's right, he mustn't be afraid of being angry. The anger had left him now for good and Craig felt strangely calm. Like an ocean going vessel that had been tossed about so long on storm filled waters suddenly sailing into a still sea, with the prospect of a smooth voyage ahead.

"I'm sorry I missed Mum's funeral," he said.

"And I'm sorry for letting her grave get into such a mess," his dad said. "So that's two of us sorry, son."

Craig watched his father pick up a piece of broken glass, a wistful expression on his face. He looked like he was deliberating whether or not to say something. Maybe he wanted to explain just why he'd kept away from

Mum's grave after that first couple of reluctant visits. Well, there was plenty of time for explanations. They could talk about their feelings while they tended the grave. With Mum nearby, prompting them.

"You men," she used to say. "Why can't you just say what you mean instead of bottling it all up?"

"We could buy another vase," his dad said now, carefully collecting the pieces of broken glass together. "And flowers."

Craig nodded.

"Lots of flowers," he said.

"Shall we go home now, son?"

He held out a hand and helped Craig up from the ground.

"Do you know the way out?" Craig asked him. "Cos I don't. A girl showed me. But she disappeared soon after."

One last piece of glass glinted in a sudden burst of sunshine. It had landed on a grave diagonally opposite to his mum's.

"Look," he said, bending to pick it up. "We missed one."

Curiously, he ran his eyes over the inscription. *Tracey Davies 1995-2008. So young, so sweet, so soon.*

That strange looking girl he'd met. Hadn't she been called Tracey too? Funny that. He wondered if he'd ever see her again. He might bump into her here another day, you never knew. It was where she hung out, after all, or so she'd said.

Geraldine Ryan

Geraldine Ryan writes short stories and serials for women's magazines here and abroad and has also dipped a toe in YA fiction. She lives in Cambridge, is a mum of four, a film addict and a voracious reader. She blogs with other writers at strictlywriting.blogspot.com

The House

Although I was a city boy, I always enjoyed walking, usually on my own. I could walk away from all the things that were happening at home. I'd rather be on my own than mixed up with the fights my parents had.

It was when I met Miriam that I learned to adapt my stride to someone else's pace. Together we discovered hill-walking, and we got to know one another on those long days exploring the Pennines, though neither of us talked a great deal. We went out in all weathers, and sometimes there was no-one else out on the hills, just the two of us and the sheep. They were beginning to open long distance paths about that time, so we started to take longer walks. We walked the West Highland way the year it was opened, lugging tent and stove and dried food on our backs and taking water from streams on the way.

As we got older, we went back to day-long walks, choosing our days according to the weather, planning our walks or just exploring. I forgot what it was like to walk alone.

After the tragedy, I decided to go back-packing again, in Scotland. Although there was a time when many of our holidays were spent north of the border, on this occasion I chose to walk in an area previously unknown to us. Easter was early this year and I got quite cold on the overnight train to Aberdeen, and couldn't sleep. I took a bus after that, west along Deeside towards Braemar. From there I set off walking roughly north-west, along lanes that became footpaths, through a landscape of small farms. The journey had tired me and I took less pleasure than usual in the walk, absorbed as I was in my sadness. By the end of the day I had reached open moorland interlaced with streams, rowan trees and rocky outcrops. I could see the Cairngorms rising in the distance. I had seen no-one and had passed no dwelling, not even a derelict cottage, for a couple of hours or so. The stream I was following joined a river which now barred my way to the west. The rough trail was turning north. I felt too weary to walk further, so I stopped to set up camp. I found a level spot, above the stream, but sheltered from the prevailing wind. It took me a long time to erect the tent: I was out of practice. I began to make stupid mistakes, mislaying the mallet, knocking things over. I was too tired to go foraging for wood to make a fire. I decided I was probably not fit enough to go further and that I would return home in the morning. I had a cold supper, with water from the nearby stream, crawled into my tent and fell asleep to the soothing sounds of the river.

I woke early the next morning, feeling refreshed and my spirits were lifted by the morning light and the chorus of birds. I had escaped from the city and felt as if I had shaken off the burden of my mundane worries. I broke camp, surprised that I had not stowed my few belongings the previous day, and walked on towards the mountains.

I had good maps and, although the path had disappeared, I took my bearings from the river. I followed it until sometime in the late afternoon, when it led me into a forest of mixed trees, probably an old wood given the variety of flora. Here there was a broad track, which was surprising, as it did not look like a plantation. I had lost sight of the mountains, but felt confident that I knew in which direction I was walking. I have always enjoyed venturing into the unknown, an excitement I'd shared with Miriam.

I became aware of a change in the light. The trees were less dense ahead of me and I was approaching a clearing. The brush beneath the trees began to form into more regular shapes, almost like a garden. There was what looked like an avenue of bushes and I saw colour. There were purple-red wild rhododendrons, but there were also yellows and a bright white as well. As I got nearer, I saw the roses and the thicker trees that were screening a cottage, a house rather, just off the track.

I stopped, amazed. This was the house I had dreamed of, we'd dreamed of, all those years ago. I wasn't sure if I was hallucinating or not. I shifted my rucksack and climbed up the bank beside the track for a better view. It was an old, stone built house with a roof of red pantiles and tall chimneys. There were signs that people were living there; a wheelbarrow with a garden fork leaning against it was filled with what looked like compost and, beyond the flower beds, a pile of weeds and a pair of gloves lay at the side of a vegetable patch.

To my left was a gate and, without a thought, I went through the gate closing it behind me, and walked up the path to the front door. The door was painted green and had neither knocker nor letterbox. I put my hand on the knob and opened the door as if I had every right to do so: didn't I know this house of old?

The hallway was as I expected: tiles on the floor, a worn rug, coats, walking sticks and boots lining the walls. The staircase climbed upwards on my left to our bedroom, and a smell of cooking came from somewhere at the end of the hall. The door on my right was ajar and that room smelled of burning wood. I took my jacket off, hung it on a peg on top of an old Barbour and dropped my rucksack beneath. Then quietly, but with a confidence that surprised me, I walked through the door. The fire burned brightly and the feeling of the room was welcoming. The old sofa had its back to me, but the bookcase stood straight in front of me as I turned to shut the door. The books were all there, well thumbed, and on the table lay Huxley's "The Island". I'd never finished that book. I picked it up and sat by the fire. I was grateful for the warmth as the day was growing late and cold. Looking out of the window, I noted that the house faced south-east and so the setting sun was not visible. This room must catch the early morning light, I thought, as there was a gap in the forest to the east. The tree, the great oak stood to the north-east, masking the house, and making random walkers, such as I had been, not visible from where I sat.

I started to leaf through the book, found a marker at the place I'd got to, and settled into the armchair. After a while, and I really couldn't say if it was ten minutes or an hour, I heard a board creak and a door open. I moved the marker, put the book aside and I got up to find who else was here. I walked down the hallway and into the kitchen. A kettle had been put on the Rayburn and a teapot was warming beside it but no-one was there. For some reason I didn't call out, but went in search of the tea-maker. I felt it must be a woman. I wandered out into the yard and there she was, collecting the washing. She turned and nodded at me, her mouth full of pegs, and returned to her task. She was an older woman, tall, but not bent, with a long grey plait of hair. She seemed to know me, but I could not remember a previous meeting. She picked up the basket and walked past me with a smile.

I heard the call of a raptor, an osprey perhaps, although they are usually to be heard later in the year. I walked out into the garden to look for it as the light was beginning to fade. The path led across the lawn to the gravelled area for the garden bench, green with its high back and broad arms. As I walked towards it, the mountains came into view again and when I sat on the bench I knew that it had been positioned to catch the sunset, at least from March through to October; in the winter it would be hidden by the forest I had just traversed. This was a spot that Miriam would have loved, in her last days, when she could no longer walk, instead of the dismal view she'd had from our flat, across the roof-tops of the city.

I watched the last curve of the sun sink behind the hills and wondered again at the colours in the fading sky. I thought of Miriam, but without the weight and inertia that has dogged me. She is free from pain, I thought, and I am grateful for that.

I don't know how long I sat there, my head in my hands. My sense of time seems to have become unreliable. In the dusk, I felt rather than heard somebody sit beside me. I knew that it was Miriam before I looked up. She took my hand.

"If I am imagining you, then may my imagination go on for ever." I said, feeling a tingling throughout my body.

"Oh Tom, my love," she said, laughing and her laughter sounded like singing to me. "I've been waiting for you to come, to find your way here."

I looked up then, but what light there was came from behind her and I could not make out her features.

"Where are we?" I asked. "Where is here? I know this place, did we come here before?"

"No. Yes. This is our other place, the place we were always looking for."

"But" I shivered as a dreadful thought occurred to me, "are you alright, can you walk, here?"

Again she laughed, my wonderful Miriam laughed and she grabbed both of my hands and pulled me to my feet and we began to dance around the bench, as light as air. I wanted it to go on for ever. Then I wanted her to stop so that I could look at her properly; her face was in shadow. I pulled her to me and she was solid in my hug. I stroked her hair and then her face, tracing the small frown lines I knew so well, and the curve of her eyebrows. I kissed her eyes and her mouth, and twisted my fingers in her hair.

"Let's go to bed," she whispered, breathing into my neck, and as I released her she ran back towards the house, a solid shadow that called "follow me." I followed her through the darkened garden, into the house and up the unlighted stairs. At the top, she slipped through the door to our room and I followed her to the bed where we made love as it was in the beginning. The night was full of pleasure and sweet sighs and I cried and she cried and then we laughed at our joyful silliness.

It was the middle of the night, I think, when we lay back, cradling our bodies in one another, but I was not tired and looked over Miriam's shoulder at the room. I could make out few details, but I knew it well: the tallboy by the door, the checked curtains and the old wardrobe. I thought the wardrobe had a long mirror, but I could not see one; perhaps it too was in shadow. I turned to face the shadowy shape that was Miriam.

"Tell me about this place, my love, where are we?"

Miriam sighed sleepily and turned towards me. "I told you. The caretaker said that this is our other place, the place we always wanted to be."

"I don't understand," I said, not courageous enough to ask my question.

"Neither do I," she said, "you can ask her about it in the morning." She paused and I felt her hand stroke my face, and then circle my body, so that we were in an embrace when she continued. "But I remember dying. It was such a relief. I think you must have died too. Can you remember it?"

I could not remember dying. I remembered the terrible weight of grief I had carried after Miriam's death. It had gone now. I remembered that I had not enjoyed my walking holiday, until today. I remembered yesterday evening when I camped by the stream, when I was so exhausted that I hadn't managed to crawl into my sleeping bag. I remembered that this morning the water in the bottle had been frozen. I must have been frozen too.

I tried hard to focus on Miriam's face, but it was still in shadow. Perhaps I was in shadow. I smiled, and a warm, light feeling spread through my limbs.

"I don't need to remember anything, my love, now that I am here with you."

Jean Lyon

Jean Lyon has graduated from academic to creative writing. She has published a number of short stories recently, has written but not published poetry, and is working on her second novel. She has begun to write a fantasy novel for older children.

email:jeanlyon@btinternet.com

Cheating Death

"No," Jonathon screamed, "I can't die now. I'm supposed to live forever."

He woke abruptly in the thick, heavy darkness, the scream echoing inside his head. He had been dreaming again, the same dream but each night it grew more real. Now, the memory of that thing clawing at him, burrowing its long fingers into his rib cage, made his heart pound painfully against his chest. He struggled to sit, slipping his hand inside his shirt and rubbing at the scar. It was freezing in the room but his skin felt slick with perspiration. The nightlight was out.

Jonathon had never been afraid of anything in his whole life except for the dark. Now he had to fight down the panic that threatened to overwhelm him. He sat, huddled on the bed, trying to slow his breathing, calm himself down. But that thing was still out there, he knew it, waiting somewhere in the darkness.

Then the light beside his bed flickered to life. He blinked and stared around the room. Nothing was out of place and he sighed; it was just a dream after all, just some drug induced dream.

The following night Jonathon didn't allow himself to dream. In fact he didn't sleep. Instead he lay awake, the nightlight glowing gently beside the bed. He was aware when the temperature dropped, when the light wavered and died. He forced himself to wait.

A faint green glow came from the corner of the room and he watched transfixed as a figure formed in the dim light. It appeared to be a young man dressed in a white hospital robe. Its eyes were covered with a bandage but it seemed to stare straight at Jonathon. He wanted to close his eyes, hold them tight shut but instead he stared back, unable to move. The figure seemed vaguely familiar; he knew he had seen it before in his dreams but there was something more, something elusive that seemed just beyond the reach of his consciousness.

"Who are you?" His voice sounded weak and he forced himself to clear his throat and speak again. "Who are you? What do you want?"

"Don't you know?"

Jonathon shook his head. "You're not real," he muttered.

It laughed softly, sending shivers feathering down his spine. His stomach turned molten. He fought to control his panic, this was just an illusion, he told himself, just a drug induced illusion.

"What do you want?" Jonathon asked again when he could stand the silence no longer.

"What do I want?" The voice was filled with menace and Jonathon shrank back against the headboard of the bed. It gestured to the bandage that covered its eyes. "I want back what you took from me."

"I haven't taken…" Jonathon started to protest but the thing was fading. He stared until it was gone and the last of the green glow vanished leaving him alone in the darkness.

Why was this happening? He'd had no problems with hallucinations after his first transplant, why now? Was it just his conscience playing games with his mind? But his conscience was clear. Wasn't it?

* * *

"You know how it works." Dr. Rayburn frowned at the question. "We take cells from your body and use them to clone the organs you need." He paused his examination and looked at Jonathon with his cold grey eyes. Jonathon had never before realised just how cold they were. "I've

216

worked for you for twenty years," Rayburn continued, "and you've never questioned my methods before. You've always demanded results and so far you've got them. What's changed?"

Jonathon shook his head. He realised with disgust that what he was looking for was reassurance. He couldn't believe that he was letting a stupid dream get to him. He'd be needing a brain transplant next. No doubt Rayburn could organise one if needed.

"Nothing," he murmured. "Nothing, just forget I asked."

"And we go ahead?"

Jonathon nodded. "Of course."

He couldn't stop now. He had twenty years and a billion pounds invested in this. It was his dream. And after all, this work was going to benefit all of mankind. Eventually.

"We've proved that your research works," he said, "how close are we to being able to go public?"

Dr Rayburn frowned. "There are certain legal aspects which at the current time might cause problems. But the laws in this area are always changing. Soon, maybe."

That night he was ready, sitting up in bed when the figure emerged from the green haze. Crimson oozed from beneath the bandages wrapped about its face and Jonathon could almost smell the sharp, metallic taint of blood in the cold air. He had to force back the tide of panic welling up inside him. "What's wrong with your eyes," he asked. "I want to see your eyes."

It paced the room coming to a halt at the foot of the bed. "That might be a little difficult."

"I don't understand," Jonathon replied, but he was starting to. Horror seeped into the darkest recesses of his brain. Suddenly he knew why the figure seemed familiar.

He put his hands to his face, pressing his fingers into his eyeballs until the pain cleared his mind. It wasn't possible, he told himself, but deep down he knew that it was.

He thought back to that first transplant. His eyesight had been deteriorating, nothing drastic but definitely annoying. Dr Rayburn had suggested the operation. He had said his research was ready to be implemented. What had he done?

The figure glided towards him, coming to a halt beside the bed. It slowly began unwinding the bandage from around its head revealing empty eye sockets, gaping, blackened with old blood.

"If you want to see my eyes," it murmured, "look in the mirror."

Jonathon felt his stomach rise in protest. He swallowed the bitter tasting bile and felt the tears seep from his eyes. They blinded him for a moment and when they had cleared the apparition was gone.

"You don't understand," Jonathon said the following night. "I didn't want to die."

"Neither did I," the specter replied.

"But you never really lived. You were never *really* a person."

"Rayburn said the same thing after he took my eyes. He told me then what I was, why I was. And afterwards, he kept me alive in the darkness." A tremor ran through its form. "I always hated the dark, but in darkness I waited. Waited to know which part of me you would ask for next." It paused and Jonathon could almost sense the despair. "I prayed in the darkness, let it be a hand or an arm, a single kidney. You see, even then I wanted to live."

It slowly unfastened the robe and spread it open revealing the ruined body, the gaping wound where a heart had once beat.

"Even Rayburn couldn't find a use for me after this. Besides he didn't need me anymore."

Jonathon's hand went to his own heart. He could feel its rapid beat beneath his fingers. This wasn't true, Rayburn grew organs not people. Didn't he? But the truth was Jonathon didn't know, hadn't asked. But that didn't make him a bad person, did it?

"I'm a good man," he said, "I've given millions to charity."

The figure shrugged. "It's easy to give what you have plenty of." It turned and gestured to the photograph on the bedside table. "Would she have been proud of you, Jonathon?"

Jonathon looked at the picture of his wife, dead for over twenty years now. She had been the only person in the whole world he had ever loved and all his money and power had not been enough to save her. All his life he'd had everything he desired until that moment. And in that moment was born his obsession with the ultimate power; the power of life over death. He had poured millions into the research, hired the best scientists on the planet and never asked for the details, never allowed himself to think about the price he might have to pay for cheating death

No, he realised, Margaret would not have been proud of him and with that knowledge he felt a sharp pain as though his heart was breaking. He forced himself to calm his breathing to slow the rapid thump of his heart before it could explode in his chest.

"What happens now?" he asked.

"I'll be your constant companion," the ghost replied. "You'll come to hate the sight of me, come to hate those eyes until one night you tear them from their sockets with your own fingers, just so you can't see me. Just for a moment's peace. But I'll still be here."

"You're evil," Jonathon muttered.

It laughed softly. "I'm you," it replied, "and you will remember that with every beat of my heart."

"What do you want?"

"Think about it," it replied and was gone.

Throughout the remainder of the night, Jonathon lay in the darkness and thought. Was the apparition really a ghost or was it somehow another part of himself? He didn't believe in ghosts, and he didn't have much of a conscience either. He went over the words it had spoken and one thing stuck in his mind. Why wasn't it needed any more?

*   *   *

"Show me."

"I really don't think…"

Jonathon slammed his hand down hard onto the metal table. "Show me."

Rayburn frowned but pulled open a metal drawer in the wall and stepped back. Jonathon felt the chill of the frozen air wash over him. He shivered and forced himself to look down. The body of a young man lay on the shelf. Jonathon recognised him immediately; even with the wounds it was like looking at a replica of himself as a young man. The nausea rose thick and hot in the back of his throat. He swallowed then closed his eyes for a moment.

"How old was he?"

"Eighteen." Rayburn replied with a frown. "Why are you asking this now? Isn't it a little late to be getting a conscience?"

"Is it?" Jonathon replied bleakly. He remembered himself at eighteen, his whole life ahead of him. Had this boy ever felt the same?

"Look," Rayburn's tone was conciliatory, "whatever you might be thinking, this was not a person like you and

220

me. He spent his whole life in the lab, he knew nothing else and let me assure you that absolutely no unnecessary suffering is caused to any of the specimens we produce here."

"What are those marks around his wrists?" Jonathon asked.

Rayburn's skin tightened across his cheekbones, his eyes turned a shade colder. "Towards the end, he got a little," he paused as if searching for the right word, "disturbed. We had to restrain him. Prevent him damaging the organs before they could be harvested." He was silent for a moment before continuing. "Jonathon, you have to understand, this," he gestured to the body, "doesn't matter. What we are doing here is groundbreaking. When it all comes out, do you really think anybody will care about what happened to a few laboratory specimens?"

Jonathon continued to stare down at the ravaged body.

Rayburn's eyes narrowed on the other man. "You do realise," he said, "that most of what we do here is illegal and I have plenty of evidence that it all happened with your full knowledge and co-operation."

Jonathon ignored the threat. "I want to see the rest," he said.

"The rest?"

"Of your laboratory specimens."

Rayburn looked about to argue, then shrugged and led him out of the room, down a corridor and stopped in front of a metal door. He slid back the grill and moved aside. Jonathon peered into the dim cell-like room.

"So," Rayburn asked from beside him, "are you prepared to spend the rest of your short life in prison? Or do you want the immortality I promised you? All you have to do is keep quiet, like you've always done, and everything you ever dreamed can be yours. Are you willing to give that up? Are you ready to die?"

"You know, I never believed in heaven or hell. I always thought that death was the end. But it isn't, is it?" Jonathon paused. "I've sent Rayburn away," he said. "I'll take the consequences for whatever he might do and one day I'll take my chances on the other side."

"Good. And…"

"Follow me."

He led the way out of the room, down a corridor and opened a door into a large bedroom. A night light glowed in the corner of the room.

"I was always afraid of the dark," Jonathon murmured.

The light showed a small boy curled up on a large bed. He woke and sat up, blinking sleepily.

"Go back to sleep," Jonathon murmured then turned to the figure at his side. "Do you see?"

"I see. He has our eyes."

"I found him in Rayburn's laboratory," Jonathon said. "He's your replacement isn't he? The reason you weren't needed anymore? Well, he'll be safe now." He stood looking at the child for long minutes. "Perhaps, one day he'll have children," he continued, "maybe that's our way to immortality. Yours and mine."

He turned but he was standing alone.

Nicola Cleasby

222

Nicola Cleasby is an ex-chartered accountant who has now settled down to a life of writing and almond farming in the remote
mountains of Southern Spain. Nicola has recently had short
stories and novellas accepted for publication and is currently
working on a novel.

The Ghost of Bony Ridge

"I know who you are," the woman said. "You that ghost woman from the Yoo Kay. You come all the way 'cross the 'lantic Ocean to talk to folk about the ghost of Bony Ridge. Ain't that right?"

Alison's mouth suddenly felt dry and she felt more out of place than she had in her entire life and she'd been to all kinds of strange locations in the past year.

The woman was sitting on a wooden veranda, rocking back and forth in a creaky chair, regarding Alison closely with hawk like eyes. She had grey hair drawn tightly back from a small round face that was remarkably unlined.

"That's correct," Alison said, struggling to keep her voice level. "The ghost of Bony Ridge is to be the subject of the last chapter of my book about ghosts around the world."

"I know about your book, honey," the woman said. "I read about it in what passes for the local press round here. That is, Martha McLachlan's weekly newsletter."

She gave a low, dry, throaty chuckle.

"You ever been to the States before?"

"My first time," Alison smiled and took a step up onto the veranda.

"Like it? What do you think of Bony Ridge?"

"Well, I've only just got here," Alison said. "But from what I've seen, it seems very peaceful."

"So where'd you hear about this ghost then?" the woman asked. "I thought it was just a local legend."

Alison found herself on the veranda now and the woman was patting the wooden bench beside her rocking chair.

She hurried along to the seat, as if she feared the offer would be withdrawn if she didn't sit down quickly.

"That's just it," Alison said, her eagerness now overtaking her awkwardness. "Everyone knows about the famous ghosts such as the one at Hampton Court Palace and of course, Borley Rectory."

"I've never heard of none of them places," the woman said, chewing her lip thoughtfully. "But then, I never done much readin' about ghosts. Martha's newsletter is about all I read. That 'n the signs on the passing trucks."

She nodded towards the road that swept by the town some distance away.

"But anyway, you come to talk about the ghost, then you happened by the right person."

Alison stifled a smile. It was quite extraordinary how many people she had met during her travels claiming to have seen ghosts. But many of the tales that had seemed so promising had proved to be just silly stories at best.

She'd been looking for tales to chill the blood, but had found precious few of those. Enough to make a small moderately interesting book maybe, but not quite the groundbreaker she'd imagined when she set out on her quest.

"You need to go on up the hill a ways," the woman said, pointing a bony finger up the hill.

It was a rough dusty road up that way, flanked by trees and bushes.

"Why? What's up there?"

The old woman chuckled.

"No what, honey, who," she said. "I'm getting to that. It's quite a steep hill and you might get achy legs, but it'll be worth it, I guarantee you that."

Alison looked up the road again and shivered. It looked spooky enough up there with the deep shadows cast by the trees.

"About half a mile or so up that road there's a house. Bit like this one, 'cept it's back off the road more and a whole lot bigger."

Alison fumbled in her bag for her notebook. She didn't use a tape recorder too much because it tended to put people off their stride. They didn't seem to notice a notebook quite so much.

"Put that away, honey," the old woman said. "Once you've been up to the house on the hill, you'll have plenty to write in your little book about."

"I'll still make a few notes, if you've no objection," Alison said.

The old woman shrugged.

"Up to you. Just trying to save you a bit of time is all."

"Could I have your name, please?"

"My name? Oh my. You're going to put my name in your book?"

She looked delighted.

"If you don't mind?"

"Mind? I don't think I've ever had my name in no book before. Well, if you're sure, then I'm known as Katie Waylon."

"Alison Thompson," Alison smiled, warming to the woman.

"I know," she said with a mischievous grin.

"Mrs Waylon…"

"Katie."

"Katie. Please. Tell me about the house on the hill. That's where the ghost is isn't it?"

226

The old woman settled back in her chair and began to rock gently, hands folded neatly in her lap.

"The house on the hill was built a long time ago by the Petersen family. They were from one of those Scandinavian countries originally so I believe. They certainly had the fair looks which they never lost down the generations.

"They were nice enough folks and they sure had the gift of making money. Mr Petersen, he owned several stores by the time he died. That's the Mr Petersen I knew of course.

"I went to school with his daughter, Lois."

She broke off and stopped rocking and a shudder went through her whole body. Alison's skin began to prickle.

"She was a bad girl," Katie said. "A bad, bad girl. I wasn't much to look at in those days no more than I am now."

She laughed and began to rock again.

"But that Lois, she never let me forget it. My mamma told me to ignore the jibes and the insults and to say that thing you say to folk that like to call you names. Sticks and stones will break my bones, but words will never hurt me. You heard of that?"

"Yes," Alison said. "I have."

"Well, my mamma was wrong about that. Those words, they cut me like a knife and they ate away at my insides like a worm crawling round inside me."

She drew an imaginary circle on her stomach with her finger.

"But you don't want to hear about how bad Lois was, do you, honey? You want to hear about the haunting."

Alison moved to the edge of her seat. Her palms felt moist. She wasn't making notes because her hands were making her notebook greasy so her pen wouldn't work.

227

She didn't want to be distracted by pens not working, so she slipped the book back in her bag.

"I wasn't the only one that hated Lois Petersen. A lot of folks round here did. She was unkind. She was the kind of girl who kicked cats for fun and pulled the wings off butterflies... oh you may flinch at that thought, honey, but people like that exist. Cruel people.

"Anyway, there was a terrible accident. No one was rightly sure how it happened, but they found the body at the bottom of Bony Ridge. All bust up it was, twisted and broken. The town changed after that.

"See, they suspected foul play, but no one saw or heard a thing and nothing could ever be proved. But healthy young women don't drop off paths they've known all their lives by accident."

"No," Alison murmured. "I suppose they don't."

"Anyway, life went on apace like it does, years passed and I decided to go up to the house on the hill and knock on the door."

She made a knocking motion in the air.

"I didn't expect no answer, so when a thin strangled sounding voice called out, 'Who's there?' I damn near wet my pants.

" 'It's me,' I said. 'Katie. You gonna open this door? Or you gonna leave me standing out here in the cold?' But I got no answer. It was Lois though; I know it was, hiding out in that dry old house.

"Seemed she'd come back to Bony Ridge and had taken up residence in her old house. But no one ever saw her. She didn't step outside, but they knew she was there all right. Same as I did.

"So every day, I walked up the hill to the house and knocked on the door and every day she yelled at me to go

228

away. They say there's no rest for the wicked and I made sure Lois Petersen didn't get any rest."

"And she's up there – now?" Alison swallowed hard, aware of the fading light. "How long does it take to get dark round here?"

"Long enough. You thinking of walking up there? You won't see no ghost at this time of day. There's been kids, teenagers you understand, camping out up there hoping to catch a glimpse of something, but they never do."

"Still, I'd like to take a look at the house. I'll go up there now and if you don't mind, I'd like to drop in on my way back to see you."

"Sure, honey."

Alison stood up, smiled down at the old lady and hurried up the dusty road. She could hear the creaking of the rocking chair for some time and then all she could hear was the crunch of her own feet treading the path.

The house on the hill was big and would have been quite imposing in its day.

There was a dim light burning inside the house when Alison knocked on the door.

"Who is it? Who's there?"

"Alison Thompson," Alison called, her throat dry. "I'd like to talk to you about the ghost."

There were a few moments silence, then the sound of rusty bolts sliding across and keys clunking in the locks. Eventually the door opened and an old wizened face looked over the top of a thick chain.

Alison had expected a ghost, but the woman before her was flesh and blood.

"All right," the old woman muttered and slid the chain free, then she opened the door and showed Alison into an old fashioned parlour. It was like being in an old sepia photograph, Alison thought, like stepping back in time.

Lois Petersen bustled about, shutting the curtains, checking all the windows were locked.

Finally she sat down.

"Miss Petersen…" Alison began.

"Shush," Lois said. "Listen. It's dark outside now. She'll be here any minute."

Alison's hair stood on end as she heard the sound of footsteps on the gravel outside, then footfall on the wooden veranda.

After what seemed an eternity there was a knock on the door.

"Wh–who's there?" Lois called, her voice strangled and full of terror.

"It's me," a voice said. "Katie. You gonna open this door? Or you gonna leave me standing out here in the cold."

Alison laughed. "That's just Katie Waylon from down the road," she said. "You don't need to be afraid of her."

But Lois's eyes were wide with terror and she was trembling from head to toe.

"That's Wailing Katie all right," Lois said. "She comes every night to torment me. Sometimes she's old like me and sometimes she's a girl like she was that night… the night of the accident."

Alison felt a shiver run down her spine.

"Accident?"

"It was an accident I swear," Lois cried. "I didn't mean to push Katie over the ridge. I just pushed a little harder than I meant to and she went over. I heard her scream all the way down… and she's been tormenting me ever since."

The knocking continued.

"Very good," Alison said, her heart sinking with disappointment as she realised the most promising story for her book so far had turned out to be an elaborate hoax.

She hurried to the door and despite Lois's screams of protest, flung it open.

There was no one there, but a cold wind blasted into Alison's face, knocking her backwards.

She spun round in time to see Lois backing up against the wall, the back of her hand flung across her gaping mouth.

Then she dropped lifeless to the floor and Alison could have sworn she heard the words, "Thank you, honey…" on the warm breeze that wafted past her towards the open door.

Teresa Ashby

Teresa Ashby's stories and serials have been published in the UK and abroad and many of those have been ghost stories. She lives in a town steeped in maritime history and rich with atmosphere, the perfect place for getting in the mood to write a ghostly tale.

teresaashby.blogspot.com

Caroline

Dear Jessica,

We called her Caroline; it seemed appropriate. I only knew her for a night but I've never been able to go back. You wanted to know, so I'll tell you. Please don't throw this away; I can see your hands twitching to scrunch this up right now. No more lectures from the wizened mountaineering guide; just your father, wanting to apologize for making a fuss when you couldn't understand why.

It's ten years ago since Rob and I intended to summit Mount Cook from the Bull Pass. The crossing was no real trouble but in the afternoon the wind picked up, gusting so hard it nearly blew us off the ridge; then it snowed, and there was a complete white out. The forecast had been for clear weather and we were unprepared for snow. We detoured, hugged the rocks, and got disoriented. And there was something terribly wrong with my altimeter – it kept trying to convince me we were below sea level. We had to rope ourselves together and inched onwards. But you know Rob – his 'army training' kicked in and after fumbling around for a few hours we stumbled exhausted into the Caroline Hut, which was full of food, and prepared to wait it out.

We waited and waited. It carried on for hours. The wind howled round the hut, and the avalanches roared like canon. The light faded and we realised we'd be there for the night. The hut shook and rocked on its foundations and the generator kept spluttering, making the lights flicker. It was a terrible evening and as we sat around our beef stew (I remember very clearly that it was beef stew) we wondered about the other climbers who might be caught. As usual, we radioed Mount Cook Base, and luckily it seemed like most of the groups were accounted for.

So we ate, and Rob fiddled with the altimeter. I found a bucket because both of us were wary of making it back from the toilet hut ten metres away, and we re-planned our route for the next day. You've been up there in storms, but this one was truly ferocious. There were no lulls between the gusts – they just kept going on and on and on. I've never experienced anything like it. We were both a little nervous and left the flickering lights on, talking longer than we should have. I've often wondered whether this made any difference, whether we were punished for being scared, whether we attracted anything with our lights. I don't like to think so.

Rob was talking about Amy, about her school – I don't know if you remember her changing school at about that time. I was only half listening and wondering who was reading your bed time story. And then his eyes froze, transfixed with shock.

"Jeeesus," he whispered, pushing his chair from the table. I followed his gaze warily. And there, melting their way through the ice on the window above the sink was a pair of hands.

We couldn't see anything else due to the reflection from our lights, just two unmoving hands. They were planted flat against the glass, and then began twitching slightly.

"Jeesus," Rob said, "they must have got lost, poor bastards."

I said we should let them in, but even as I said it something told me to leave the door firmly shut. But we couldn't leave a climber out there, without gloves. It did seem strange to me that they didn't have gloves.

Rob and I stared at each other, knowing what we had to do, neither of us daring to admit that we didn't want to let them in. In the time we were staring, the hands had

233

started to move, inching their way across the windows. It was Rob who finally battled the door open and began shouting.

"Over here, the door's over here!" But his voice was lost in the weather. Later we both thought we'd heard a shriek, a wail, but I don't know. I doubt anything could have carried in that wind.

After a minute of shouting a figure emerged from behind the water tank, looking like a snowman. I don't know what I'd been thinking but I was hugely relieved to see just two arms, two legs, and almost cheerful when we pulled it into the hut and saw that it was a woman. Her face was round, moon like, and her dark eyes filled with terror. I remember I scrambled for the first aid kit and Rob tried to take off her coat. But before we had time to begin to help her, she tipped her head back and screamed, drowning out the weather.

"I've lost her, I've lost her."

Rob did his best to calm her and asked me to put the kettle on. He's always believed a cup of tea cures all women's problems. But she flailed her arms around and began tearing at her long black hair, screaming all the time, "I've lost her, I've lost her."

Rob wrapped his arms around her to control her and started shouting as well. "Who've you lost? How many are missing? Where were you heading when you lost her? And where the hell is your pack?"

I have to hand it to him; he was more awake than me. She'd come in wearing a jacket and over trousers with leather boots. No ice axe, no crampons, no pack, rope or harness. As I fumbled with the radio she seemed more like an animal than a woman, throwing her head back, thrashing in Rob's arms and screaming. The louder she screamed, the louder Rob screamed. And I tried to concentrate while I radioed the base. The few seconds it took them to respond willed me with terror; it felt as if we were all alone in the world. Tim was on duty and sounded incredulous when I said we'd found someone. He said that everyone, remarkably, had been accounted for. 'All climbers tucked up,' as he put it. I think that's when I realised something was seriously, seriously wrong. And she and Rob just kept screaming.

I tried to stay calm. Tim promised to have a team standing by for when the weather cleared, if we could only work out where to send them.

Rob exhausted himself shouting eventually but still struggled with her arms. She was wriggling herself free only to find her limbs re clamped to her side. "Get the rope," he barked. I hesitated for a moment before he yelled me into action.

We wrestled her into a chair and tied her down at the waist. We left her arms free as we assumed she'd want some food. As soon as we'd secured her and moved away, still screaming, she stared at me in utter terror and raised her hands to her face. I know I have a go at you about the length of your nails, but hers were way longer than that, and none of them broken. She dug them deep into her plump cheeks and dragged them down, streaking her cheeks with red.

"I've lost her," she wailed.

Rob turned pale and shuddered. I felt sick. Rob and I each grabbed a hand and wrestled it from her face. After a guilty glance at each other over her upturned face we joined her wrists behind her back and tied them there.

"I've lost her," she sobbed this time, "lost her." Her hands twitched as she tried to free them. Gently at first, then aggressively as she realised we'd imprisoned her. And she began to wail again, rocking back and forward in the chair. It was horrible to watch, like an animal in the zoo or something.

I promise you, we tried. We really tried to help her. I tried to feed her some stew but she snarled and bared her teeth. Rob continued with his interrogation. Who had she lost, and where? But she carried on wailing and moaning. After a couple of hours it was hard to stay sympathetic. We were tired, but I promise we tried.

Rob looked at me wearily through half closed eyes. And then inspiration hit.

"Maybe," he whispered, "maybe her partner fell, maybe she had to cut her loose."

I stared at the woman and shuddered; I couldn't say what state I'd be in if I'd had to cut a rope, leave Rob for dead. It's crossed my mind before that I'd rather be the dead one than face his family.

"Poor thing," mumbled Rob.

"Is that what happened?" I asked her calmly. "Did your friend fall?" I was greeted by a cavernous mouth screaming in my face, and my terror of her returned.

Meanwhile Rob scoured the hut for sedatives. There was nothing useful. I think it was me who muttered something to the effect that I couldn't spend a night like this; it was driving us both mad. We sat for a few moments with our backs to the wailing, rocking creature.

We've made many decisions in our climbing career without discussion, without words, and this was one. If we'd said anything I doubt we could have gone through with it. I grabbed blankets from the spare beds, hastily boiled water and poured tea into one of our flasks. Rob donated bars from his hoard of chocolate and we bundled it all up. Then we tied her up again with more rope so she wouldn't be set free when we untied

236

her from the chair. She struggled like some kind of mutant caterpillar, bound up in her rope, her screams piercing my brain.

With one of us on either side we hustled her to the door, letting ourselves out into the ferocious storm. Her wails seemed to merge with the wind, became a part of nature's assault on us. We made slow progress, hugging the side of the hut; our head torches barely penetrated a foot in front of us.

It seemed an age before we reached the metal door of the emergency shelter. It used to be attached to the back of the main hut. I threw the bundle in, and through a half closed door we untied her, trying not to let her escape. She didn't. My dear Jess, we didn't mean to be cruel. There were enough blankets to keep warm, we left a warm drink and plenty, plenty of food. I promise there was nothing else we could have done.

And so, we made our way back into the hut, had some tea and tried to talk. We heard banging through the wall, like a boxing match locked up in a tin. We started talking about ludicrous, stupid things, rugby, planning permission for the leisure centre. And when the thumps resounded through the wall we tried to hide our flinches with scratches and coughs. I didn't dare sleep, but eventually we snatched a few moments of rest, our heads resting on the table and the light still on.

I guess at some stage the banging must have stopped because what woke me up later was not another onslaught of noise, but total silence. Rob and I stared at each other and watched the pink glow of dawn seeping across the face of Mount Cook. It was a beautiful, clear morning. There was utter peace, silence, as the pink expanded, filling the sky and staining the snow. I felt rested, like I'd awoken from a bad dream. Then the radio crackled into action. Rob stumbled across the hut and gave his re-hearsed explanation.

They were clearly surprised she was in the emergency shelter. I thought I detected a hint of suspicion in their voices and it made me nervous. It all seemed so ludicrous with the wind gone and the sun streaming through the window.

Despite the sun, neither of us had the courage to check on her before the rescue party arrived. I don't know what we should have done but there was a flicker of fear in both our eyes and we did nothing.

We even ate porridge while we waited, but not much. My hands shook as I stirred it and it almost choked me when I tried to eat. It wasn't long before we heard the helicopter, not long either before the doctor emerged. I was scared when I saw him; it didn't feel like help had arrived. We led him and some other man to the entrance of the shelter and opened it for them.

There was no screaming, no wailing. Silence.

We crept forward and peered behind the door at a scrunched up bundle of a woman. I tiptoed forward as the doctor began uncovering her. He freed a bloody hand from the blanket and laid it gently aside. And then he uncovered her head. I felt sick. The scratches she'd made on her cheeks in front of us had been multiplied hundreds of times; her face was covered with long red streaks. Her eyes were disfigured by deep red gashes across her eyelids and hair was matted with blood.

"Is she alive?" I whispered. The doctor grunted.

I tried to explain that we hadn't hurt her. The doctor grunted again and stared at me with loathing. I foresaw police, law suits, all sorts of bad things; our actions seemed thoroughly ridiculous. I shouted at her, shook her. Her body was warm so she wasn't dead. In desperation I grabbed the hand mirror from the shelf and shoved it in her face. I'd wondered for years what a grotty pink mirror was doing in the shelter, Dan told me one of his vain American clients had brought it but I don't know.

"Look what you've done. Why did you do it? Tell them we didn't hurt you."

As the doctor prepared the stretcher her eyes flickered into life. At first there was the panic from the night before, and then, as she stared at me and the mirror, calmness replaced it. She stared hard at the mirror for a few seconds before trying to touch it with her bloody fingers.

"I've found her," she whispered, "I've found her," before closing her eyes again with a hint of a smile on her lips.

I don't understand what happened. She checked herself out of hospital two days later without giving her name or anything. The only thing she ever said to the doctors was that she needed to get back to the mountains. No other bodies were ever found. Rob and I abandoned our trip, and I've never been able to go back. I'm sorry but it scared me when you said you were going to 'find yourself' with Abbi, and doing exactly that route.

I know you'll have had a great time when you get back and read this, though I heard tonight that the wind is picking up and it's beginning to snow. So I hope you're being safe. I didn't mean to doubt your ability. I hope you're being careful. Stop by when you get back and tell me all about it, please.

Love
Dad

Catherine Greene

Catherine Greene has been writing short stories for a number of years but only began trying to get published recently. She has just finished a novel and is planning to begin her second. She currently works in the City and is expecting her first baby in November.

The Attic

Anna stomped up the stairs, stepping over the missing tread and avoiding the hole where her brother, aged eight, had experimented with a chisel. The dust made her nose twitch. *I don't need this,* she thought, *not on the only weekend I've got off this month. Paul will be at home right now, the children will be in bed and he'll be pouring himself a glass of wine, while I'm* – the sneeze nearly blew the top of her head off – *while I'm clearing out my Mum's attic.* She switched on the light and groaned. She knew the attic would be full, that had been its charm when she was a child, but she hadn't realised… she stared at the piles of boxes and trunks, of upended dining room chairs, a broken guitar, piles of rugs rolled like cigars, of heaps covered in dust sheets and… well, Anna wasn't sure.

"What on earth is all this stuff, Mum?" she called.

"What stuff dear?" Anna could almost hear her mother's hands flapping, wide and soft and white, anxious as moths.

"This!" She lifted a dust sheet. There was a telephone, avocado, with a dial, circa 1978. "There's a phone here, does it work?"

"Oh, I wouldn't think so, it wouldn't be up there if it worked, would it? It's probably waiting to be mended."

It's been waiting a while, thought Anna. She blamed the War. All this hoarding. There must be things up here her mother hadn't seen for years, particularly now that her knees were bad.

"It's going to take some time, Mum," Anna called.

"Shall I make tea?"

"No, thanks. I'll see what needs to be done, then we can make a plan."

A plan to hire a skip, Anna thought, and she took a deep breath, which was a mistake. Once she'd finished coughing, she grabbed the nearest dust sheet and pulled. Underneath were some removal boxes, carefully tied, their contents noted in her mother's spidery handwriting: 'Crockery misc: Wedgewood, cups etc. Glasses – green, peculiar.' Anna peeped into the box. There were indeed carefully wrapped bundles the size and shape of cups. *Charity shop*, she thought, and stuck a bright pink post-it note onto the box. It looked efficient, modern, brisk. Anna was pleased. Maybe this wasn't going to be so hard.

The next box had more spidery writing. 'Gramophone', it read, 'assorted records'. Anna opened flaps and there was the black square case she remembered from her grandmother's house. She took it out and set it on the floor – it was heavy and she staggered slightly. Also in the box were a pile of thick black '78s. *Might as well have some music while I work,* she thought. The winder was taped to the lid of the gramophone and she screwed it in, wound up the old player and put on Glen Miller's 'Moonlight Serenade'. I haven't heard this since Granny died, she thought as she bent over the next box, 'Linen misc'.

As she opened it, she caught a whiff of cigar smoke. *Odd,* she thought. Her mother didn't smoke, and her father, now long dead, had never touched cigars. Anna put her nose into the linen and drew back sharply at the pungent mix of lavender and moths. She must be mistaken. Glenn Miller came to a crackling end, and she turned the record over. She went to open the next box: 'Ornaments: broken' and she smelt the cigar smoke again. Abandoning the box she walked to the top of the stairs.

"Mum," she called, "Is anything burning?"

"No, dear," her mother called back.

"Are you sure? I'm certain I can smell something."

"Quite sure dear," her mother trilled, in her 'don't patronise me, I'm not senile yet' voice.

Anna turned back. She felt a flicker of uneasiness. Maybe she'd leave the boxes. Probably the smell came from the bulb as it heated up its thick layer of dust. Perhaps she should listen to Acker Bilk, distract herself... She changed the record and turned to a tin trunk, shoved under the eaves. As she pulled it out she dusted the lid. A torn and faded label advertised the Shepherds' Hotel, Cairo, with a picture of pyramids. Her mother had lived in Egypt at the end of the war. The trunk wouldn't open at first, but she used a sliver of wood to lever up the catch. The hinges squeaked as it swung open.

On the top was a sheet of browning tissue paper. When she lifted it off there was more underneath. As Anna scrabbled through the layers, she smelt the cigar smoke again, and another, different, smell. *Gardenias,* she thought, *or... what was it?* The paper parted to reveal a dress. What a dress. Anna lifted it gently from the trunk. Thick cream satin, cut on the bias, tightly fitting from shoulder to hip and then swirling out into a glorious wide skirt. Anna held it against herself and smoothed it over her body. She'd never seen it before. She loved it. She hesitated for a moment, she was after all here to do a job, and then she gave in. She put the dress down and unbuttoned her jeans, then stripped off her fleece and shirt. *Odd,* she thought, *it's not cold. It's December and the attic isn't heated, but I'm actually... hot. It must be because I've been working hard*, she thought, and she slithered into the dress. It fitted her like skin. *Frangipani,* she realised, *that's the smell.* It was strong now, in the heat of the warm dark tropical night. Acker Bilk played on, but the static and crackling had gone, the sounds of the clarinet and the sax were clear, as if he were playing at the bottom of the stairs. She heard the sound of low chatter, the clink of glasses at a party. A shiver ran down her spine, and then she realised it must be the telly. *The volume Mum has it at these days it's a surprise she doesn't blow the tubes,* Anna thought. She smoothed the dress over her stomach, down her thighs. It made her feel different: flirty, voluptuous. She tossed her hair and wished it was not cut so ferociously short. *Bright red lipstick,* she thought, *that's what it needs. And dark kohl-lined eyes.*

She turned back to the trunk, wondering what else lay in amongst the tissue. There were three more layers and then her hand brushed against another material, harsher, scratchier, thicker than the silk. Anna snatched her hand away as her body broke out in a cold sweat, every hair on her arms stood up and her nerve ends tingled. She frowned. What on earth was the matter? She was being ridiculous. She was in an attic in Wiltshire in December, looking at some old clothes. Her mind was playing tricks. She leant back over the trunk and pulled out the material that her fingers had touched. It was the khaki uniform of a soldier. As she held it, she felt an electric shock of sheer terror. A rush of water filled her mouth. She tried to swallow and then to spit it out, but she couldn't get rid of the water, every time she spat more water filled her mouth. She shook her head from side to side but it made no difference, she coughed and choked and vomited up water. What was happening to her? She dropped the uniform and fell to her knees gasping for breath, spitting and choking. She couldn't breath, she scrabbled at her throat, her lungs were filling with water, her vision was blurring, a black mist was clouding her eyes...

Then, it was over. She gasped for breath and instead of water, she gulped air. She drew deep breaths into her lungs, coughing. She licked her lips. They were salty. Her breath was still ragged, but she could breath. She was inert for a moment, then she began to shake and cry. She must get away. She crawled to the top of the stairs, her legs a rag doll's. She stumbled, half falling, scrabbling at the banister, down the stairs from the attic, and then down again to the ground floor of the house. She dragged herself into the sitting room where her mother was sitting and knitting. When she saw Anna she stood up, her face twitching.

"Mum—"

"Take it off," her mother said, her voice guttural. "Take that dress off, right now."

* * *

As Anna searched through her weekend bag to find more clothes – there was no way she going back upstairs to retrieve her jeans – she tried to rationalise what had happened. She'd nearly drowned on dry land, in her mother's attic. She licked her hand – she could still taste the salt water, and the front of the dress was soaked. She was forty-one, she was a solicitor and she was not given to flights of fancy. It had happened. She had not made it up. Perhaps – and she was not one to believe in these things, but given the last half hour maybe she'd have to reassess her beliefs – perhaps there was some kind of memory embedded in the clothes. Perhaps if you felt a very strong emotion it lingered like a stain on whatever you were wearing at the time. Perhaps – she shivered and decided she would wear two pairs of socks – perhaps the soldier had drowned and that's what she had experienced. Anna was pleased with this idea. It was good to find an almost rational solution. Well, perhaps not exactly rational. Now she needed to speak to her mother.

Her mother had retrieved her knitting when Anna came into the sitting room. She had a blanket over her knees and her white hair floated halo-like around her head. Her skin was deeply wrinkled, with a few brown liver spots on her cheeks. She looked old. She looked frail. Anna wanted to protect her. Her mother looked up. Anna noticed the new milky sheen around the blue irises.

"That's better dear. Very nice," said her mother.

"Mum, about the attic."

"It's a terrible mess up there. I was thinking that maybe we should get one of those house clearers in—"

"I had the oddest experience…"

"They can be a bit pricey, but it's probably worth it—"

"There was a trunk of clothes—"

"You don't want to be spending your weekends sorting out a lot of old rubbish—"

"There was a uniform."

The knitting needles picked up speed. "They'll say if there's anything worth selling but I doubt it, just a lot of broken bits and pieces—"

"Mum! Stop it. I nearly… well, I think I nearly died up there. I was choking on salt water. I think you owe me an explanation."

The needles stilled. Slowly, her mother looked up.

"Oh, you do, do you? An explanation. Well. So, what do you want to know?"

"Well, that dress for instance."

"Was a dress of mine, yes."

"Why did you react so strongly to it?"

"I hadn't seen it for a while. I was … surprised."

Anna paused to let her mother continue. When she didn't, Anna put on her most sensitive face.

"Was he your boyfriend? The soldier."

"Not … exactly."

"And did he die?" There was a long pause. "Did he drown?"

Anna's mother bent over her knitting again.

"Yes. He drowned."

As she said this, Anna's throat contracted as though a hand had grasped it and squeezed. Her mouth filled once more with water. Falling on all fours she spat and choked and heaved and vomited water all over the carpet but still her mouth filled. As she was about to black out she heard her mother shout "All *right*! I'll tell her." Anna spat and no more water filled her mouth. She gasped, drawing glorious cold air into her mouth. She swallowed, the pain in her throat making her wince. She rolled onto her back and let herself breathe. Her mother bent over her, stroking her head.

"I'm sorry dear that you had to go through that. I really am sorry."

"Who were you talking to? What's going on mum?" Anna was weak now. She wanted comfort, like a toddler. Her mother sighed.

"I didn't think anyone needed to know, but maybe … that's not to be." She paused so long that Anna thought that she had fainted. She sat up. Her mother had started her knitting again.

"I met him at a dance. He was a soldier, on leave. It was a beautiful night, hot, very hot. I remember the frangipani. The smell still makes me retch. The band were playing Acker Bilk and we were dancing. He was handsome. Oh you young people, you think you invented romance. Let me tell you that there's nothing like war to sharpen the senses."

"You must have looked stunning in that dress."

"I did. Yes, I did."

"So he went away and then he never came back?"

"What? No, not at all. I was just telling you. It was a hot night. He suggested we went for a walk. The dance was at the Club and it had its own private beach. We used

247

to swim there a lot. Well, we strolled down through the gardens. He took my arm. I'd had a couple of glasses of what passed for champagne in those days and I was laughing. We got to the sand and I took off my shoes. They had sling backs and I hooked both of them over one finger I remember. I wanted to cool my toes in the sea. Then I felt his hand. He ran it down my spine, smoothing it, like stroking a cat. I turned around and he kissed me. At first, it was perfect. I was lost in his mouth—"

Anna shifted uncomfortably. This was her mother. Old. Respectable. A little bit dull.

"And then it changed. I tried to push him away but he just held me tighter. His tongue – I couldn't breathe. I tried to turn my head, but his hand held it firm in place. I stepped backwards and I was in the water. I struggled to push him, but he was strong, he was a trained soldier, it was like pushing steel. I stepped back again, the water was up to my knees, he grabbed me and I fell, right in, right under. He threw himself on top of me. His hands grabbed at my dress, pulling it up. He held my head down. My mouth filled with water. I was choking. I couldn't turn my head, I couldn't breathe. I was feeling with my hands under the water to find something, anything, that I could push him with. I was losing my strength, my lungs were bursting. I felt a stone. My fingers clutched it and I brought it up—" Anna's mother stopped.

"You hit him?" said Anna.

"Yes. On the temple. I think I knocked him straight out. But I carried on, hitting him I mean. I think when I'd finished he was quite dead. What with the stone and the water. Yes, quite dead."

There was a long pause. Anna couldn't take it in. She didn't know which question to ask first. Then:

"You must hate him."

"During the war, you know, it wasn't all heroics. Men were still men. Some of them charming and gentlemen, and some of them... not. And training men to kill, well, they'd call it adrenaline these days I expect. It's hard for them to turn it off when they come away from a battlefield. You can't blame them."

"How did you get away with it?"

"Oh, I made up some story about him going back to barracks. The currents were strong around that coast, I knew the body – he'd – be carried out to sea. There was a bit of a fuss and a search, but it was wartime. They were only on leave for a few days. One soldier more or less ... I think he might have been reported as missing ... but everyone had other things on their minds."

"You seem so calm."

"It was different in those days. You didn't paw over every emotion like you youngsters do. You dealt with it."

"And that's what you did?"

"Yes. Although..."

"Although?"

"Recently... I've been thinking... When you're old and there's nothing to distract you, you do return to your memories."

Anna sat back. She looked over at the fluffy white head bent over the needles, click clicking like Madame Defarge at the guillotine. She didn't know what to think.

"Just one thing Mum," she said. "Why did you keep the uniform?" Her mother looked up.

"What do you mean, uniform? I didn't. There is no uniform." And she went back to her knitting.

Clare Reddaway

Clare Reddaway writes short stories and scripts for adults and children. She performs in the South West with live fiction group *Heads and Tales*. She is currently writing a novel for older children, trying to sell a radio play and creating bespoke historical stories for festivals and other venues.

Index of Authors

Sally Angell, 119
Teresa Ashby, 231
Rosemary Bach-Holzer, 189
Adam Bealby, 143
April Bosshard, 17
Nicola Cleasby, 223
Carol Croxton, 66
Paul A. Freeman, 152
Danny Gillan, 28
Catherine Greene, 240
Alyson Hilbourne, 36
Rebecca Holmes, 52
A.J. Humphrey, 74, 182
Boo Irwin, 171
Sophie Jackson, 44, 196
Jean Lyon, 214
Susanne Martin, 160
Clare Reddaway, 250
Geraldine Ryan, 207
Glynis Scrivens, 111
Amanda Sington-Williams, 87
Mark R. Smith, 131
Paul Starkey, 101

Other anthologies by Bridge House

Alternative Renditions

Have you ever wondered why the ugly sisters hated Cinderella so much? Or asked yourself what drove a young woman to treat her step-children so cruelly? Or pondered what a beautiful young woman living with a lot of vertically challenged bachelors may have looked like to a concerned neighbour?

Sometimes we also feel the need to know what happened after the "happily ever after" and indeed if the after was ever happy.

"Alternative Renditions" challenges your normal perception of some very well known stories and gets a little further behind the scenes.

This collection of witty and well-crafted stories will give you several hours of entertainment and food for thought.

Order from www.bridgehousepublishing.co.uk

ISBN 978-0955791-03-1

Bridge House

In the Shadow of the Red Queen

The Red Queen's shadow falls upon us in all sorts of circumstances. She may help us to play tricks on each other while she plays tricks on us. She has a streak of cruelty and can make us cry. Yet she also has a sense of humour and being the wily female that she is, she excels at making us fall in love.

A story for everyday of your holiday – and the day before you go and the day after you come back.

"This is a delightful and entertaining collection of stories, ranging from the heart-warming to the humorous, from action-packed to downright bizarre. There is one for every mood and an abundance of great characters. I think Bridge House is doing an excellent job of bringing together this group of talented writers for us to enjoy. A must for anybody's holiday luggage."
(*Amazon*)

Order from www.bridgehousepublishing.co.uk

ISBN 978-0-955791-06-2

Bridge House

253

Do you have a short story in you?

Then why not have a go at one of our competitions or try your hand at a story for one of our anthologies? Check out:

http://bridgehousepublishing.co.uk/competition.aspx

* * *

Submissions

Bridge House publishes books which are a little bit different, such as *Making Changes, In the Shadow of the Red Queen* and *Alternative Renditions*.

We are particularly keen to promote new writers and believe that our approach is friendly and supportive to encourage those who may not have been published previously. We are also interested in published writers and welcome submissions from all authors who believe they have a story that would tie into one of our themed anthologies.

Full details about submissions process, and how to submit your work to us for consideration, can be found on our website
http://bridgehousepublishing.co.uk/newsubmissions.aspx

Lightning Source UK Ltd.
Milton Keynes UK
13 November 2009
146237UK00001B/19/P